# REVELATIONS

**Rissa Watkins**

**Library of Congress Control Number:**
**ISBN-10: 1939776163**
**ISBN-13: 978-1-939-776-16-7**

*Watkins, Rissa*
**UNREVELATIONS:** Adult Fiction, Urban Fantasy, 2015
Trade Paperback, First Edition, USA

**Author:** Rissa Watkins

**Editors:** Accentuate
**Proofreaders:** Lynn Hunter, Kaira Jackson

**Cover Design:** Rissa Watkins
**Matt and Sara Character Images:** Sladjana Milojevic

The author respects trademarks and copyrighted material mentioned in this book by introducing such registered items in italics or with proper capitalization. This book is a work of fiction. Names, persons, places and incidents are all used factiously and are the imagination of the author. Any resemblance to persons, living or dead, events or locales is coincidental and non-intentional, unless otherwise specifically noted.

10 9 8 7 6 5 4 3 2 1



Published in the United States of America
By Desert Ninja Publishing

# ACKNOWLEDGEMENTS

This is the closest I will get to an Academy Award speech, so please be patient and don't try to play me off the stage. Seriously, they would have to drag me kicking and screaming—evening dress and all—off the stage until I was finished.

There are so many people who made it possible for me to create this book. First, I need to thank Kellie Ann Barker who donated bone marrow to a complete stranger (at the time) and saved my life. You are my own personal super-hero, and I am honored to carry a part of you with me forever. Also, thanks go to Dr. Lisa Sproat & Kristen Lee C.RN at the Mayo Clinic and to Dr. Mazen Khattab of Arizona Oncology for helping me stay alive. I am blessed to be under your care.

I want to thank Michelle Devon: friend, editor, and mentor. If it weren't for her encouragement a decade ago, I would never have been brave enough to write a novel. She has helped me through the worst moments of my life and shared the joys with me, too. I love you, Michy.

I also need to thank my friends in my critique groups: David Nelson, Vaughn Treude, Ron Friedman, Angee Stonehouse, Clint Opine, Dharma Kelleher, Denise Ganley, Tina Wahl, Carl Wilson, Nanor Tabrizi, and David Waid. They suffered through many painfully written chapters offering suggestions to polish this baby up.

A huge thank goes out to Jami Nord who chose to be a mentor for my book when I entered it in a contest. I didn't land an agent, but I got something much better- her friendship.

Another shout out goes to my Beta readers: Rik Miller-Smith, Cindy Gunnin, Angel Sharum, Melissa Snark, Kim Morgan, Emily Henderson, Lynn Hunter, Christine Brody, and Kaira Jackson. Without your help and encouragement I wouldn't have been brave enough to publish this novel.

Finally, thanks go to my family, especially my husband,

De, who made me so mad one day, I wanted to kill him. So I did… in my novel. Don't worry, he remains unharmed in real life and should remain so, if he stops hogging the covers and dumping food into the side of the sink that doesn't have a garbage disposal. My husband and Chase (my baby-boy who isn’t quite a baby anymore) put up with me running out to crit group meetings and leaving them to fend for themselves for dinner, being cranky from editing, and making them act out action scenes so I can visualize them better. I love you.

~~Rissa Watkins, Author

# CHAPTER ONE

*And the Lamb Broke the Fourth Seal*

Some people thought the world would end in a zombie apocalypse. They would swear their friend's sister's boyfriend was eaten by a zombie. It would take more than some fifteen-year-old's shaky phone video to convince me. Don't even get me started on vampires or werewolves causing the End of Days. Just because there was a meme or news story on some website didn't mean it was real.

It might look like a duck and quack like a duck but I wouldn't call it Daffy. Take, for example, the vampire who currently sat outside my door and was begging me to invite him inside. I could have looked at him and thought, *Huh, my cheating husband was turned into a vampire tonight. Vampires have taken over the world. It's the End of Days.*

Except he looked like a man playing a vampire. David's razor-sharp teeth and the blood on his face looked real enough, but he was the embodiment of a bad actor with poor timing. His director—the dude in the yard who wore what looked like a black dress and a smirk on his face—sat astride a pale horse. At first glance, you'd think he was cosplaying Death, but something told me he was the real deal. The monsters on the news were merely the opening act for that guy.

"Please, baby, I need you to let me in," David said. His whiny voice grated on my nerves, but it was a good move on his part. I mean, it might have worked on me before. I would have welcomed the thought of eternity with the man I loved, my soulmate. We could have gone off into the night, biting and loving, *la la la.*

But the douche-viper had left his cellphone at home when he went off tonight to his 'business meeting.' Mandi, a blonde he worked with, had texted him to say she couldn't make it to dinner, but she would meet him at the hotel later. **Kiss kiss**

A bottle of wine, a whole lot of tears, and a couple of hours later, he'd shown up at our door. One glance at his current dead—or rather, undead—state, and the fact that he looked and smelled like he had been dumpster diving in his favorite power suit, led me to believe he hadn't made it to the hotel for their rendezvous. At least the garbage covered up the smell of smoke permanently ingrained in the Armani Exchange suit he'd bought at a fire sale shortly after the store literally had caught on fire and burned half their stock.

"Sara, we can be together, forever, young and beautiful lovers eternal."

Really? His promise to be faithful to me hadn't even lasted ten years of marriage, and he was talking about eternity?

"Screw you, your blonde tramp on the side, your little costume-wearing friend back there, and the sickly-ass horse he rode in on."

Not used to me standing up for myself, David stood there with his mouth open. Throughout our marriage, I'd sacrificed everything to make him happy. I worked overtime at a job I hated to maintain the lifestyle he wanted, sucked up to our snooty neighbors because he thought I needed to make more of an effort to fit in with them, and I'd even moved away from my only friends to this town so he could get the job he wanted.

And this was what I got. I was distracted with disgust at myself for letting people walk all over me all my life, so I'd missed when the Horseman went from looking at me with a startled expression at the end of my driveway to standing right in front of my door. I gave a little yelp and stumbled back.

"You can see me?" From a distance I thought he could have been related to me, with the same dark-brown hair and eyes and

Asian flattened nose, but up close, I realized there was nothing average about this Rider. We shared some features, but while my eyes were brown with flecks of gold, his were one solid color, black. If they were a window to his soul, he didn't have one. This guy oozed darkness.

*I remember you.*

*Where the hell did that thought come from?* "Hello? Not blind here. Yes, I can see you."

"That is not possible. No mortal can see past my veil." He was handsome and self-assured, usually an attractive quality in a man, but looking at him made my knees weak, and not in the good way.

"Veil's lifted buddy. Rose-colored goggles disappeared a few hours ago with a text message. Now get the hell out of here and take your little puppet with you." His astonishment at my being able to see him was the perfect opportunity to slam the door in their faces. I started to close the door, but stopped out of reflex when my husband tried to stick his hand in to stop me. His fingers were frozen at the threshold. He looked like a mime trapped by an invisible wall.

Huh. Guess the CDC was right when they said the monsters hunted at night and couldn't come in unless invited. Even if they were former owners, they lost legal ownership once they died so they couldn't cross the threshold uninvited. I wasn't really sure why legalities would matter to a monster, but it did add a ring of truth to the government's claims the monsters were actually humans on some new illegal drug, hallucinating and becoming violent when they think they've been turned into zombies, vampires, werewolves... and I think the latest was a Yeti. They called it Draino because when you used it, you and everything around you gets sucked down the drain.

Most of mainstream America bought into the government's spin of a new drug on the scene, but I wasn't fooled. Knowing this didn't really help me with the problem on my doorstep though.

"Sara, baby, please? Let me in. I love you. Nothing happened,

I swear. She didn't mean anything to me." He was pathetic in his rumpled, blood-stained suit. He still wore that stupid skinny tie that made him look like a wanna-be hipster. The fingernail scratches on his cheek hadn't been there when he'd left the house. God, there was lipstick on his collar. Even as a vampire the bastard couldn't put me first. He'd already fed off someone else. I hoped it was the bitch he went off to meet.

"Fuck you, you unfaithful prick. I bent over backwards to make you happy. No more! At least I won't have to file for divorce since you're all vamped out. I'll save a shitload of money in lawyer's fees."

Speaking of bending over, a pink VW Bug with daisy hubcaps pulled into my driveway. There were flowers and butterfly stickers all over the hood and a familiar blonde behind the wheel. She damn near hit the horse, who looked to be on his last legs anyway.

She screamed before she unfolded her long, thin legs out of the car. "I knew it. You stood me up, for her. How could you do this to me?" I couldn't decide if it was more a whine or wail. Either way she didn't sound happy. Not that I really cared. She had been screwing my husband, after all. Who knew a man's taste could vary so much? We were polar opposites. She was tall, thin and could only be described as cute. Almost perky. I'd hated her from the first day I'd met her, ten years ago in his office.

I saw the moment when the Pale Rider realized what was happening. He looked at her, then at David, and finally to me. "Three women? He must have been quite the Lothario."

Lothario, cheating bastard. To-may-to To-mah-to.

*Wait, did he say three?* I shoved that tidbit to the back of my mind.

"He loves me. We're soulmates. He's leaving you. We're going to be together for eternity, bitch." Mandi-with-an-i still hadn't figured out something was amiss in her little fairytale life. This might be fun to watch.

The Rider turned from me and looked at my husband. It was

as if the Horseman reached out and gave him a little shove. David turned to Mandi and I realized I had to warn the little ditz. "Mandi, get back in your car and drive away. He's a vampire. He'll hurt you."

She actually stuck a hand in the air and shook her head back and forth before she said, "Talk to the hand, 'cause the head ain't listening. He told me about you. You're the only vampire here. You're always nagging him and sucking the life from him and spending his money. He would be successful if it wasn't for you ruining his life. The only one who sucks around here is you."

My mouth opened, but no words could form. Me? Sucking the life from him? Was she kidding? My salary paid the bills. He had never held a steady job throughout our relationship. If it hadn't been for my working my ass off to pay the mortgage, he wouldn't have been able to go to school and get that insurance sales job where he had met the little home wrecker.

So, yeah, I would like to think it was shock and hurt that stopped me from warning her again, but I have to admit a small part of me wanted that bitch to get what she really wanted: Him. He walked over to her... no wait... yuck, he glided, like some cheesy vampire in a B movie.

She squeaked "Baby!" before she threw her arms wide open for him, but then jerked away in horror when she saw his fangs.

I didn't want to save the traitorous bitch who'd slept with my husband. Sure I felt bad for her, just not bad enough to risk my neck, no pun intended. I mean, I had tried to warn her about him. She was the one committing adultery with David.

But did she deserve to die for her sins? My conscience nagged at me.

David yanked her to him. Her arms flailed uselessly. She screamed but was unable to stop him. He sank his teeth into her neck.

Damn it. Her little whimpers were too much. I had to do something.

I looked around for a weapon and my eyes settled on the iron cross on the wall. We had bought it more as an art piece than for religious reasons; it went really well with the rustic decor of the room. I ripped it off the wall and held it up in front of me before I stepped out the door.

"Get off her, asshole." I tried to keep from turning my back on the Horseman who hadn't strayed far from my door, but I needed to get closer to save the little idiot. To my surprise, when I turned the cross in his direction, the Horseman disappeared and ended up back on his horse.

I swung the cross back towards my husband and he looked up and hissed at me. The man was a walking, breathing (okay, not so much anymore) punch line. Mandi's body made a surprisingly loud thud on the driveway for such a little thing. Silicone must be heavier than I thought. Her whimpering let me know she was still alive.

"Mandi, get up. Put your shirt on your neck and apply pressure to stop the bleeding. Do it, now."

Kneeling down, I reached out for Mandi with my left hand while the right held the cross up high. I didn't dare take my eyes off my husband or the Horseman who now looked almost bored at the end of my driveway. Hopefully, she had listened to me and wasn't bleeding out all over the place.

Miraculously, she was still alive and able to stand. She clung to my hand like we were besties out for a day of shopping, and we backed toward the house.

"I thought he loved me," Mandi said with a pathetic whimper.

"Yeah, join the club. Now shut the hell up and get into the house." I yanked her hand, and we stumbled up the steps.

"You can't escape me. I will be back for you. You are mine. Our love is eternal." The man tried, he really did try to be threatening, but in his disheveled, stinky and clichéd shape, he just wasn't.

"You talking to me or to her? Cause you know, your eternal love seems to be going around." I was so on with the snappy comebacks tonight. Usually the snarky replies came to me hours too late. I felt for the doorknob behind me and shoved Mandi through the door, nearly tripping over her in my haste to get inside.

Mandi yelled, "You used me, you bastard. I hate you! Stay the hell away from me. I hope the sun comes up and fries you in your sleep."

Whoa. Mandi had a mean streak. Who knew the little blonde had it in her?

"No need to wait for the sun. He's useless to me since neither of you would succumb to him now. One out of three." He ruefully shook his head. "Usually I collect all, but I'll see you again. Time to face Hades, David." The horse reared up and a burst of flame flew from the Horseman's hand toward my now screaming husband.

He was on fire. Song lyrics popped into my head, one of those old disco songs from the seventies: *burn that mother down* was all I could think while I watched the unfaithful bastard I married turn to ash.

# CHAPTER TWO

*The End of the World as You Know it*

"We have no reports of vampire attacks in this area, ma'am."

Ma'am? I was only thirty-seven. Wasn't it illegal to call someone under fifty ma'am? That had to be police brutality. Okay, I shouldn't antagonize the police, but after the night I'd had, I was done. "Well you do now, officer." I had forgotten the name of this police officer who didn't look old enough to drink yet.

"So, you're saying your husband, David Reynolds, was a vampire who tried to attack you last night, and he burst into flames, but not before attacking a Miss Mandi Dumas."

Dumas? More like Dumb Ass. Oh well, at least he didn't call me ma'am that time. We were making progress. Cop number two, who I think had said his last name was Espinoza, turned away from snooping through the piles of magazines and mail on the table by the door to add his two cents.

"So what you're saying is you saved her when she was sleeping with your husband?" No ma'am or nicely pressed uniform from this guy. He didn't even have on a belt, and there was a half-moon of a coffee stain on his knee that was a little darker than the color of his skin. It looked like he had missed a few spots while shaving, but his dark, curly hair was cut with military precision.

"Well, she wasn't screwing him at that moment so technically I didn't save her *when* she was screwing him." The cop snorted and tipped an imaginary hat to me. Hmmm, a man who appreciated grammar jokes. Very nice.

"Just because she shares my shitty taste in men doesn't mean she should die for it. It's not like she wasn't awake and talking when the paramedics got here. Ask them. Ask her." I rubbed my arm where Mandi had gripped so tight it took both paramedics to pry her hands off me. She'd been a hysterical mess. They had to give her a sedative just to get her outside so they could load her into the ambulance.

"These are just routine questions. We need to establish the exact chain of events. We've only had a few reports of monster attacks in town, most turning out to be false alarms. We're not like the big cities. Our crimes are the standard ones. Nothing like this, not even in Phoenix, ma'am." Great, the pup was back at it again.

Officer Espinoza covered a yawn. There was a flash of bright yellow on his wrist when he glanced at his watch before he blew out a breath. "And, most of those are probably BS too. Vampires, zombies, they sure makes a convenient excuse to kill someone. Most people would have a heart attack if they came face to face with one of 'em for real. They sure as heck wouldn't be able to survive an attack. Homicide is homicide." He blew out an impatient breath and continued. "So you save the girlfriend and your husband bursts into flames, even though sunrise is still hours away? Did he stumble into a campfire or something?"

A button was missing on his shirt. I glanced up at his dark eyes, framed by impossibly long eyelashes. They seemed to catalogue my every twitch, so I tried to look innocent.

Here was where things got tricky. Lying to the police was probably illegal. However, by the skeptical looks they gave me when I said David was a vampire, and their repeated questioning about it, mentioning a mythical being on a horse would have been too much for them to handle. No way they'd believe me, especially since Mandi hadn't seen him at all.

"I don't know what happened to him. Maybe he tried to light a cigar or something and set himself on fire. He wasn't the brightest guy, no pun intended. Maybe Buffy found him. I was kind of busy trying to save my life, and the slut."

Okay, I probably shouldn't have called her a slut and maybe I was a wee bit snarky, but it was late and the wine I had indulged in after reading that text was giving me a monster headache. The adrenaline surge that had helped me through my night of hell had long since passed. My husband was dead. I should have been upset, but all I felt now was numb. I was probably in shock.

"It's not like we can tell that pile of ash is your husband, could be from your barbeque grill and you dumped his wallet, wedding ring and keys on top. Maybe you caught your old man with blondie, then you killed him and hid him somewhere, and only called us so you could file the life insurance claim."

Before I could answer, he continued. "Yeah, but why leave a witness alive, especially if you caught her with your husband?" He rubbed his hand across patches of unshaved chin and along the back of his head absentmindedly.

I wasn't sure if he was asking me a question or if he was just thinking out loud. So I asked, "Can't you test his ashes to check his DNA or something?"

Officer Espinoza laughed. "Yeah, right. We'll have the crime lab analyze it right away. Even if they could get DNA from some ashes, do you have any idea how much those tests cost? The guy was just some insurance salesman, screwing around on his wife. No offense."

The young cop looked scandalized by what the older officer had said and cut him off. "Usually the first suspect is the spouse in cases when the man has, uh, indiscretions."

I liked Espinoza's word choice better. Indiscretions was much too civilized a word. It trivialized what that scumbag had done to me. The older cop checked his watch again. I did a double take when I recognized a cartoon character from some show David liked to watch. I expected beat up stainless steel with a stretchy band, not this touch of whimsy.

Officer Espinoza caught me smiling and shoved his sleeve down to cover the pineapple owner's spongy image. His embarrassment softened the hard lines of his face, and I realized he was kind of hot under that crusty exterior.

"Except we got a witness who corroborates her story. We're wasting time here. Dude got what he deserved, if you ask me, unlike my cheating ex who'll probably take me back to court if I'm late taking our daughter to school again. We've got the other vic to talk to and paperwork to file. If we need anything else, we know where to find Mrs. Reynolds. Let's just chalk it up to karma and get out of here."

The young officer hesitated but didn't seem to have the nerve to argue. "We might be back with more questions. The crime scene guys are finished gathering evidence outside. We can send a cleaning crew in later today, but you're responsible for their fee."

He was a pile of ash in the driveway. Like I would pay someone to clean it up. At least the Nazis at the Hillside Homeowners' Association couldn't blame me for a messy yard this time. I shook my head. "I'll hose it down in the morning, thanks."

"Understood, and Mrs. Reynolds, don't leave town."

The older cop rolled his eyes at the rookie's parting line. "Been practicing that one in front of the mirror, huh?"

I grinned while they walked out the door. Always nice to meet another person fluent in Snarkanese.

I deadbolted the door behind them and then double checked that every window and door in the house was locked, again. Though I felt a little foolish, I left a light on in every room. When I walked into the bathroom, I flinched at my reflection. I can't believe I spilled so many tears over that bastard. The red in my bloodshot eyes matched Mandi's dried blood on my sleeve. It clashed horribly with the wine spilled on my collar.

*Oh shit!* I was out of wine. *Will this nightmare never end?*

I washed my face and stripped off my clothes, so tired I didn't even bother crawling under the covers. Ah but sleep, that fickle bitch, would not come to me. I turned to the other side, flipped my pillow around and closed my eyes. The thought I had shoved away crept back in: The Horseman had said there were three.

David had another girlfriend who he had apparently already killed. Once I let that thought in, others clamored to join the noisy crowd in my head.

"Shit. Shit. Shit. Shit. Shit!"

Normally when I couldn't sleep or was stressed, I would bake. I hadn't been grocery shopping, and I was out of milk and eggs. The thought of eating chocolate chips straight out of the bag flashed through my mind. No, not going to allow David the satisfaction of me leaving me alone and fat. Mandi was a skinny little thing. I bet his other girl was thin too.

I sat up and turned on the TV, to try to ignore the flash of glee I had at the thought of one of his girlfriends dying. It was wrong to want her dead, even for a second. I was a horrible human being. My fingers flipped through channels faster than I could register. There wasn't much on at that late hour. I paused when I saw a man holding a Bible to a young girl's head while she sobbed and begged for forgiveness for her sins. I changed the channel to a reality show about garbage men. What the hell. Better than the televangelists. At least these guys were upfront about the garbage they dealt in.

I knew exactly how that young girl felt. When I was fourteen my parents died in a car accident. I had to move across the country to my only kin, my aunt. She dragged me to the front of her church and declared me a sinner in front of the whole congregation.

Every night before bed, she would hold her well-worn Bible open to read me yet another lecture about eternal damnation. I'd had to live with the old witch for three years until I could escape by graduating early and going to college. She said my parents and Rachel, my half-sister from Mom's previous marriage, had been punished because their marriage was a sin. It was her mission to save me. I learned that, if I wanted to keep from being locked up at home the whole time, I'd better know The Book from cover to cover.

Because of that, I would have known who the Rider on the

pale horse was even if I had never seen him drag my parents and sister away from me while I lay trapped in the crumpled metal of the burning SUV. I had thought he had been a hallucination all these years, but I was wrong.

It was Death.

You know, the Fourth Horseman of the Apocalypse. I should have been really freaked out. But really, why? My life had ended years ago, even before David destroyed our marriage. What should I care if Death came for me?

The weird stories on the news made kind of twisted sense now. When the lamb broke the fourth seal, Death was supposed to have the power to kill a quarter of the earth by war, famine, plague, and wild beasts. It seemed like every other night I'd heard about someone going crazy and killing a bunch of people. Officially, it wasn't called a war but lots of people dying seemed like a war to me. Famine sounded an awful lot like the vampires always thirsting for blood. Plague could be the zombies and wild beasts had to be the werewolves.

I'd be happy and patting myself on the back for my cleverness in figuring out what so many others hadn't, except for one thing. If the lamb were breaking seals, it meant the end of the world.

Crap.

My aunt had been right. The world was going to Hell, and apparently I would indeed have front row seats. Where did I put my handbasket?

# CHAPTER THREE

*No Good Deed Goes Unpunished*

My car steered almost instinctively to the nearest drive-thru coffee place as if it sensed my need for a cappuccino with two extra shots of espresso. Sleep-deprivation hangover: all the misery of an alcohol hangover without the night of fun first. After handing me my coffee and a muffin, the guy yanked his hand back as though he were afraid I would bite it off. I must look more desperate than I thought.

I still couldn't believe I was doing this. It seemed like I had just fallen asleep when the phone rang. Eight in the morning and guess who was on the phone? Yes, Mandi, who naturally was a perky morning person. It must have been the lack of sleep and the stress from the night before—or maybe residual effects from the wine I'd gulped after finding it in the back of the pantry—that made me agree to pick her up from the hospital so she could get her car from my house.

Most people would think it was pathetic she didn't have any friends or family who could help her. I wasn't most people. This pot wasn't going to call that kettle black. Apparently, despite our outward appearances, we were more alike than I'd thought.

I had manhandled my hair into a scrunchie, washed my face and brushed my teeth. Wait, did I brush them? I ran my tongue over the fuzzy fronts and grimaced. Oh well, the coffee breath would hide it.

I was stuck taking bunny sips of my coffee because it was still at the molten lava stage. If I slammed it like I wanted, I wouldn't be able to taste anything for the rest of the day. Hmmm, maybe that would help me lose weight. I took a bite out of the muffin and made a face. Mine were so much better, which reminded me that I needed to swing by the store to get some baking supplies. I had a feeling this week was going to be a heavy baking week.

Naturally, there were no parking spaces available at the hospital. I decided to splurge on valet because picking up my dead husband's mistress from the hospital seemed like a good time to treat myself.

My coffee had finally cooled enough to gulp while I waited for the world's slowest elevator to arrive on the third floor. The aroma helped dilute the plastic, burnt coffee, and bad cafeteria hospital smell. I stepped out into the dreary beige hall and found room 302. Mandi sat on her bed while she whipped a mascara wand through her lashes with super speed. If I'd tried to do that, I'd have blinded myself.

"Took you long enough to get here. Wow, you look like crap."

You'd think in a hospital they would have a scalpel handy, maybe some needles or something that could inflict bodily harm. Nope, nothing but hand sanitizer dispensers and a plastic water pitcher. I fantasized about blinding her with the sanitizer, then braining her with the pitcher. I somehow resisted the urge. "Take a cab home for all I care. I don't know why I agreed to this."

She put her hands over her mouth and looked contrite. "Sorry, the painkillers make every thought pop straight out of my mouth before I can stop them."

I bet that was an issue before the drugs. "Whatever. Let's go."

"They won't let me yet. Something about paperwork and doctor's orders. They said it should only be a few more minutes."

A few more minutes in hospital lingo meant at least another twenty. Twenty minutes trapped in a room with her. I wondered if they could give *me* some painkillers.

"The police came by to talk to me. I told them how David…" she paused and touched her bandaged neck, "tried to kill me and that you saved me like a super hero or something. It was amazing."

It was probably the closest I would get to a thank you from her. "Did they say anything about his first victim?" I had avoided thinking about who his first blood donor might have been, even though I had wanted to Google for other victims. I just didn't have the strength to face it.

"First? I thought I was his first!"

Her jealous tone made me smile. *Poor baby. Hurts finding out you're not his one and only, doesn't it?*

I was still trying to be nice for some reason, so I said, "No, there was someone else. He had blood and lipstick on his shirt when he got home. I thought it was yours, until you pulled up. Two girlfriends and a wife, no wonder David was always tired."

Okay, I said I would try to be nice, but come on, I wasn't Superwoman.

"He cheated on me? That bastard. How could he do that to me? He said he loved me." She broke down into hysterical sobs, messing up the makeup she had artfully applied.

You know how some girls are pretty even when they cry? Not Mandi. It made me like her just a teensy bit, but not enough to contain my anger. "Really? You're really going to go there? With me?"

I was spared her response by a nurse who came into the room. One look at Mandi's art deco face and she gave me the stink eye. Wow, did everyone fall for Mandi's helpless girl act?

"What is going on in here? Who are you?" Nurse Ratchet didn't wait for my answer. She turned back to Mandi, handed her some tissues, and said, "Calm down, Miss Dumas. If you raise your blood pressure too high or you tear open your sutures you won't be able to leave. Don't you want to go home?"

She said the magic words, because Mandi's waterworks immediately dried up. With one last sniffle, she said, "Yes, please. I just want to put this nightmare behind me and move on with my life."

Before I could say something snarky, the tyrannical nurse

turned to me and said, "She needs to sign some forms before she can leave. Don't upset her anymore."

I meekly nodded. I'd faced down a vampire husband and Death two times but no way would I mess with that lady. She had access to scary drugs and a license to use them. I gave her my brightest smile and even patted Mandi's hand in a comforting gesture. I must have looked properly cowed, because she bustled out of the room.

"She is so sweet. Just like a mom or something," Mandi said wistfully.

"Mom? If your mother's Mommie Dearest maybe. That lady is scary as hell."

Mandi pulled her hand from mine and reached for her compact. She carefully fixed her face before mumbling, "Better than mine. At least she seems to care."

Damn. I didn't want to feel sorry for Mandi. I shouldn't have to feel anything but disgust for her. I could see the chinks in her armor and they were a little too much like mine for comfort. I didn't want to think about her being alone in the world, just like me.

Get her out of here, get her to her car, and never deal with her again. That's the plan. The nurse arrived just in time to help move things along. I tuned out what the nurse was saying and waited for Mandi to sign the damned paperwork already.

"Do you have any questions about her care?"

I looked at Mandi and waited for her to answer, until I realized the nurse was staring at me. Oh shit. She was talking to me? She didn't think I was planning on taking care of her, did she? "What? I, uh, missed the last part."

"The bandage should be changed after twenty-four hours. I will pack a few dressing kits for you to take. She needs to follow up with her doctor within forty-eight hours. Did you understand all that?" She enunciated every syllable like she was talking to a child.

"Me? I'm just giving her a ride. I never said anything about taking care of her. I don't do bandages."

The nurse gave me a stern look that would put any schoolmarm to shame. "She can't take care of herself. Someone needs to stay with her for the next few days. She lost a lot of blood. If she starts to bleed again she could die."

I wilted under her look. "But I, she...I thought she just needed a ride. It's not like we're friends or anything. I'm just not good with taking care of stuff. I don't even have a goldfish."

Could I sound less like a lunatic? Luckily, Mandi came to my rescue.

"It's okay. She's just nervous. We'll be fine. I'm really good at following instructions." Mandi turned up her thousand-watt smile and nodded her head.

The nurse smiled back. "Fine, sign here and here and then you can leave as long as she signs a form stating she will be driving you home. The hospital doesn't want any liability if you drive while taking these painkillers."

I heard the word 'leave' and didn't dare argue in case she changed her mind. I signed where she said and even pushed Mandi in a wheelchair out to my car. I waited for Florence Nightingale to safely go back into the hospital before I let out a shaky laugh. "Man, I thought she was going to go all Terminator on my ass."

Mandi didn't make a sound and I looked over at her. She looked pale and exhausted. Poor thing looked like she was about to pass out. I decided it wouldn't kill me to get her prescriptions before taking her home to her car.

Mandi fell asleep on the drive home and didn't wake up when I stopped to get her prescriptions. Luckily, the drug store had her insurance information on file. While waiting for it to be filled, I did some shopping.

I drove onto my lawn to detour around her VW bug, which

blocked most of my driveway. The damage to my yard from David's immolation, the crime scene guys, and me trying to pull out of the garage without hitting her car was pretty bad. I doubted the peonies would recover.

"Okay, there's your car. Here are your prescriptions. Take them when you get home so you can drive." I tried for a cheerful tone to try to cover up the fact I was all but booting her ass out of my car and hopefully out of my life for good.

"What? Wait. I can't drive. Remember what the nurse said? Gotta stay here. You agreed on the form."

Form? What form? Surely her groggy ass didn't mean the hospital paperwork? I thought we both understood I was just playing along to get her out. She didn't think I was actually going to take care of her, did she? I took one look at her washed out face and her unfocused eyes and had my answer. What was the old saying? No good deed goes unpunished.

I was going to have a house guest for the day. Yay me.

I let her in the house, and she stumbled upstairs and right into my bedroom. Uh, no. I followed her upstairs.

"Get out of my room. You can stay in the guest bedroom. Here's your pills." I didn't bother getting her something to drink. She could get water from the bathroom faucet if she needed something to wash them down.

As the bedroom door closed I heard the water running. Another pain pill should knock her out for a while. Too wound up to go back to sleep, I headed out to the garage to get the groceries.

Drowning my sorrows in a double chocolate cake seemed like a good idea. I'd made this cake so many times, my body moved on auto pilot. The mixer was running when I heard the doorbell. Dammit, now what?

I shut it off and heard Mandi's caveman like snores from all the way upstairs.

My porch light was set to come on automatically at dusk. I opened the door while I said, "Look, I told you guys everything, why-" I choked on my words at who waited on my doorstep.

Death had come for me. The thought of dying while that bitch slept soundly in my house, really pissed me off. The last few moments of my life would have been spent as chauffeur for the slut who had screwed my husband. That was so fucked up.

I slammed the door shut and screamed, "Go away. I have my cross. I'm calling 911. You're not invited in."

Death snorted like a ten-year-old boy laughing at a fart joke. "You do realize the crucifix is a tool of mine. After all, they killed Jesus on the cross. And the police will not be able to see me, which brings me to the reason for my visit. I want to know how I am visible to you."

"Yeah, well you are still not invited in." I hoped he was like a vampire and couldn't come inside without an invitation.

"Come now, Sara. No need to be afraid. I simply came to talk. I swear no harm will come to you from me today. I give you my word."

Death gave me his word and for some reason I believed him. How absurd was that? I reached for the doorknob before snapping back to my senses. Was I an idiot? "If you just want to talk, then send me a text or an email. You don't need to talk to me in person. Now go away."

Death sighed deeply. "This is getting tiresome. I can enter at any time without your invitation. I grow weary of talking through your door."

"If you're so mighty and powerful then let's see you do it. I bet you're full of it." Okay, I know, taunting Death wasn't the brightest idea, but I hadn't slept more than a few hours last night and was feeling punchy from everything that had happened. I remembered Mandi sleeping upstairs and screamed her name, screamed for help. Bitch owed me. Maybe together we could fight Death off.

"I think she has taken too many medications to be able to hear you right now. Besides, she can't see me. Only you." Death said calmly after appearing in my dark living room. He smiled a perfect Tom Cruise-like smile, all his teeth alabaster white. It upped the creep factor big time.

I'd like to say I faced him bravely like a warrior going into battle. I'd also like to say I'm a size six, but neither of those things were true. I screamed like a little girl, turned and threw open my door.

One foot made it to the first step before I was face to face with Death once again. Backpedaling, I managed to fall on my ass back into the house. I swear that damned horse of his laughed at me in a wheezy breath.

Death reached out a hand to help me up, but I flinched away. Didn't anyone who touched Death die? Was that why he was here? A thought crept into my head. I'd finally get to see my mom and dad again and laugh with Rachel. I wouldn't be alone anymore.

I reached up and grabbed Death's hand.

There should have been a bright light, or a tunnel maybe. Instead I was yanked to my feet by Death's strong grip.

"You might be a little bruised, but it doesn't look like you suffered any major injuries. Do you feel all right?" The concerned look on his face was more fitting for a doctor, rather than the Fourth Rider of the Apocalypse.

"I think I'll live. Though I guess you would know that better than me."

Death gave another hearty laugh. For a guy sent to destroy the world by slaughtering millions, he was pretty jovial.

He stopped laughing, and we awkwardly stood by the doorway. I realized he had changed from the black hooded cloak he wore the first two times I saw him. Tonight he was looking quite dapper in a suit. His freaky eyes were covered with Versace sunglasses. I knew they were Versace because David had a pair just like them.

In fact the whole outfit was the same one David was wearing when he died. Except Death's looked like it was made by Armani himself, whereas David's was a cheaper suit with a designer label slapped on. Death even wore one of those stupid, skinny ties

David tried, and failed, to pull off, whereas Death looked like a model in a magazine.

What did it say about me that I was both attracted and terrified of him at the same time? I wasn't sure if I was supposed to offer him a seat in my living room or if we should remain standing. Was I supposed to offer a drink or maybe a snack? Somehow I doubt even Emily Post would have the answer for this etiquette question.

My aching ass made the decision easy. "Fuck it. Have a seat." I turned on the lights before I perched on the edge of my favorite recliner, too nervous to get comfortable.

"No human should be able to see me. Yet you can. You are human, correct?"

It seemed stupid to be insulted by his question. After all, he had turned my husband into a vampire and tried to kill me just last night. Twenty-three years ago he destroyed my life by taking away my family. Why should I care what he thought of me?

"Yes, I'm human."

Death cocked his head to the side and furrowed his brow. "Do you have the sight?"

I gave him my best, 'what the hell are you on' look.

"You are not a witch?"

I rolled my eyes and sat back in my chair. I had a feeling this might take a while.

"How is this possible? In thousands of years, few mortals have been able to see me, until it is their time."

Their time. Who the hell was he to decide when it was a person's time to die? He may have the power, but what gave him the right to pick and choose? My ears rang from the blood rushing to my head and my vision blurred. Anger and grief made it impossible to stop the words from ripping out of my mouth.

"I saw you. I fucking saw you the night you took my family from me. I lay trapped in that SUV trying to claw my way out so I could be with them. But you left me. You took away my mom, dad, and sister. Rachel was my best friend. You took away my whole fucking life and left me there alone." I choked on a sob.

Death, froze for a moment and stared at me intently while I tried to stop crying.

"I remember now. A car accident. The others were killed instantly, but not you. I was supposed to acquire you too, but your families' pleas to let you live distracted me. I hesitated and in that moment another stepped in to save you. The scale had been tipped and I could no longer collect you."

It was too much for me to process. They saved my life, but left me to live alone and hollow all these years. My soul would have been happier with theirs.

"And last night with your husband, it was your time again. Yet, you eluded me. Tell me, how did you know about his transgressions?"

"Text message from Mandi on his phone." Exhaustion and sorrow made my voice sound robotic. Maybe if I answered all his questions, he would finally go. I could crawl into bed, steal some of Mandi's pills and hope for oblivion for a little while.

"Without that knowledge, you would have welcomed him back."

He was right, though I hated to admit it. Even though our marriage wasn't ideal, David was all I had in the world. I probably would have let him in if it wasn't for Mandi. Weird how pride and anger had saved my life.

"I don't often lose someone once, much less twice. There must be more at work here than I know."

Though I couldn't see his eyes, I could feel his eyes inspecting me. I felt like a slide under a microscope. "Are we done? I have a cake to finish. If you aren't here to kill me, I want you out of my house."

Death stood and brushed imaginary lint off of his black pants. "My apologies. I shall let you finish your dessert. Though, perhaps you should rethink cooking in your current state. The kitchen can be a dangerous place when you are tired. You look...what is the saying? Oh yes, you look like me warmed over."

I blinked, and he was gone. His laugh echoed in the room.

"Must have been hard to ride that horse in a dress, though riding in a suit is a bit over the top, don't you think?" It was a lame parting shot.

The horse outside chuffed. I parted the blinds to look out the window. Death was back on his steed. He nodded at me through the glass before he turned and rode down my driveway for the second time.

The blinds snapped back into place with a metal clang. What the hell did he mean the kitchen was a dangerous place? Was it a warning or a threat?

I'd been baking since I was a kid. I could do it in my sleep. Screw Death. I went back into the kitchen and tasted the batter before I re-started the mixer. It needed more chocolate. I used the measuring spoon on the counter to scoop out some cocoa. When I added it to the batter, the spoon got jammed in the beaters. Wrenched from my hand, it flew past my head and knocked over my salt shaker on the table.

What the hell?

Death's warning came back to me. Had he done that? I unplugged the mixer with a pot holder, just in case it tried to electrocute me. I hesitated to use my oven. What if it blew up?

Screw this. It's not like I could spend the rest of my life being afraid of the kitchen.

I poured the batter into a pan and gave it a little shake so it would bake evenly. I slid it into the preheated oven. Easy peasy. When I shut the door, I burned my hand.

"Dammit!" I yelled and slammed the door shut.

"Hey, can you keep it down and turn off some of the lights in the hallway? It hurts my eyes, and I really need to rest," Mandi yelled from upstairs.

Unbelievable. All my screaming and now she wakes up? Morning and her exit from my life forever couldn't come fast enough.

# CHAPTER FOUR

*Money, Money, Money*

Two days. Two whole days this woman had been in my house. The first day hadn't been so bad, because she was mostly unconscious. Yesterday, however, she was awake and whining. Whining about the pain. Whining because her stomach hurt from the antibiotics, which I had to pick up for her. Whining about how she was lactose intolerant and needed organic soy milk.

All her whining had helped keep my mind off Death, but I still regretted not letting my husband finish her off.

Live and learn, I guess. When I broached the subject of her leaving, she would either cry pathetically or pretend to be asleep. Ever since lunch, her ass had been parked on my favorite chair while she watched some show about child beauty pageants. One more day, and then I'd boot her out the door if I had to drag her out by her not-so-blonde roots to do it.

"Oh my God, look at this." I had no idea why Mandi would want to watch that show. Little girls made up to look like middle-aged cougars were just nauseating. I sure as hell wasn't going to subject myself to it.

"No, thanks. I'd rather get a root canal." I turned back to the book I had been unsuccessfully trying to read while I tuned her and the TV out.

"No, Sara, look. They're talking about a vampire attack. I think it's about David's first victim." She turned the volume up, and I set my book down spread open, which had always driven David batty.

`Cordero Roto experienced what might have been its first legitimate vampire attack three nights ago. The Cordero Roto Police Department has refused to confirm or deny a vampire was involved, but an inside source at St John's hospital tells Eye in the Sky news there is one person confirmed dead and another possible victim in critical condition. Police are keeping a round-the-clock watch on the survivor in case the vampire comes back to finish the job.'

"Round the clock watch? On what? Your empty hospital bed? Morons."

"Shhhh! I'm trying to listen." She gasped and pointed at the screen.

"Oh my God, look, that's a picture of me. I look like shit. How could they get my work ID photo?" Mandi covered her mouth in horror.

I grinned.

`The survivor has been identified as Mandi Dumas. Unconfirmed reports claim she may have worked with the unknown assailant.'

"We were more than co-workers. He loved..." She bit off the end of that sentence and gave me a guilty look. "Sorry."

I rolled my eyes and turned back to the screen where a new picture was up of a pretty brunette with blonde highlights. She had a twinkle in her eyes and the kind of smile people automatically returned. The next image was of a body bag being loaded on a stretcher in front of an apartment complex. My chest tightened.

`Twenty-five-year-old Stacy Tiffany moved from Indiana only months before meeting her terrible fate at the hands, or should we say, fangs of her own boyfriend.'

The news station cut to a couple being interviewed by an unseen reporter.

`Stacy was the sweetest girl. She loved to laugh, and she was such a good little cook. We hadn't seen her in a couple of days, and something smelled awful in her apartment. I sent Darren over to check on her, 'cause we had her spare key. I reckon it was that boyfriend of hers who never got out of his car when he picked her up. Something shifty about him. It's just so awful.' The woman shook her head sadly.

The man put his arm around her and nodded his head. `I were the one that found her. She had big ole bite marks on her neck and looked like one of them zombies. But not moving. I about puked right there. Damn shame. She sure did know how to fry a catfish. I hope that bastard pays for what he done. Hey, when are we gonna be on TV? Can I get a copy of this for my momma?'

The footage cut off and the news anchor's face filled the screen with a calculated sadness in her expression. `While there is no official confirmation this was a vampire attack, authorities are urging residents to remain alert and cautious when going out after dark. Experts say holy water and crosses seem to repel vampires but civilians should not try to stake one on their own. Never invite them into your home, even if it is someone you know. Remember, contrary to popular belief, garlic has no effect on vampires. We will have more on this story as it unfolds. This is Selena Martinez from Eye in the Sky news, Cordero Roto.'

Mandi shut off the TV and turned to look at me with a pained expression. I almost fell out of my chair in shock. Genuine emotion about someone else? An empathetic Mandi? It rattled me.

"He was a monster. You know, even before he turned into one of those things. I know you thought I was just some slut, screwing a married man, but he told me he loved me. I had just turned twenty-one when we met. I thought we were soulmates. He said he couldn't get a divorce until after ten years because of money or taxes. Only a monster would do that to someone. Nine years together, but it was all bullshit. He probably told her the exact same thing. I wish I'd never worked at that damn insurance company. God, I'm such an idiot."

She looked so pathetic I almost felt bad for her, but I was spared the need to console my husband's girlfriend by a ringing doorbell. Saved by the bell.

Speaking of the insurance company, who should be on my doorstep but my husband's manager, Dan, along with the VP of Operations at Presidential Insurance. I was shocked. They must have heard what happened and had come over in person to console me. I didn't know they had it in them. They usually seemed so standoffish.

"Steve, Dan, wow, you came all the way out to The Hills to see me." I stepped back ready to invite them in, but hesitated before I could issue the invitation. What if they were vampires? Yeah, it was daylight out, but still. Who knew if sunlight was another false myth like garlic?

"Sara? What are you doing here? The message said this was where we could find..." Dan let his words trail off. He seemed confused to see me. Weird.

"What do you mean? This is my house. Where else would I be?"

"We were supposed to meet— "

"Perhaps we should have this conversation somewhere private?" Steve Michaels, the VP of Operations, cut Dan off as he eased his way inside.

I guess they weren't the undead since they didn't need an invitation to walk through the door. But why was Dan so surprised to see me here? If they didn't come to see me, why were they here?

"Danny, Steve, finally. You would not believe the horrors I have been through." Mandi jumped out of my favorite chair and pulled them both into a hug.

Both men awkwardly returned the hug and took a step away from her. She looked at me and froze.

"Sara, we were all very sorry to hear about your loss. If there is anything you need from us, please don't hesitate to contact me." Steve's smile seemed sincere. Yet why did it feel like he just told me to get lost in my own home?

"So why exactly are you here?"

"We are here to discuss David's life insurance policy. We need to go over beneficiary information and some other items before we can issue payment." Dan answered.

"Wow, you guys are efficient. I didn't even call yet or anything." An alarm rang in the back of my mind, "Wait. Why would the company send out a VP to handle a claim? What's going on?"

Dan and Steve traded weighted looks. Apparently Steve lost out on their ocular tug of war because he cleared his throat, turned to me and said, "The, uh, beneficiary called earlier today to file the claim. As this wasn't a standard policy, the company thought it best if we both handled the matter in person to be sure there weren't any misunderstandings or mistakes."

He directed the next sentence to Dan in a hard voice. "Like not checking personal records for correct addresses."

I felt like I had walked into a pop quiz on the first day of school. My brain was trying to understand, but I didn't get it. "I didn't call you earlier today."

Then it clicked. They were surprised to see me because they hadn't come to see me. They had come to see *her*, the beneficiary who had called while I was out getting her freaking soy milk.

"Perhaps we can go into another room so as not to disturb you any further?" Smooth Steve tried to soothe the murderous-rage monster building inside me.

"No, this is *my* house, and he was *my* fucking husband. That bitch is not his beneficiary. I am. I deserve every penny of that policy."

You could practically hear the steam come out of my ears in the awkward silence.

Dan's voice came out slightly higher in pitch than normal when he said, "But you signed the waiver forgoing your rights to the policy, giving all benefits to Mandi."

Was this some weird joke? I understood every word they were saying but my brain couldn't process it. Why would they think I would ever do that?

Mandi put in her two-cents' worth. "It's *my* money. David wanted me to have it. You didn't even want him to get the policy with the undead clause, but I understood he needed it. How could he sell the policy if he didn't have one himself? It's mine. That million dollars is mine."

She was more alive at that moment than I had seen her look in days.

Undead insurance. The good ole boys at Presidential Insurance had wasted no time trying to capitalize on the monster reports over the past year. They had duped the conspiracy theorists into buying expensive undead insurance in larger cities. Out here in the sticks, people were more practical, and extremely skeptical of monsters. David had told me claims would probably never get paid out because it was so hard to prove someone was undead after they were killed for good and there were rarely any survivors left alive. Which is why we had decided not to get it, or so I thought. "Did she say a million dollars? I thought the company only provided a hundred thousand dollar policy."

"Yes, well, this was a supplemental policy we encourage our employees to purchase in addition to what we provide. You are listed as the beneficiary of the company policy, but waived your rights to the undead insurance."

"I didn't sign a damned thing. If you pay her one cent, I will sue the shit out of your company, so help me God!" I pointed a finger in Dan's face as I threatened him.

The top of Dan's bald head turned red and splotchy. He huffed out. "But you can't threaten us. We have your signature right here on the paperwork, and it's even notarized."

Steve glared daggers at Dan, and I knew why they had sent out the big guns to handle one life insurance claim. They were covering their asses. "Who? Who notarized my signature?"

Dan clenched his jaw like he was afraid I would pry it open to get my answer.

"Let me see it, right now." I didn't recognize my own voice it was so deep with rage.

Dan glanced at Steve who nodded. I noticed Mandi was doing her impersonation of a statue again. Dan reached into his suitcase and pulled out a copy of the form. The flowing signature of my name looked absolutely nothing like mine but looked awfully similar to my husband's. Mandi Dumas with a heart above the i was listed as both the witness and the notary.

Stealing my husband wasn't enough for the bitch. Oh no. She was trying to steal my money, too. Over her dead body.

I looked up at her across the room and felt a savage growl bubble up from my throat. "Get the fuck out of my house. Now."

She stuck out her chin, narrowed her eyes and said, "Not without my money."

My heartbeat pounded in my ears like drummers sending me to war. My eyes settled on the heavy cross still on the ground after it fell of the table. I snatched it up, and lunged for her. "Let's see if you have life insurance, bitch."

# CHAPTER FIVE

*A Deal with the Devil*

A metal cross makes a pretty good weapon, like a sword without the long, pointy tip. Unfortunately, without that extra length I couldn't quite reach Mandi once Dan and Steve jumped between us.

They were pretty strong and surprisingly fast for insurance guys. They must work out at the company gym a lot more than David did. I fought to reach the screaming Mandi, but it was no use. Their hold on me was like iron. The cross fell from my hands with a loud clang. "Fine. Uncle. I give. I'll behave."

Mandi was still screaming and crying. Geez. I hadn't even touched her. "Shut up!" I yelled at her.

Dan jerked in my direction again, but Steve put a restraining hand on his arm. "Dan, perhaps you can calm Ms. Dumas down while I speak with Sara in the other room."

He placed a light hand on my back and guided me out of the room and into the study, then closed the door behind him. I could still hear Mandi's sobs and Dan's soothing voice, but at least the screaming had stopped. Drama Queen.

"I know this is a difficult situation, Sara. Losing someone you love is devastating, even under better circumstances."

"Do you think the fact my husband was a cheating

bastard makes the circumstance of him turning into a vampire and trying to kill me better or worse, Steve? 'Cause I'm not really sure."

The man would make a great politician. He didn't even react to my sarcasm. Instead he gave me a sympathetic smile before he calmly walked to the couch and indicated I should sit beside him.

How nice of him to invite me to sit on my own couch in my own house.

"I understand why you're upset. And I don't wish to upset you further, but you must understand the delicate predicament the company is in. We would like to take care of this matter in the most expedient and reasonable manner possible for all parties involved."

All parties? Was he kidding? No way was he including her in this. "I was his wife. She forged my signature on that waiver and your company allowed it to happen and now you are trying to cover your ass. If you think I am going to let her have one penny of his life insurance, you're dumber than she is."

Steve let out a sigh and sat back in his seat. "I was afraid you would say that. Look, the fact of the matter is, you're right. If this goes to court it would reflect badly on the company."

"And I care because?"

"Although Ms. Dumas didn't follow company procedure, she was apparently paying the premiums for the policy. Unfortunately, that gives her a reasonable claim on his estate. She could tie up your inheritance for years. She would lose, but most of your money will be lost to the probate court costs."

She would do it, too. Mandi might play the dumb

blonde but inside that peanut head was a shrewd brain. I would have to see her over and over again in lawyers' offices and courtrooms while attorneys burned a hole through my settlement. David was probably laughing his ass off in Hell right now. Bastard.

"Besides, without a body it will take some time and effort to procure a death certificate. The reason these policies pay out so much is because meeting the criteria to claim them is quite difficult. We have yet to pay out a single claim."

I blinked back the tears that filled my eyes, which always happened when I am really angry. I couldn't believe that bitch was going to make money off of this. Steve placed a hand over the fists I hadn't realized I'd formed.

"Honestly, if I had my way, we wouldn't pay her anything and file formal charges against her for fraud. But you would be the one who would suffer the most from such an action. Quite frankly, you've suffered enough being married to that sleaze ball."

Wow, Steve actually showed real emotion. I wasn't sure if he was outraged on my behalf or the company's, but it made me feel a little better that he hated the thought of her getting paid for this, too.

"So what's the plan? I know the second you saw me open the door instead of her you started making plans for a deal. Spill it."

Steve pulled his hands from mine and brushed imaginary lint off his suit. "As an insurance company, we are heavily regulated by the State Department of Insurance. We are also a publicly traded company, so our financial reports are subject to meticulous audits. Therefore the most we can pay on this policy is the one million dollar amount. I propose we divide it up between you both, five hundred thousand each. The company provided policy amount would all go to you. We will waive the need to have the death certificate before payment as long as it is provided before the end of the year so it can be added to the file before audits. There would be a standard non-disclosure settlement agreement both of you would have to sign, and a waiver against any future claims, of course."

Half a million dollars. She screwed my husband, forged my signature, and had left me to fend off Death while she slept nice and cozy in my guest bed. And *she* was going to make half a million? Hell no. I glared my answer.

"Perhaps two hundred-fifty thousand for her? If you both agree we can have a check in your hands in a few days. You would never have to see her again."

I felt something break inside me. It was all too much. David was all I had in the world. I didn't have any close friends. My aunt was the only family I had left. I had walked away from her when I turned seventeen. The emotional roller coaster I'd been riding the last few days had sucked the fight out of me. I just wanted to crawl into a ball and hide from my nightmare life. "Fine, do it."

Steve didn't move for a minute, and then he gently patted my shoulder before he stood up. He walked to the door and opened it. He left the door open behind him so I could hear everything that was being said in the other room. After he cleared his throat he said, "Ms. Dumas, I have spoken with Sara and we have reached an agreement on the policy division."

"Division? That money is mine, all mine. David wanted it that way. And you know you have to pay me that money. I'm listed as the beneficiary. Don't make me file a complaint with the Board, Steve." Gone was the soft kittenish tone from before. Now there was steel in her voice.

"Now, Mandi. I know you are upset. You've suffered a huge loss, but you must be reasonable." Dan's syrupy voice made me want to puke.

"I don't have to be reasonable, do I, Steve?" She sneered his name. "You know I'm right. I'll get what I'm owed. Won't I?"

I bet she wouldn't be voted Miss Congeniality at the company picnic this year. And I wasn't the only one pissed at her attitude.

"You'll get what you're owed, Ms. Dumas. However, since you obviously forged Sara's signature to commit insurance fraud, don't expect to be paid the full amount of the policy. As I stated, Sara and I have negotiated an agreement. We will pay you," he paused for a few seconds before continuing, "one-hundred-fifty thousand dollars. The balance of the policy will be paid to her. You will sign an agreement accepting this settlement in lieu of any other payment or claim you have on his estate. If you do not accept this offer, it will be our fiduciary responsibility to press fraud charges against you and also contact the state to have your insurance license revoked."

I did a double take. Did he say one hundred-fifty thousand? Guess she pushed Steve into playing hardball. Her pissy attitude cost her one hundred thousand dollars, or if she didn't take the settlement, could end with her wearing an orange jumpsuit.

I heard her gasp, and she said in a little voice, "But I didn't know. David told me she had signed it. I swear I didn't do anything wrong. You have to believe me."

I couldn't stand to listen to another word from her. Who

cared if she took me to court or not? I was throwing her ass out the door.

"You didn't do anything wrong? Are you kidding me? Take the money like a good little whore and get the fuck out of my life. Now! Or so help me God I will make David's attack seem like a walk in the park."

This time Steve and Dan didn't make a move to block me. I stalked toward her, ready to beat out all the pain, fear and anger I had repressed deep inside myself the last few days on her pretty little blonde head.

Her survival instincts must have kicked in because she held up her hands in the air and said, "Fine. I will take the hundred-fifty K."

Steve stepped in front of her, blocking her from my view and held his hand out to me. I shook it without thinking. "Good, then the matter is all settled. I will have the lawyers draw up the contracts in the morning. Dan, why don't you escort Ms. Dumas out while I say goodbye to Sara."

Mandi must have gathered her medicine and other things while I was at the store. She was smart enough not to say goodbye when she walked past me to grab her things. Dan put a protective arm around her shoulder. Thank God I would never have to see her again.

"Oh, and Ms. Dumas," Steve said, "You are terminated as of today. You can pick up your final paycheck and your personal items tomorrow. I suggest you don't try to use our company as a reference."

Her face screwed up like a toddler that had her sucker taken away. Before she could let loose with a wail, Dan pulled her out the door.

Steve turned to me and smiled. "I'm truly sorry for your loss. If there is anything else you need, please feel free to call me directly." He turned and walked out the door behind them.

I locked the door and then leaned my forehead against it. I know I should have been jumping for joy because I was going to be an almost millionaire, but what really made me happy was the thought of finally being alone after days of enduring Mandi's company. A shaky laugh escaped my chest. Finally, some peace and quiet.

# CHAPTER SIX

*The Devil's in the Details*

The problem with being home alone with your thoughts for the first time after a shitload of drama is it gives you too much time to think. Thoughts run around in your head making you crazy. I knew the fact that David cheated on me was minor compared to the other shit that happened, but it really bugged me.

I never thought I would be the type of woman who was completely clueless about her husband's lies. What else had he been keeping from me? Mandi flashed into my head with her expensive clothes and organic demands. No way could he have kept a woman like that happy on the small discretionary amount we put aside for incidentals.

At first, I was calm while I looked through the files in the study. Nothing. I moved on to the garage, David's other domain. Nothing. I went upstairs and started going through his drawers. Calm had left the building. I dumped the contents on the floor and even turned the drawers upside down to see if anything was taped underneath them. My bedroom looked like a tornado had blown through it and had only touched down on David's stuff, and I still had nothing.

Then I remembered his phone. It had revealed one lie, wonder what other secrets it held? I raced downstairs to the kitchen to get his phone that I'd left charging out of habit. I scrolled through his messages and saw some from a bank we didn't use. There were texts notifying him of charges and large cash withdrawals. It was like a connect-the-dots puzzle to his affairs. Dinner at a nice restaurant on a night I'd had to work late. Expensive lunches. Hotel charges. I noticed three charges to a jewelry store for the same amount on my birthday. He must have bought the other two the same ugly pearl bracelet he'd bought me. Asshole. No wonder the clerks had looked at me weird when I went to return it. There were thousands of dollars worth of charges listed. Holy shit. How much did he owe?

I checked his email on his phone and found a few other statements from other cards. One was even in my name! Son of a bitch had forged my signature on more than just the life insurance policy. It looked like he had gotten cash advances from one card to pay the others and just kept going around and around every month to hide it from me.

We never would have been able to pay these off. What a fool I had been to think we only had a little debt from student loans and his car. I wished he were alive so I could kill him again. Thank God I would be getting life insurance or else I would have had to file bankruptcy. What a dickweed.

Crawling into a wine bottle sounded like a good plan. I'd replenished my stock on one of my shopping trips for Mandi. I grabbed a bottle and a corkscrew and didn't bother with a glass. I stumbled out of the kitchen still clutching his phone and sat on my recliner to finish the bottle. When it was empty, I threw it at the fireplace and enjoyed the destruction so much that I tossed his cellphone after it.

*Someone was screaming at me.*

No. Something. I fumbled with my left hand for my alarm clock, but all I got was air.

I cracked an eyeball and realized I was on my couch in the living room. The caterwauling continued and I looked at David's smashed phone in confusion.

My brain finally kicked in, and I realized the ringing came from my phone on the coffee table. Who could possibly be calling me before seven in the morning, and why did they hate me?

"What?" I tried to growl it but my parched, tired voice sounded more like Rip Van Winkle than Rip Your Head Off.

"Sara! Oh, thank goodness you're up. So sorry to bother you. I know you're taking a little break, but we have some questions about the P&L report for the RBA account."

Only Colleen, my boss, could make it sound like taking a few days off after the death of my husband was me milking sick days. Yes, how irresponsible of me to get attacked and widowed at month end. Senior accountants are supposed to know better.

"What? The RBA account?"

She took my mumbled questions as a sign to continue. "Yes. We need to close their books ASAP. You know their fiscal year end is this month. We don't have time to waste. Given the urgency of the situation, perhaps you can come in to work on it this afternoon?"

"This afternoon? But I am on bereavement leave."

She sighed like she was dealing with a difficult child. "Yes, but today will be the fifth day. You know the handbook only gives five paid days off. If you take more, they are unpaid and frowned upon. Quite frankly, it's somewhat irresponsible to expect your co-workers to pick up your slack, especially during this time of year."

I had always known she was a tool. She had called me the morning after my wedding to ask about an account and then had expected me to postpone my honeymoon until after month end, which I did. I had even delayed gall bladder surgery until after the books were closed, though it meant I could only drink broth for days because I was so sick. David had encouraged it because we needed the money for the down payment on this stupid house.

"David just died on Friday. You don't count Saturday and Sunday toward bereavement leave. Only business days. I'll be back next Monday."

"Monday? But you missed Friday. That makes today the fifth business day. Surely you don't plan on taking more than five days?"

Her voice got that sickening 'I'm your best pal' tone that made me want to grind my teeth when she said, "Sara, honey, I know you've had a bad time. But you have to think about your career now. You don't want to lose your job along with everything else. You need the paycheck and the benefits. I'll tell you what. I'll have George look at the bank rec and see if he can figure out why the balance sheet doesn't balance. You go ahead and take Friday off too. I understand how hard it can be, we're not heartless after all. Take the extra day, but we have mandatory OT on Saturday starting at 10:00 AM. You come on in and I'll even bring you a donut."

A donut? Really? The woman just offered to quell my grief over losing my husband with a baked good. It would probably be glazed too, not even jelly filled.

She didn't wait for my response. She was used to me caving in and taking one for the team. "Great, we'll see you then. Rest up and we'll see you on Saturday. Oh, but don't stray far from your phone in case George can't figure this out. Thanks, Sara."

I knew as soon as she hung up she'd told George she was graciously letting me take Friday off. I hated that job.

The phone made a satisfying crunch as it crashed against the wall and landed beside David's. I turned over to go back to sleep but was too angry to get comfortable.

I had been working as an accountant at that job for ten miserable years, ever since David got the job at Presidential and was transferred out here to Arizona. My co-workers were self-centered jerks who expected me to pick up the slack for them because they all had busy lives with kids and family. As if I didn't have a life of my own.

Could I blame them for thinking that? I was a thirty-seven-year-old widow who even, if he were still alive, couldn't keep her husband happy enough to be faithful. Tears turned the couch cushion damp while I thought about how pathetic my life had become. I had worked too hard to be the perfect wife for David, I hadn't had time to do anything for myself or even make my own friends.

I should quit. I had the money now. Last night's discovery seeped through my wine-addled brain. Except I had no idea how much money David owed. It could eat away a large amount of his life insurance and then I still had the mortgage and his car to pay off.

Can't quit my job, because I had to pay for a house that I

had never wanted in the first place. I wanted to live downtown in those cute condos not too far from my job. But no, they weren't nice enough for David. We had to buy a house out in the sticks so David could tell everyone we lived in the town's only gated community, The Hills. I had a longer commute to the job I was stuck in because my salary had to pay the bills.

My co-workers were right. I didn't have much of a life at all.

The emotions I had sealed off since I was fourteen flooded out of me in a waterfall of tears. I cried for my family. I cried for my broken marriage. Most of all, I cried for that little girl who should have died that one awful night so long ago.

I must have dozed off because I woke up in the late afternoon. My head pounded. My eyes burned, but I felt lighter than I had in years. And hungry. Bears probably felt like this when they woke from hibernation.

A search of my kitchen turned up fruitless, literally. My options were limited to condiment soup or a questionable meat item in the freezer. Was it a rib or a chicken breast? The ice crystals hid the answer.

If we lived closer to town I could order a pizza, but no one would deliver all the way out here. I was going to have to venture out of the house if I didn't want my stomach to cannibalize itself.

If you ever tell yourself it was okay not to wear a bra, change out of your raggedy pajamas, or even wash your face, because no one except the kid at the drive-thru window would ever know, don't listen.

I was halfway down my driveway before I noticed the crowd of people in front of my house. What the hell was going on? Had the homeowners' association formed a lynch mob to force me to fix my landscaping?

No, they were reporters, and cameramen with lots and lots of cameras, running up my driveway to snap pictures of me in my unwashed glory.

Where was Death when I needed him?

# CHAPTER SEVEN

*Every Dog Has His Day*

My tires screeched and left black skid marks on the driveway when I slammed on my brakes. Several voices screamed my name. Microphones and cameras were jammed into my open car window. I fumbled with the button to roll it up. Damned thing moved in slow motion while the sharks jockeyed for the best position.

Thankfully my garage door was still open or I would have plowed right through it in my rush to get away. I put the car in drive and sped forward, hopefully crippling some of those bastards as they dived out of the way. Once inside, I hit the button on the remote and hid in my car while I waited for the garage door to meet the concrete.

Of course, it couldn't be that easy. One of them stuck his leg in front of the sensor when there was still two feet left and the door bounced back up. Dammit. Stupid safety sensors. It would have been so cool to see the asshole's leg squished under the garage door.

I stepped out of the car and looked around for something I could use to get rid of them, and my eye fell on the weed killer. Perfect. I channeled my inner curmudgeon and yelled, "Get off my lawn!"

Making my meanest face, I grabbed the weed spray and

ran toward the nearest reporter. You know what's not a good idea? Spraying poison and then running through it. My eyes teared up and I choked on the fumes. I pulled the collar of my shirt up to block my mouth and waved the nozzle in their direction. The crazed lunatic act must have worked, because I was able to close the garage door while they scurried down my driveway.

How had they found me? How had they gotten past the gate without a code?

More importantly, how was I going to get food?

The police. I should call the police. This subdivision was private property and only residents and their guests were allowed.

I dropped the weed killer and ran inside to call for help. Before I could make that call, I heard a siren out front.

*Woohoo, the cavalry is here!* One of the neighbors must have already complained. For once I was grateful for those nosy busybodies.

I washed my hands and my face in the kitchen sink to try to get rid of all the weed spray and waited until I heard the sounds of the news vans driving away before I risked a peek out the window. Standing at the end of my driveway, looking fierce was a familiar person. Cop Number Two from the night David died scowled at the last retreating reporter.

No cameras were in sight, so I poked my head out the front door and yelled, "Are they all gone?"

The cop ambled up my driveway and nodded. "Yeah, cleared the last of the blood suckers out of here. You okay, Mrs. Reynolds?"

"Call me Sara. Officer... Sorry, I forgot your name. I'm really bad with names."

"Espinoza. Mateo Espinoza. I hoped the gate would've

kept them out long enough for me to get here first, but they got in somehow. Probably some idiot hoping to be on TV let them in." He rubbed his chin like he had the first night I met him. Today it was clean shaven though. I missed the stubble.

"How did you know they would be here?"

He blew out his breath and stopped trying to rub a hole through his chin. "Guess you haven't seen the news. The chief couldn't put the buzzards off any longer. He released your husband's name. I knew it wouldn't take them long to hunt you down. I tried calling but kept getting your voicemail. Figured I better get out here and warn you before you walked into a shitstorm. Guess I was late."

I should have realized they would find me eventually. A vampire attack with survivors was news, even in the big cities. Here it was probably the biggest news story in a decade. Hell, probably a lot longer than that. Cordero Roto wasn't a huge metropolis, but it was big enough I'd hoped to hide out in suburbia without drawing attention to myself. There's a word for that: delusional.

"I'll never be able to get my pizza in peace now. I'm so hungry," I said mournfully. Maybe it was my broken spirit, my tear-swollen eyes or possibly my mismatched pajamas that reeked of weed spray, but I must have looked pathetic enough that he felt sorry for me.

He sighed and said, "I should probably stick around in case those parasites try to come back in again. Food would be good though. I'll get the pizza; you get the drinks. You got something other than that diet stuff?"

"Negative, Officer Espinoza. The only straight stuff I have is booze, but I do have some ice cream hidden in the freezer."

"Stay inside until I get back. Shouldn't take me too long,

I'll use the siren." He gave me a mischievous grin that would have been right at home on the face of any twelve-year-old boy doing something he knew he would get busted for but was going to do it anyway. He headed back down to his car.

I waited until he sat behind the wheel before closing the door and running upstairs to change and shower off the poison before my hair started to fall out.

When I eventually got back downstairs there was a noise out front. He must have blown through every stoplight and taken someone else's pie to get back that quickly. Just to be safe, I peeked out the window to make sure it wasn't one of the reporters sneaking back. The sun had set while I was upstairs. I flicked on the front porch light. The street was empty. Considering everything I had been through the last few days, it was no wonder I would hear mysterious noises.

I chalked it up to my imagination, until I heard it again. This time it sounded like whimpering and scratching by the front door. I cracked it in case there was a wild animal outside and saw a little brown bundle of fur, feet and ears. The puppy tripped over his long ears and a little blue bow fell off. He gave the bow a ferocious yip and then stumbled over his oversized feet to run away from it. The little fluff ball was the most adorable thing I had ever seen. What the heck was he doing out here by himself? The coyotes would eat him for sure.

"No, come back here, little puppy. Here, boy." I whistled and patted my legs but the puppy ignored me and ran around my front yard chasing imaginary butterflies. I went to go pick him up. He wagged his tail, but then ran away from me down my driveway. He stopped and barked as though he wanted me to play.

"Stupid dog. Come back here before something bigger

comes to eat you. I won't hurt you. Come on." He sniffed with his nose in the air and took off at full speed down the street.

For a little guy, he sure was fast. I followed him and made it to the end of my driveway before I heard the growl from the bushes across the street. Oh shit. A coyote must have been tracking the poor little guy already. I ran to save him.

The puppy's whine from the other side of the dark street made my feet pump even faster. The overgrown bushes on the sidewalk surrounding the subdivision sign scratched my arm when I ran past. Not for the first time, I cursed the idiot who put this giant blind spot right beside my driveway. It made backing out a game of chance.

A dark SUV with its driver-side window rolled down was parked illegally on the corner. There were a bunch of cigarettes littered on the ground outside the door. I had just cleared the bumper when I saw it.

Across the street, where I'd last heard the puppy, was a monster I'd seen only in horror movies. Standing on all fours, he was about chest height, big as an ox, and covered in brownish-black hair. When I skidded to a stop, he turned to face me and stood on his hind legs, like a man, dwarfing me by several feet.

*Get in the car! Get in the car! Go! Go! Go!* were the only thoughts that screamed in my brain. I knew I wouldn't have time to get away if I tried the door and found it locked. I ran at the SUV as fast as I could and dived through the open window, screaming the entire time.

Stars filled my vision when my nose smashed into the steering wheel. A salty, metallic taste hit my mouth when blood exploded out of my nostrils. I jerked my legs through the window just when something huge slammed into the side of the vehicle and lifted it up on two wheels.

Tears streamed down my face when I collided with the passenger door. A glance at the keyless ignition told me I was screwed. I couldn't even roll up the window. I scrambled into the back seat as far away from the werewolf as possible, while he tried to claw his way into the SUV. Thank God he was too big to fit through the window.

Where the hell were my neighbors? Fuckers complained if I dared to play the radio too loud in my own backyard, but they turned a deaf ear to this? Cowards probably didn't want to risk their precious necks for someone like me. That didn't stop me from screaming for help anyway while the werewolf tried to force his way inside.

His black-clawed hands shredded the leather seats like they were made from rice paper and his frustrated growls echoed through what might turn out to be my metal coffin. Warm slobber splattered all over the windshield, some landed on my cheek.

I used my shirt to wipe it away and noticed my shirt turning red. Oh, God, was he drooling blood? I looked at the window and expected it to be crimson. No, it was my blood. For some reason, that made me feel better.

The werewolf had moved from the open window to the back door and was throwing himself at the glass. It broke on the second attempt and I plastered myself against the opposite door to stay out of his reach. I looked around for a weapon, something, anything I could use to defend myself. All I found were empty chip wrappers and soda bottles along with an empty camera bag.

I threw the bag at him and the werewolf shredded it with one swipe. Cotton from the lining flew right into his snout and he sneezed. He yanked his head out and sneezed again.

He loped around the back of the car and rubbed his nose in the grass by the passenger side before he noticed me gaping at him. I scrambled over to the door with the shattered window when he lunged.

The suspension on the SUV screeched in protest while he scrambled to fit into the now empty window frame. No luck. He was too big to fit through the side windows. Was he smart enough to try the windshield?

*Oh God, please don't let him try it.*

I needed to distract him before he made it to the front. I grabbed the debris in the car and threw it at his head. A soda bottle hit him right in the eye, and he went nuts. He gave a deafening howl, and then shoved his head through the window. His hair ripped in several places from the broken edges of the frame. Blood matted the remaining hair. My teeth chattered with terror.

The putrid smell of his warm breath filled the car as he panted heavily while he tried to shove his shoulders through the hole. I could hear the sockets pop as his arms were forced out of joint. He howled again, but he didn't stop.

I opened the opposite door and tumbled to the ground. The werewolf frantically thrashed back and forth as though half of his body wanted to go farther into the car and the other wanted out.

*Get up and run!* my brain screamed at me, but I was paralyzed.

The werewolf stopped his inner war and started working on getting his head and shoulders back out through the door. With me back on the street, I would be easy prey. My timing had to be perfect. He needed to get almost out of the window, but not free of the car before I got back in and closed the door.

*Wait for it.*

His right shoulder crunched back through the frame.

*Wait for it.*

His left followed without as much damage.

*Now!*

I jumped back into the car and slammed the door just when he leapt over the car. I didn't manage to yank my hand back in time and felt the red hot fire of his claws ripping down my arm.

*Fuck!*

I wrapped my arm in the bottom of my filthy t-shirt and wondered if the monster would soon finish the job.

I heard the siren before seeing the flashing lights. Help was here.

*Finally!*

I looked out the back window expecting a fleet of cop cars, but it was Officer Espinoza in a lone cruiser.

*Oh shit.* He was going to get killed.

"Run! No! Help me! Shoot it. It's a werewolf. Kill it. Kill it!" I hysterically screamed. The SUV no longer rocked because the werewolf had stopped his assault and turned to the new threat.

"What the... Get down, Sara!" I heard something fall to the ground and three loud shots rang out. The werewolf let out a howl of pain and the back window glass shattered. A bullet ripped through it and out the front windshield.

I scrambled out the door to get away from any stray bullets and the monster howling on the other side. I ran for the police car.

"Holy shit! Holy shit! Do you see that thing? Is it for

real? The sun just freaking set. Is it a full moon? It can't be real. Is it dead? Can it come back to life?" The words seemed to rattle from my mouth as my whole body shook.

"Get in the car. Now!"

He didn't have to tell me twice. I leapt into the car right on top of the pizza sitting on the passenger seat, while he got in on the other side. He put the car in drive, lined up the tire with the werewolf's head, and stomped on the gas.

The front of the car lifted like he was trying to run over a boulder, but he managed to bounce over it. When he reversed and ran over it again, I tried to keep my head from hitting the ceiling. He stopped for a moment, looked at the squashed head, and then he drove the car forward and parked it on the werewolf's carcass. The driver's side sat slightly higher than the right side.

"Just in case it isn't dead, since I don't have silver bullets. Doesn't matter what it is, not much can survive being roadkill, right?"

He looked over at me and noticed my bloody shirt. "Sweet baby Jesus! You okay? Did it get you?"

His hands ran over my stomach while he looked for wounds and I pushed them away. "Stop it. That tickles. I'm fine. Yeah, I... shit... Yeah. There was this puppy. He was all cute with a bow. And then that thing jumped out at me. Cars aren't supposed to park on the street. A freaking werewolf. They are real." I pulled out the pizza box and tried to pop it back into shape. "The pizza is toast."

He chuckled and guided the pizza box onto the dashboard with one hand and used his other to turn my face to his. "I think you might be in shock. I should probably call an ambulance or take you to the hospital."

I didn't get a chance to protest before seeing the flash of

a camera. Some intrepid soul had managed to sneak back in and take a picture. One look at Officer Espinoza's face and the guy bolted between houses, and scrambled over a fence.

Officer Espinoza threw open the door and leapt out of the car to chase after the cameraman. The dude was fast, but Officer Espinoza didn't give up and vaulted over the fence like it was nothing.

I looked over at the trashed vehicle that had saved my life. I bet it was that reporter's SUV. *Hope he has good insurance.* The blood and various other nasty parts of the werewolf were all over the front of the car and the street. I forced myself to look away from the carnage and thought about the little puppy. Was it still wandering around out here?

I stepped out of the car and looked for the puppy down the street. Having no desire to see a close up of the blood and gore, I walked to the trashed vehicle.

That was where he found me after the reporter had eluded him. I was clutching my hands to my chest examining the bullet hole in the shattered glass of the back window that was held together by the tint.

"That's gonna be a hell of a picture. The Chief will have my ass in a sling for this. He hates when we make the press with stuff like this. You okay?"

I pointed at the bullet hole and said, "You missed one, sharp shooter. Hope he has glass coverage."

He snorted and said, "Hard to shoot straight when you jump from a moving car to shoot a monster while holding on to your Coke at the same time. Dang. Can't stand that diet shit. Now I don't have dinner or a drink."

I looked at him while he worried a small patch of stubble on the side of his head and noticed his left leg was soaked where he spilled his soda. That must have been what I heard hit the ground before he took the shots. I burst out laughing.

"You look like you peed your pants. And you're doing that nervous tic thing where you rub your hair."

He dropped his hand. "I had to shoot and run over a freaking werewolf, then chase after a reporter who is Mr. Olympian. Be happy I'm not ripping my hair out in chunks. Hell, I'm not so sure I didn't piss my pants."

We walked back to my house, and he paused outside the door.

"Want to come inside for some ice cream now, Officer Espinoza?"

He snorted and said, "Let me just call the station first. Don't know if I should call the ME or Animal Control to get the body. Oh, and after all this, you can call me Matt."

# CHAPTER EIGHT

*Five Uh-Oh*

"I think I love you right now."

Matt snorted at my declaration of love.

Over the top? Maybe. But I was starving and he had lied to dispatch and told them my blood sugar was low so they would have one of the rookies stop for food on their way over. No way would I be able to get food by myself tonight.

Some asshole had let the reporters back in and they had multiplied like gremlins in a swimming pool. It sounded like the crowd at a baseball game with all the noise they were making.

"Yeah, chicks always love you when they want something."

He tried to make it sound like a joke, but I sensed the bitterness in his response. I remembered he'd said something about a cheating ex the night we met. I guess men weren't the only ones who couldn't keep their zippers closed.

"Can I wash up, or is that like, destroying the evidence?" I had convinced him not to send an ambulance out, and I desperately wanted to shower the pungent animal stench of the werewolf off my skin. That and the sweat from being scared shitless made me smell pretty rank.

"Don't worry about it. There's plenty of evidence you were attacked, plus the dead werewolf under my car backs up our story. Be sure to disinfect those scratches really well."

Scratches! I looked down at my arm, and my heart started pounding. Oh, shit! I'd been scratched by a werewolf. I gulped to try to swallow the fear, but it clamped a vice-like grip around my chest. Holy crap. Did that mean I would turn into one, or did it have to bite me? No, this can't be happening. I raced up the stairs to look at myself in the bathroom mirror.

No facial hair or tail had formed. My wounds had stopped bleeding and looked shallow. My hair was snarled and matted in places with slobber from the beast. *Gross*. I looked pretty savage, but not like a werewolf.

I hoped.

The hydrogen peroxide was all the way in the back of the cabinet under the sink. Bottles of shampoo, lotion and hairspray scattered on the floor while I dug it out. I dumped almost the whole bottle of peroxide on the werewolf scratches and watched it bubble up.

I bit my lip to keep from screaming. They say hydrogen peroxide doesn't burn. They fucking lie. I blew uselessly on my arm, through clenched teeth until the burning finally stopped. I could feel the bubbles tickling the skin around the cut.

Was the burning normal or did it hurt because I had been infected? Why didn't I read more werewolf books? I would know if I were turning into a werewolf, wouldn't I? I wasn't craving raw meat, but my hair was looking pretty wild. Had it grown longer? I couldn't tell because it was so snarled. *Oh, God.*

I gulp air and tried to not hyperventilate. Maybe I

should wash it some more? I turned on the water as hot as I could stand and stuck my arm under it and squeezed some antibacterial soap on it, just in case.

I cried out from the pain and, I'll admit it, a little panic. I didn't want to turn into a monster.

Pounding on the door brought me back from the edge of hysteria. Matt called out. "You okay in there?"

I turned off the water and tried to sound normal.

"Yeah, just cleaning up. I'm fine." It came out high pitched and shaky.

"You don't sound fine. I'm coming in." He didn't wait for my agreement. He opened the door and stepped over the bottles that littered the floor.

"Can you help me bandage my arm?"

He reached down to pick up the first aid kit and pulled out supplies.

I shut the toilet lid and sat while he unwrapped the gauze. "Did you sterilize it?"

"What, afraid I am going to go all wolfy on you?" My high pitched laugh made me sound like a crazy person.

Matt didn't laugh.

He grabbed the antibiotic ointment out of the first-aid kit and gooped it all over my arm. After the peroxide, soap and hot water, the ointment felt like lava.

"Oh, my God. You do. You think I am going to turn into one of those..." I couldn't say it. I tried to suck it up and blinked back tears so Matt wouldn't think I was a baby, but he wasn't paying attention to my face. He rolled the gauze around my shaking arm a few times and then taped it shut.

"No. It didn't bite you, right? They have to bite you to make you turn and sometimes it takes more than one bite. You're not gonna turn into one."

"You're just saying that to make me feel better. How would you know? It's not like there's some guide book about these monsters out there."

Matt slid his hand down my arm to inspect the road rash on my hand. "I'm not at liberty to give you details, but let's just say… I got a lot of specialized training in the Marines. I know what I'm talking about. You'll be fine."

"Then why did you use that stuff before you put the bandage on?"

"You aren't going to turn into a werewolf, but you were still scratched by an animal. Who knows where that thing has been?"

My heart slowed down under his ministrations. For a big guy, he was surprisingly gentle.

"That should be good. Let me see your nose." He held my face carefully in his large hands while he inspected the damage. He used a wet wash cloth to wipe the blood and dried slobber off my face.

"Doesn't look like it's broken, but it's gonna be bruised and swollen. You should probably put ice on it. Your face will look pretty again in a few weeks."

His face was inches away from mine. If I just leaned in a little bit I would be lip to lip with him. Was that what I wanted? Maybe it was what he wanted. He did call me pretty after all. He leaned down and his necklace slid out from under his collar, nearly hitting me in the mouth.

I jerked back and said, "Um, nice necklace."

"Sorry about that." He let go of my face and tucked the necklace back under his shirt, pausing to kiss it first.

"My mom gave it to me before my first deployment. St. George is the patron saint of soldiers. She thought it would keep me safe."

I smiled and grimaced when it made my nose throb again.

"I could use one of those," I mumbled.

He chuckled softly and stepped back, letting me get a good look at myself in the mirror. Pretty in a few weeks? Pretty messed up was more like it. No way he had wanted to kiss me when I looked like that.

The bruising, which covered my nose, also spread out halfway under each eye. It was already swelling. I looked like I had gotten my ass kicked in a fight. I had, but at least I survived.

"How can you tell it isn't broken?" I asked him. I put my face right in front of the mirror for a close-up inspection.

"Ex-Marine, remember? You see a lot of broken noses in the Corps."

*Duh.* I should have figured that out. "Iraq?" I asked him.

He barked out a laugh and said, "No, most enemies don't bother throwing punches. Those puss- uh, wimps just shoot from a distance or blow you up with IEDs. Broken noses come from cramming a bunch of young, hot-headed Rambo wannabes together in close quarters, and adding alcohol. Someone was always fighting. Course no one wanted to get busted, so if there weren't any serious injuries, no one reported it."

I imagined a younger version of Matt, in uniform, busting some heads. I teased him with "I bet you were the champion of the bar fights."

He crinkled up his forehead. "Me? Nah. I was the one who usually broke up the fights. The only heads I busted were the ones who didn't realize the fight was over after knocking the other guy down. You don't kick a man when he's down."

"*Unit 26. Uniforms are on the scene requesting your location,*" his radio squawked.

"10-4, I'm inside the premises. I'm on my way down," he answered. He turned back to me. "I already gave them a report about what happened, but they're going to question you pretty hard about it."

"Well, as long as they bring me food, I don't care how many questions they ask. This will be my second time surviving a monster attack. I'm becoming an old pro."

"When I radioed it in, they had a hard time believing me, especially since it isn't a full moon. The evidence is pretty clear, though, so they won't be able to deny what happened and claim it was some mutant dog. Thank God the monster didn't turn back into human form. They'd never have believed me then."

"I'm sorry you have to deal with all this, but I'm very happy you were there." Not used to giving or getting affection, I awkwardly squeezed his arm in a not-quite-a-hug-but-more-than-a-handshake move.

He gave me the same what-the-hell-was-that look he gave the werewolf after he ran it over. "That's right," he said, "You've been through this before, huh? What's up with that? Can't imagine a nice lady like you would have such bad karma. First a vampire, now a werewolf. You should talk to a priest to bless the house or light some incense. My abuela would say you've got bad juju."

I snorted. My aunt would have died in shock if she heard I'd had a priest—or any kind of holy man—in my house.

We shuffled out of the bathroom, careful not to touch each other too much, and he paused to look around my bedroom. I hadn't picked up David's clothes and some of the drawers were still pulled out. Matt raised an eyebrow but didn't say anything before we headed downstairs.

I followed him while I wondered if I'd told him about Death's little visit, would he raise both eyebrows or just lock me up for good. "I was a married accountant living in the suburbs. My life should be boring. Hell, it was boring until this week. I have no idea why this is happening to me. I don't believe in that superstitious crap."

Matt rubbed his head and shifted to his other foot. "Trust me; I've seen some stuff that would make you a believer. You really should consider moving closer to town so help doesn't take as long to arrive next time. You'd have been toast if I hadn't already been on my way back with the food."

"I'll have to find a way to pique your interest so you keep coming out here, huh?" I was going for a flirty little joke. It came out creepy, with a hint of desperation. My people skills sucked. No wonder I didn't have any friends.

He cleared his throat but was spared making an awkward reply by the uniformed cop at the door with my food. "Okay, here's your food. Someone should be over soon to question you. I better go. There's always a crapload of paperwork when you fire your weapon. I left my card on your hall table. It's got my cellphone number on it; call me if you need me. Anytime."

My mouth watered from the smell of the greasy fries and burger in the bag. I managed not to snatch it from his hand and devour it on the spot. Who says I don't have self-control? "Thank you. Go book 'em, Danno."

Really? Did I just quote some cheesy line from some cop show? Hopefully he thought I watched the cool new one, not the one from the seventies. I stuffed some fries in my mouth so it would shut the hell up.

He raised his eyebrows at me and chuckled before he turned to walk out the door.

I had the sudden desire to ask him to stay. I reached out to put my hand on his shoulder to stop him but didn't want to make a fool of myself. He was just doing his job; he wasn't interested in me. Besides, I was through with men, even hot ones who had saved my life.

I was too hungry to offer to share my food—or even to stop eating—when his captain showed up to question me a few minutes later.

The annoying captain kept asking me the same questions over and over, distracting me from figuring out if Matt meant anything special when he added I could call him if I needed him, anytime.

"So, Ms. Reynolds. You saw a puppy?"

Was this the second or the third time he asked me that same question? After having given him complete sentences the first go-round, I decided to stick with grunting, nodding, and unintelligible words around a mouthful of burger.

"And where did the puppy go? Had you seen this animal before?"

How was I supposed to know where the little monster bait had run off to after luring me to my almost demise? I shrugged my answer while I stuffed the rest of the burger in my mouth.

He either decided I was telling the truth or was disgusted watching me masticate my dead cow. I didn't really care which because the end result was that he left me alone.

The next day would be Friday, and it was the last day I could hide out completely undisturbed before having to go back to work and deal the world. I reached into the freezer to pull out the frozen mystery meat to hold to my throbbing face. In the cabinet, there were some leftover pain killers from when David had his wisdom teeth pulled.

*He won't need these in Hell.* I popped a couple on my way up to take a shower.

# CHAPTER NINE

*St. George of the Urban Jungle*

You know what's worse than a plain glazed donut? An old-fashioned one purchased from the day-old bin. I had to dunk the damn thing into my coffee to make it soft enough to chew. I looked at my boss, Colleen, supplier of the donut abomination, and wondered if I threw one hard enough at her head, if it would knock her out. Her hair-sprayed helmet head of dyed red hair would probably deflect it. Thankfully, it was almost noon and I could leave.

"Whoa there, Sara. Do you think you need another donut? You know, all those carbs go straight to your thighs." She whispered the last part and pointed down at the chair. Yes, as though I had forgotten where my thighs were located.

Did I need another donut? I don't know. Did she need me to punch her in the face? I didn't want another one of those stale donuts, but I grabbed one and took a huge bite out of it while I stared right in her eyes, crumbs falling down my chin. *Yeah, that'll show her.*

It sucked all the moisture from my mouth so I couldn't swallow. Before I started to choke, I took a big swig of coffee.

"Alrighty then. You know, we tried calling you several times yesterday but you didn't answer. They talked about your unfortunate incident on the news. They claimed your husband was some sort of vampire, and he attacked you. Like anyone would be stupid enough to believe that."

"Uh, he actually *was* turned into a vampire and he *did* try to kill me." I wasn't going to bring up Mandi. Colleen didn't need more acid to throw in my face.

"Oh, really? Well, I'm sure it was very traumatic for you," she said in a snippy voice.

My co-workers smirked and someone outright snickered. I pretended to be completely focused on dipping my donut into my coffee.

"Moving on. Listen up everybody! Today is going to be a full day, rather than a half-day, because we are so behind. But we'll try to get everyone out by three so you can enjoy the weekend."

That announcement knocked the ridicule right off their faces. Now everyone blamed me for ruining their weekend. They were going to really hate this then. "Oh, sorry there, Colleen. No can do. I have to meet with the, uh, funeral home at one." Not that I had any plans on having a funeral, but she didn't know that.

Colleen flared her nostrils like a bull about to charge. I wanted to tell her not to do that because it would wrinkle her botoxed face, but I didn't have the guts.

"We have a deadline. If you don't stay today, you and everyone else will have to come in Sunday."

Oh, clever, trying to use peer pressure to make me stay. No one in this meeting had bothered to offer me condolences over the loss of my husband. Not even a hasty email. I suppose that was partly my fault for not socializing with them. David never wanted to go to company parties, and I was embarrassed to go alone. They had stopped inviting me out for lunch, because I always said no when I couldn't afford it. They gossiped and stared at my bruised face and now they had laughed at me. Why should I care what they thought of me?

"But tomorrow is the Sabbath. Surely the company doesn't expect us to break God's law of not working on Sundays?" Widening my eyes in shock, I was the picture of moral righteousness. Somehow I managed not to crack a smile.

"Of course not. We would never interfere with the practice of your religion, but this account-"

"Thank you." I cut her off mid-sentence. "I guess I'll see you all on Monday. Bye."

I jumped up, shut down my computer and grabbed my purse in one fell swoop, even gave a little finger wave while I walked out the door.

I had never done anything like that before. It was always me stuck there, carrying the slack for everyone else. Was it losing David that had made me brave, or the thought of his life insurance money? No matter. The air smelled sweeter outside, the sun brighter. The birds chirped happily, the flowers were in bloom. I rolled down my car window to let the wind dance with my hair. I brushed it back behind my ear and it reminded me of Matt.

I should bake him some brownies as a thank you for saving me. The grocery store was coming up on my right, so I braked and pulled into the parking lot. While I was there I remembered how empty my fridge was, so I stocked up. Normally I hated to shop, but today I browsed each aisle while I hummed to myself. Ditching out on work gave me a little high. I felt better than I had in days.

Naturally, the high didn't last long. When I arrived

home, I suffered from déjà vu. A horde of reporters were packing up and leaving from the front of my house. Matt must have just chased them off. He leaned against a dirty blue truck with his arms crossed, accenting how muscular they were. That man could sure wear a uniform.

The truck was a regular truck, not a police one. They must not have fixed his old one yet.

I hit the garage door button and pulled up my driveway, braking only when I was safely inside. My antenna was nearly ripped off from the slow moving door, but I was able to park unmolested.

The garage door rolled down in feeble spasms, like it was being cranked by an arthritic hand. It creaked the whole way down but finally closed. I gathered my grocery bags, then strained to carry them all in one trip. I managed to get inside in time to see Matt walking up to my front door. The reporters had fled the premises.

"What the hell is going on now?" I demanded as I opened the door for him. A few bags slipped from my grasp, but I ignored them and turned to head for the kitchen.

He grabbed the bags and a letter that was on the floor, and then he followed me inside. "You really should answer your phone. I tried calling you several times. You ever check your messages?"

Was he worried about me? It seemed so strange that someone cared enough to actually worry about me. Hell, one time I'd gotten home three hours late because of a really bad accident. My cell was dead so I couldn't call. David was playing video games and hadn't even noticed.

"Sorry, I had to work. What happened? Why are they back here?"

Matt put the groceries on the table. His freed hand crept

up to his head and absentmindedly rubbed. He must be stressed again. With all the time he had been spending with me, I was surprised he wasn't bald.

"That picture of us in my car after I ran over the werewolf went viral. Congratulations, we beat that pissed-off-looking cat in views. Too bad we won't make any money off of it. I could use it since I got suspended without pay today while they investigate me for improper conduct."

"Oh, shit. I'm so sorry. You want me to call someone? I would be dead now if it wasn't for you."

"Nah. It's all a bunch of bullshit. My Sergeant happens to be my ex-wife's new boyfriend's brother. Said since I already shot the thing, running it over was excess force and caused unnecessary damage to the police car."

"That's stupid. Like you ran over it for fun."

"He said I did it to impress you. You know, `cause nothing gets a girl in the mood like running down a monster with the squad car. You calling would just make it worse. Asshole. My Captain's back from vacation in a week. He'll take care of it. He's always got my back. It'll work out."

I had never heard Matt cuss before. Even when he was killing the werewolf. He must be getting comfortable with me, or else I was just a bad influence.

He handed me the letter he'd picked up before he reached into the bags and pulled out items. Without saying a word, he put the cold stuff in the fridge. David had never helped with the groceries.

He must have noticed my raised eyebrow because he stopped emptying the bags and took a seat. "Oh, uh, sorry. Habit. My mom needs help putting away groceries. So why weren't you answering your phone?"

I threw the letter on the table and took over putting

groceries away. I stopped with the ice cream in my hand and said, "Yeah, had a little accident with my cellphone. I need to get a new one."

"Accident?" he asked.

I pantomimed with the ice cream throwing the cell at the wall. The carton was wet on the side from the condensation, making it slippery. It flew out of my hand toward the table. Matt caught it before it hit the floor.

"Easy there, slugger. Huh, Chunky Monkey. Haley's favorite." He stood and put it away in the freezer, then went back to putting the remaining groceries away.

*Haley?*

I ripped open the letter, tearing the envelope in half. I was hit with a stab of jealousy I had no business feeling. I barely knew Matt. It wasn't like we were dating or anything. "Good thing I stocked up on food on the way home. Looks like I'm going to be under siege yet again. I was just going to make lunch. Hungry?" I didn't give him a chance to answer between my babbling. "Hey, how bad was the pic? What website posted it?"

Matt froze in the middle of closing the freezer door. You know that face guys make when they hate your new haircut but are afraid to say anything bad about it? Matt made that face. "Not sure. I saw the one in the newspaper."

"What? How bad is it? Spill it."

He was a brave man; I'll give him that. He didn't say a word, just closed the freezer and drew out the folded up newspaper he had tucked in his back pocket. It was beyond bad.

I looked like a mental patient. My mouth was open, my hair looked like some weird origami and it looked like I was fighting Matt for the pizza rather than putting the smashed box on the dashboard.

Matt's other hand was on my face in what looked like a caress. From the angle of the shot, it looked like he was leaning in to kiss me, rather than checking to see if I was in shock. The car was splattered with blood and gore. The remains of the werewolf were mostly under the tire, except for an arm that was no longer attached to the body. It still gripped the top of the wheel well.

"What did I do to deserve this? Why is all this shit happening to me? And look, the HOA sent me a letter saying they are fining me for 'my guests'. What guest? The reporters? It's not like I let them in. I was supposed to be at some meeting today to discuss other violations."

Matt pulled the paper gently from my death grip and set it on the table out of sight behind the cereal boxes. "I think you got bigger problems than a bad picture or an HOA meeting. I saw one of the reporters punch in a code for the gates. That means they aren't just piggybacking their way in when another car goes through. Someone gave them a code. Did you give it to anyone?"

I plopped down in the seat next to him and shook my head. "No, we didn't really have friends over or anything. Who would want to drive out this far and have to worry about driving all the way home?"

Matt reached out and touched my arm. "What about your, uh, late husband?"

Why would David have given the code to anyone? Any repair people would come during the day when the guard was at the gate. You only needed the code at night and on weekends.

*Weekends.*

Like the ones he had encouraged me to work to help my

career.

I remembered how Mandi had walked straight up and into my room as if she had been there before.

I was such an idiot.

The HOA letter crumbled into a ball in my fist. Matt retrieved the opened bottle of wine from the fridge. He looked around at the cabinets and spotted a wine glass in the drying rack by the sink. A full glass was in my hand within moments.

I took a big drink and tried to remember those deep breathing exercises I'd learned in yoga a few years ago. Just like in class, I must have looked like a woman in labor, because Matt grabbed my shoulders.

"You okay? You're not having heart attack, are you?"

I laughed at his worried face. "No, I'm trying to balance my chi, or is it my chakras? I don't know. Screw it. I hate yoga. More wine, please."

He refilled my glass and sat down slowly. A man who puts away groceries and pours wine on demand? I might have found the perfect male.

"I figured it wasn't you. But hoped your husband wasn't that big of an asshole. She probably sold them the gate code. You need to change your locks too, just in case she has a key."

I wrinkled my nose as if smelling something bad. "No, even he wouldn't have given her a key to our house. No freaking way."

Matt stood up and patted me on the shoulder. "I thought the same thing, until I came home after meeting with her at our couple's therapist and realized my mint-in-the box Star Wars action figures that Dad gave me when I was kid had been opened and Boba Fett was missing along with all of her stuff. Screwing another cop's wife wasn't bad enough; he had to take my stuff too?"

His hands were clenched into fists and he looked like he wanted to hit someone. I wonder what pissed him off more: Her cheating with a cop or the stealing. I put my hand on his arm and squeezed. "Assholes. I don't understand how people can be so selfish. Hope you kicked his ass."

Matt grimaced. "Had to give up custody of my daughter, Haley, so he wouldn't press charges after I beat the crap out of him. People can sink lower than you ever think possible."

I gave him a sad smile. He looked into my eyes a beat too long and my heart sped up. My smile twitched like it does when I get nervous, and his eyes darted to my mouth. He licked his lips and his weight shifted like he was going to lean in.

The theme from Jaws played from his pocket and he jerked away from me. When he pulled it out, something fell out in a flash of gold.

"What?" he answered, and his face screwed up though he had smelled something bad.

I knelt to pick up the gold necklace from the floor while Matt stood to take the call.

"No. You can't do that. I'm supposed to have next weekend." Matt said into the phone, "But this weekend is already half over. You can't switch on me like this."

I tried not to eavesdrop and focused on the charm on the necklace. It was a St. George medallion like the one Matt wore, except this one was delicate with filigree scrolls around it and the words "St. George Pray for Us". It was beautiful.

"Fine, but I'm keeping her until Tuesday." He ended his call and shoved it back into his pocket.

"Interesting ring tone. Jaws?" I asked him.

Matt nodded. "Thought it fit. Look, I'm sorry. I gotta go pick up my daughter. If the reporters come back, call the station. If dispatch hassles you, call me."

I nodded and tried to hand him back the necklace.

"No, actually that's for you."

For me? "You bought this for me?"

His hand went up to rub the slightly grey patch of hair above his ears. "No. I didn't buy it. It was my Mom's. She saw the picture in the paper, so I had to tell her about what happened. When she heard about the werewolf and the vampire attack, she took it off and told me to bring it to you. She says you need protection."

I floundered and tried to think of what to say. How could a complete stranger show such kindness? "Oh, no, I couldn't accept it. Please, tell her thank you, though. It was so nice of her to offer though."

Matt stepped away from my outstretched hand like I was holding a bomb. "No way. Mom said I was to make sure you put it on and you aren't ever supposed to take it off. I go back home with that, Mom would," he paused and shook his head, "I'd rather face that werewolf again. You're keeping it. And get a new phone."

He nodded his head at me and turned to walk out of the kitchen. I heard the front door open and close while I stared at the necklace and sipped my wine. I nearly snapped the stem in my hand when Death appeared in the seat Matt had vacated. What was he doing here again?

"He was the one who saved you from the werewolf, no? What was he doing here again?" Death sounded like a girlfriend wanting to dish.

I poured more wine into my glass with a shaking hand.

Death had changed out of the power suit and was going for something a little more casual. He was dressed in black jeans and a black hoodie. I was so thankful he was still wore the sunglasses so I wouldn't have to look at those depthless black eyes.

I put the necklace on and prayed Matt's mom was right about it protecting me.

# CHAPTER TEN

*The Bitch is Back*

"How did you know about the werewolf?" I avoided his question about Matt. It was bad enough that Death seemed fascinated by me; I didn't want to draw that kind of attention to the one person in my life who seemed to care.

He flashed his pearly whites and tilted his head to the side a little. "Because I sent him, of course. You have escaped me not once, or twice, but three times."

"...a lady," I sang to him. They must not hear a lot of Lionel Richie in Hell judging from the furrowed brow and scrunched face he gave me. The wine was having that lovely sedating effect, so it took me a minute to realize what he'd said.

"You sent him? You sent that monster to eat me? Why? You said you wouldn't kill me. Liar. Lying bastard, just like all men. But not Matt. He's nice. He hasn't lied to me. Not yet anyway."

The smile left Death's face. The room grew colder. My eyes widened as the shadows in the room seemed to grow. Oh shit, I wasn't supposed to talk about Matt.

In a booming voice that hurt my ears, Death said, "Do not compare me with mortal men. My word is never broken. Mankind is the one practiced in lies and deceit. Not me.

Humans brag all the time about cheating Death, but never do you hear about Death cheating them."

"Well, duh. Be hard to hear from someone who is dead." The wine made my mouth work faster than my brain.

The chill left the room, and the shadows in the corners disappeared. Again, Death smiled, perfectly straight little enamel soldiers, ready in formation to go to battle. It never stopped being scary as hell.

"You aren't afraid of me, are you? I find that refreshing. Usually the only ones who aren't are lunatics or the elderly. Intriguing."

I realized I had consumed about three glasses of wine and all I'd eaten were those stale donuts from work. Food would help absorb the alcohol in my system and hopefully clear my head.

As graceful as a hippo on roller skates, I stumbled to the fridge and grabbed some ham, salami and cheese. I set it on the counter next to the bread. I wondered if Death liked cold cuts? "Want a ham and salami sandwich?"

He shook his head and said, "No, thank you. I don't eat."

I waited for him to finish his sentence. "I don't eat...what, salami? ham? carbs? what?"

"Food. It keeps you alive. Well, not the genetically modified kind. I don't need sustenance to exist."

Oh. Creepy. I guess it wouldn't be rude to eat in front of him then. I opened the bread and put it right on the counter, not bothering with a plate, and then I walked back to the table with my sandwich. David always liked everything neat and tidy. He would have had a cow if he had seen me.

I shook my sandwich toward the floor. How do you like the crumbs now, dick?

"So why'd you send that werewolf after me when you

said you wouldn't kill me?" I was careful not to call him a liar this time.

"I promised you would not die that night. I didn't say I wouldn't come back for you."

I choked on a bite of my partially chewed sandwich when a vision of Death in sunglasses doing an impersonation of Arnold's famous catchphrase, 'I'll be back' popped into my head.

Death leaned forward and watched me carefully. He nodded when I managed to swallow and leaned back again.

"Wait, were you just waiting for me to choke to death? Did you make me do that?"

He huffed out a breath. "No, it was your choice to take such a greedy bite. I cannot make you do anything. People think I have the ability to take them on a whim, but it is not so. Your choices determine if you live or die. God is big on free will. All I was doing was waiting to see if that sandwich would succeed where the other attempts failed."

I was confused. Free will? Choices? He made it sound like you could live forever if you just decided to do it. "You're Death. You make the decisions of who lives and who dies."

"A common misconception. I just collect the souls after people have made their choice."

Made their choice? "So what? My parents made the choice to die when they got in that accident? I made the choice to almost get eaten by the werewolf? You're fucking nuts."

"Your parents made the choice to drive that night knowing the risks involved. You made the choice to go outside and get attacked by the werewolf."

"You sound like an insurance company trying to deny a

claim, saying my parents were at fault for being in their car. That's bullshit. They didn't ask to get in that accident. And I only went outside to save the puppy. It's not like I knew there was a werewolf out there. Wait, where did that puppy come from?"

He turned his head away from mine and looked across the room. Fucker! "You did that? You put that puppy there to lure me outside? Thought you couldn't make people do anything."

Death stood and put his hands in the hoodie's pocket. "I cannot make someone choose to put themselves in harm's way. However, I can entice them in that direction and take advantage when they do. You made the choice to go after that puppy. We all have our parts in this play. I just wonder what your role will be." He paused a moment. "Ah. You have company. And I have to follow up on a plague in China. I shall see you soon."

He walked a few feet toward the door and faded until he disappeared before my eyes, but not before I noticed the pink cat-shaped skull with a bow on the back of his hoodie. Goodbye Kitty? I did not understand Death's flair for fashion.

The squeak of the mail flap on the door caught my attention. Wait, the mailman had already been here today. A little white envelope with the dreaded HOA return address greeted me when I left the kitchen. I recognized Elise Travino, the HOA President's, handwriting on the front. I'd seen both plenty of times in the past.

My back cracked several times, sounding like those obnoxious people in the movie theater who chew popcorn with their mouth open, when I bent over to pick up the letter. I ripped open the top and braced myself. Time to read the verdict.

It was a form letter but hand written on the bottom was a list of my infractions, and the total fine amount. A fine? Those bitches were going to fine me $250 for an unauthorized gathering and another $250 for my "guests" parking in restricted areas.

There was a note under the total that said this was just for the previous incident. Today's violations would have to be reviewed at another committee meeting and more assessments could be levied at that time.

*Those motherfuckers!*

When we first moved in David insisted I volunteer for committees to help run different events, but they'd always turned their noses up at me and said all the positions were full. Assholes wouldn't even eat the cakes I brought to potlucks. And I made damned good cake.

My clothes had the wrong label. My hair wasn't expertly styled. But my worst offense: I dared to speak my opinion even when it differed from El Presidente, Mrs. Travino.

David blamed me for not making an effort, despite the fact my tongue practically bled from how many times I had to bite the poor thing. David wasn't around to restrain me any more. If they wanted to get petty and nasty, they could bring it. They'd poked this sleeping bear, and they're going to get one pissed off grizzly with PMS.

## CHAPTER ELEVEN

*Keep the Home Fires Burning*

It was Sunday morning and the vultures were out in front of my house again in full force. I had forgotten to change the passcode on the gate like Matt had warned me to do. The HOA was going to put on a helluva Christmas party this year on my tab thanks to Mandi.

I suddenly realized she had been in my bed. My skin crawled when I wondered if she had slept in the same sheets I had last night. Well, I guess she probably hadn't actually slept. *Ewww, nasty.*

I gathered the bedding, wrapping everything up inside the comforter. Not even bothering to remove the pillows from the pillowcases, I dragged the whole thing downstairs. It was warm for a fire, but I was going to be rich soon. The air conditioning bill wouldn't break me.

I threw the whole thing into my huge fireplace, wedging the comforter in place with the fire screen. After I hit the ignition button, the fire made a satisfying *woosh* sound when it lit the whole thing ablaze. I had some second thoughts while I used the poker to force the pieces of smoldering comforter that hung over the top of the screen back into the fireplace. A fireplace should be the safest place for a fire, right? The screen should keep it from spilling on the floor and burning the house down.

The heat sucked all the moisture from my eyeballs. I dropped the poker and stepped back. It didn't take me long to start to sweat. I paused on my way to turn on the air conditioner when I heard a loud pop coming from the fire.

*Oh, shit.* I forgot about the candles David put in the fireplace. The votive glass was shattering from the heat. The man hated having an actual fire because he was such a neat freak, but insisted on having an oversized fireplace in Arizona.

Smoke was pouring into the living room. What the hell was wrong with the chimney? I turned off the gas before I opened the front door and the windows to try to bring in some fresh air. Black smoke billowed out of the fireplace faster than the fresh air could blow it away.

The smoke, and who knew what other toxic chemicals from the bedding, burned my throat and made my eyes tear up. I pulled my shirt up over my mouth and ran into the kitchen to fill up a pot with water. By the time I filled it and threw it on the fire, it was too late. The material was completely ablaze and a little water wasn't going to put it out.

*Eeeeaahhhhh, Eeeeaaahhhhhh, Eeeeeaaahhhhh!*

I covered my ears, dropping the shirt from my mouth, which made me choke.

Yes, thank you for the hearing damage little plastic ear terrorist, but I figured out that there was a fire from all the smoke billowing through the house.

I grabbed the broom and swung at the plastic harpy. Too short. I jumped and I could almost reach it. My second jumped knocked the cover off, but the thing was still howling. My third jump didn't even graze it.

You know how you are supposed to stay low in a fire? It's because the smoke rises.

What you shouldn't do is jump up and down several times trying to hit a screeching smoke detector like a piñata until you are out of breath and panting, thus breathing in even more of the noxious smoke.

A wave of dizziness hit me, and I dropped the broom and crawled to the back door to get away from the smoke filling the front rooms. How could I have been this stupid? A temper tantrum might be the death of me.

*Death.* He must have messed up my fireplace somehow to try to finish me off. My head hit the door and I fumbled for the handle. *Maybe he succeeded,* was my last thought before I passed out.

I thought I was dreaming when I came to on my back porch with my head in Matt's lap and a cute firefighter hovering around me. They gave me oxygen while I coughed up what felt like embers. Tears streamed down my face.

"Maybe we should take her to the hospital," Matt told the paramedic who'd checked my vitals.

"Her lungs sound clear, and her blood oxygen levels are good. Luckily, she opened the door before she fainted. She should be okay, but it wouldn't hurt to take her in. Ma'am, are you feeling better?" The paramedic yelled over the noise from inside.

"No. No hospitals. I'll live. Stupid chimney isn't working." With the oxygen mask covering my mouth and nose, my voice sounded a bit like Darth Vader, if he had a two- pack-a-day smoking habit.

"The fire is almost out. Looks like the flue was closed, which is what caused all the smoke to back up inside the house. A careless mistake that you're lucky didn't turn deadly." The firefighter seemed to scream the last part of his sentence when the smoke alarm finally shut off. He turned to walk back into the house.

"There are better ways to kill yourself, you know." Matt joked, but he looked at me a beat too long.

"Death by comforter?" I teased. "No, I'm not the suicide type. Just needed to get rid of some things." I pulled off the oxygen mask and Matt helped me stand up.

He kept a steadying arm around me while we walked into my slightly less smoky house. The same fireman from outside walked over to us. He had the now-silent smoke detector.

"You'll need to replace these once the smoke clears," he handed me the batteries and set the detector on the hall table. "I'm going to have to cite you though. Today is a no-burn day. You'll have to go to court and pay a fine."

This guy was totally ruining my fireman fantasies.

"Actually, that's a gas fireplace. They are exempt from the no burn days." Matt stood beside me with his bulky arms crossed. Bet he intimidated many a suspect with that pose.

The firefighter made a face and said, "I'll give you a verbal warning, this time. But these fireplaces aren't meant to burn garbage. I also suggest you have it professionally cleaned before you try to use it again. You can hire a fire restoration company to come out to get rid of the smoke and clean the soot in the room. Oh and next time, open the flue."

They packed up their gear and left the house, cutting a wide swath between the reporters. Matt stayed behind.

"If this is how you cook, I don't think I want those brownies after all," he joked.

Brownies? A memory tickled my brain of me stress baking last night and finishing the wine bottle. Oh no. I had drunk dialed Matt talking about how I was a kick-ass baker and asked him to come over today to get some. Oh God, I couldn't remember if I had finished that sentence with brownies or not. "Thanks for the save, again. I thought it would be good symbolism to burn everything from the bed. Get rid of old ghosts...and their sluts."

Matt patted me on the shoulder. "Next time, try Goodwill."

I laughed and turned to look at him. He was dressed in faded, well-worn blue jeans and a t-shirt with a TARDIS on the front that read, "It's bigger on the inside."

Whoa, a fellow Doctor Who fan. "I would have never pegged you as geek."

I picked up the plate of brownies and sniffed. They smelled charred from the smoke. "Damn, these brownies are toast now."

Matt rubbed his flat stomach. "That's okay. Shouldn't eat the carbs anyway. I should probably open some windows to help air the place out." He walked over to the kitchen window and opened it, then walked out to open the windows in the rest of the house.

"Don't suppose you know a good fire restoration company?"

Matt made a face and shook his head, "Shoot, you don't need to do that. Just rent an ozone generator. Leave it running overnight, and the smell will be gone."

"Um, right. And where do I get one of those, and will they come out and set it up for me?"

He rolled his eyes and said, "I'll go with you to get it and show you how to work it."

"Cool. I'll buy you lunch for helping me."

He looked at his watch. "I gotta be back in town by two.

Haley had dance practice to go to so I have to pick her up afterward. If we grab lunch, it has to be fast."

A breeze blew in and whipped my hair across my face. I reeked of smoke. "Lemme go get cleaned up first."

I ran upstairs and stripped out of my stinky clothes. We only had a few hours, so I skipped the shower but used a soapy washcloth to wipe off grime. There was no hope for my hair, so I shoved up into a pony tail, before trying to find some clothes that didn't reek of smoke.

To cover up the smell, I sprayed some perfume from a bottle that sat on the dresser. Ugh. It was David's unisex cologne I always hated. Too fruity to be a man's scent but too musky to be a woman's.

The smell of the smoke and cologne reminded me of David and his stupid power suit. Gross. I sprayed some of my own perfume to cover the scent and realized thinking of him didn't make me want to cry or scream for once.

Time must already be healing those wounds.

I felt an independence I'd never had before. To celebrate, I decided to do something I'd always wanted to do, but knew David wouldn't approve.

Matt was shoving the contents of the fireplace into a garbage bag, when I slid down the banister. I laughed when I fell off and landed on the bottom step.

He looked at me, shook his head and walked over to give me a hand up. "And you call *me* a geek?"

Time might be the best medicine for some wounds, but having a cute guy ready to pick you up when you fall ain't so bad either.

# CHAPTER TWELVE

*Food, Shopping, and Near Dismemberment*

You can learn a lot about a person by the choices they make. I'm not talking about careers and other big life decisions; I mean the little stuff. This revelation occurred to me while I listened to Matt order a turkey sandwich on wheat, no mayo, with a side-salad, and a chocolate shake for lunch.

His choices said he cared about his health but wasn't militant about it. This was a guy who knew how to live a little. I thought about what I had ordered out of habit: a Cobb salad with an unsweetened iced tea. Did he think I was unimaginative and stuffy?

"Oh, and can you add an order of jalapeno poppers to that?"

Jalapenos say I am spicy and fun, right? Or did it say I was cheesy and full of fat? Maybe I should have ordered onion rings instead, but onions meant bad breath. Would he think I was making a statement about not wanting to be kissed? Did I want him to kiss me? I sneaked a glance at Matt to try to guess what he was thinking and came up blank. Do guys think about these things too?

"So... like the guy said, you need to be out of the house

for twenty-four hours while the ozone generator is running. Can you crash at a friend's house?" Matt asked.

"Um, yeah, sure, no problem." I'm sure my imaginary friend would be willing to let me crash at her place.

"Okay, good. I should have just enough time to get it set up for you after we finish lunch. Sorry I can't stay and help you clean up, but I gotta pick up Haley."

They called out our number and Matt walked back to the counter to pick up our order. After stopping to pick up silverware and napkins, he placed the tray on the table.

"Tell me about Haley." I stabbed my salad with a fork.

"She's ten. She's amazing. Smart, funny, pretty. Thank God she looks like her mother. She was the one thing we did right in our marriage." Matt went from sitting straight with his arms resting slightly tense on the table, to leaning back in his chair with his hands relaxed and a smile lit up his face.

He seemed like the kind of dad who would do anything for his kid. I felt a stab of jealousy and quickly shoved it away. I wondered how different my life could have been if I had grown up with a dad like that.

"She's gonna think her dad's an idiot for getting suspended without pay, again. I'm sure her mom told her all about it." He bit down hard on his turkey sandwich.

"I bet she'll be proud of you for saving someone's life. What little girl wouldn't want a superhero as a dad?" I nudged him with my foot and was rewarded with a sexy smile. I bet those lips could make a girl forget a cheating, vampire, dead husband. Oh God, stop staring at his lips.

"Just doin' my job, Ma'am," he drawled. He tipped an imaginary cowboy hat.

"Did she give you that watch?" I asked and pointed at the bright-yellow, cartoon character on his wrist.

He looked at it and nodded. "Yeah. She traded all her Halloween candy to some kid in her class for it because her mom wouldn't take her to go buy me something for my birthday. What kid does that?"

He stopped and concentrated on his food for a few seconds. He cleared his throat, looked up, and smiled at me.

While we ate in comfortable silence, the St. George medallion he wore caught my eye. My fingers brushed my neck to feel the one his mother had given me. His necklace and his watch were talismans of love. I bet when he was happily married he thought the same of his wedding ring. This man had a mother and a grandmother that loved him. A daughter who adored him. Probably a bunch of guys he was friends with from the force or the service. He was so unlike David in every way. So unlike me.

I had never really thought about how alone I was in the world. What would it be like to have people who cared about me in my life? I'd been too busy working and trying to be a good little wife to think about it before.

Hanging with Matt made me picture playgrounds and Thanksgiving dinners. Sunday mornings being lazy in bed. Figures, now I think about getting a life just when Death keeps trying to kill me.

"It's getting late." Matt interrupted my thoughts. "We better get going so I can make it to your house and back in time."

We gathered up our trash, and headed out. He cleared his throat and said, "You're awfully quiet. With women that usually means trouble."

He winked to show he was just messing around.

"I was just thinking about those Princess sheets you wanted at the mall. Maybe if you are a good little boy, Santa will get you some." I nudged his arm.

He snorted and said, "That poor clerk spent a good twenty minutes trying to find them in a King size for me."

"What would you have done if she found some?" I asked.

"After she went to all that effort? Shoot, I'd have to buy them. One sheet is as good as another. No one else but me sees them anyway."

*Hmmm, he sleeps alone. Good to know.*

"Thank you for taking me. I had so much fun today. I can't even remember the last time I had this much fun..." *Way to spoil the mood, dummy.*

Matt nodded his head. "I get it. You're feeling guilty because your husband just died. There's nothing you could have done to save him, you know?"

He didn't get it. Telling him would make me sound like a horrible person, and he would probably want nothing to do with me. I decided to go for it anyway. "No, that's just it. I don't feel guilty. I didn't want David to die or anything, but we hadn't been happy in a long time. I see that now. We met in college, and I was desperate to get away from my aunt. I convinced myself I loved him, and we got married."

"A lot of women get married for those reasons. When you realized you didn't love him, why didn't you leave? You didn't have any kids. That's the only reason why my ex and I stayed together so long."

"It was easier to stay with him than go through the hassle of a divorce. I didn't really know anyone out here, and I don't have any family, except my psycho aunt. I know it's stupid, but I guess I stayed out of habit." I sounded pathetic.

"I get that. If I hadn't found out about that bastard my ex

was screwing, I probably would've stayed married too. Guess I should thank him." Matt joked, but I could sense the pain behind his words.

"And now I get to go home and sleep in the same house where he screwed his girlfriend, and the house is probably crawling with reporters. I never wanted to live there in the first place, but the condo I liked in the city didn't have the same 'prestige' as the Hills. And those bitches out there hate me, always did. Fining me for getting attacked. Assholes."

I hadn't meant to rant like that. Poor Matt had come to my house for brownies and ended up being sucked into my drama.

"Is that why you tried to burn the house down?" he joked.

I gave him a half-hearted laugh, and he reached out to squeeze my hand. "Sucks you have to go back there, but you can't sell in this market. I got totally hosed selling our house in the divorce. Maybe you can rent it to someone."

Now would be a good time to mention the hefty check I should be getting this week from the insurance company, but I couldn't. Sharing my dirty laundry about David was one thing, but letting him know I was rich made me squirm, especially since he was losing a few weeks' pay being on suspension because of me.

Money changed the way people treated you. I'd seen that first hand after we bought that stupid house. David made sure to casually drop into conversations that we lived out in the Hills. They would get that look on their faces, like we thought we were too good for them, which was probably accurate as far as David was concerned. The irony was that our neighbors didn't consider us one of them, no matter how hard David had tried.

Matt hadn't judged me yet. I didn't want to spoil it. "Yeah, maybe I'll rent it out."

We pulled into my driveway and there wasn't a single reporter hanging around. Woohoo! Matt was right. Changing the gate code worked. That bitch could give them the old one all she wanted, but they wouldn't get back in. Finally some peace and quiet around here.

He carried the ozone generator from the car and as soon as I opened the door the smell hit us. I flipped on the lights, and Matt whistled softly.

The good news was that the smoke had settled from the air. The bad news was that it was all over my walls and furniture. The living room walls were grey from the smoke, all except the ones by the fireplace. They were covered with greasy black soot. I had hoped it would only be the smell I would have to deal with, but I should have known I wouldn't get off that easily.

I dropped the bags and headed upstairs to see if it had escaped the damage.

They walls weren't as bad, but the air was still hazy with smoke. Matt helped me open all the windows upstairs. The burnt-plastic smell lingered, but not as strong.

"You want to stay up here while I set it up?" Matt indicated the ozone machine.

I looked at the stripped down bed and a vision of David and Mandi flashed in my head. Downstairs might be a sooty mess, but it was probably less toxic than this room was to me now.

"I'll just pack a bag and be down in a second."

He nodded and turned to go down the stairs, while I gathered some clothes and toiletries to throw into a bag. By the time I made it to the living room, he had the machine all set up.

"Okay, I'll set the timer to start in fifteen minutes. It'll run for twenty-four hours then shut off. Don't come back until then. You'll probably have to rent a machine to wash your furniture and carpets, but the walls should come clean by scrubbing them. You might have to repaint that one though." He indicated the fireplace wall.

"Thanks, Matt. Don't know what I would do without you."

He shrugged and bent down to set the timer. After it was set, he walked over and picked up my suitcase and the shopping bags. "You don't want to leave these here, or they'll stink. Ready?"

I picked up my purse and led the way through the kitchen to the garage door. While it groaned and screeched in protest while it rolled open, he put my stuff in the trunk. "Just return the machine tomorrow once it's done. Call me if you need a hand moving. I'll probably be suspended for at least a week, and my ex is taking Haley away on Wednesday for vacation. So I'll have some free time."

"Okay, thanks," I said and stood there awkwardly.

Do I hug him goodbye? Cheek peck? Handshake?

I felt like a clueless teenager on a first date. Hug, definitely a hug. I was going in and reached my arms up… just when he turned away.

He turned back and saw me with my arms raised in the air. My eyes darted to the open trunk. I reached over with both hands and slammed it shut. He yanked his hand out of the way just in time.

My awkwardness had strayed from embarrassing to potentially disfiguring.

"Oh, my God! Are you okay? I'm so sorry."

"I'm fine." He rubbed his left hand with his right as if to reassure himself it was still there. "Well, we better get out of here before that thing starts up. Remember, stay at your friend's house for at least twenty-four hours. Um, see ya." He nodded at me and walked to his car.

I got in my car and pulled out of my driveway pretending I had somewhere to stay the night. If he knew I had nowhere to go, would he have invited me to stay with him, even though I almost mangled his hand? Sexy thoughts flashed through my mind of what his hands would feel like on my body. But even if he were interested, he couldn't because he would have his daughter.

A hotel it was, then. Maybe the mini-bar would have booze and a good pay-per-view movie or two.

# CHAPTER THIRTEEN

*For Whom the Bell Tolls*

After a restless night of acid reflux from the poppers, I returned home to face the massive clean-up that waited for me. I opened the door to the kitchen and took a big whiff. The air smelled a bit like it did right after a lightning strike or before a storm. Much better than the smoke.

I walked inside and dropped my stuff on the floor by the stairs. The place still looked like some idiot had tried to use the fireplace without opening the flue first, but the air seemed less toxic. I yanked the cord out of the wall and grabbed the machine to put in my car and ran right into Death.

"Ahhhhh!" I screamed and dropped it at his feet with a loud clang. "You scared the heck out of me. You need a bell around your neck."

"A bell? Might be a good idea. One would hear it before I arrive to collect them for their journey and I can say, 'the bell tolls for thee'." He laughed.

Can a laugh be off key? It made my skin crawl. "Happy I could be of assistance in accessorizing your wardrobe."

He gave me that perfect gleaming-white smile and my bravado turned into an iceberg in my stomach. I brushed past him and flopped down on my recliner. Leftover smoke and dust puffed around me and caused me to cough.

"Interesting changes you have made to your decor. Reminds me of when I visit Hades." He looked around at the sooty walls and my ashy floor, before he settled down on the couch and sat back.

Great, he was making himself comfortable, which meant he probably wanted to have another heart to heart. Maybe if I joked around with him he would be happy and would leave faster. "Yeah, I bet this reminds you of home now, huh? Though it probably isn't nearly as hot."

Death tilted his head to the side and I could see creases on his brow. "Hot? Ah, you think I reside in Hell? No, that is Hades' domain."

The Book of Revelations flashed into my mind, and without thinking, I blurted out something that had always bothered me. "You know, they talk about the four Horsemen of the Apocalypse all the time, but really there are five, right? Because you and your buddy Hades would make four and five. Unless you share a horse or he walks, but that would make it hard for him to follow close behind you."

Death stopped playing with the cuff of his black button-up shirt and laced his fingers together. "Buddy? I think of Hades as more of a partner."

Whoa. "I know the Bible says you and Hades ride together, but I didn't realize you *ride* together. Man, the Catholic Church would have a field day with that knowledge."

Maybe that explained Death's quirky fashion sense. I turned in my chair to look at him and Death was still as, well… you know. "Not that there is anything wrong with that. Everyone deserves love, right? It shouldn't matter who you're with, as long as you are happy. I mean, shit, you guys have been together way longer than my sham of a marriage."

I had forgotten how fast Death could move. He stood up and loomed in front of me before my next cough could escape my mouth. "You have mocked me in the past, and I have allowed it, but do not forget to whom you speak. I will brook no further insult from you about me or Hades."

Cold anger radiated from his body. I gulped and shook my head. "Insult? I wasn't insulting you. I thought you were a couple."

The chill left the room as quickly as it had arrived. Death stepped back and cocked his head to the side. "Couple? You think Hades and I are together in a sexual way? That might just be the most ridiculous thing I have ever heard."

Death gave me an amused grin, which was so much better than his horrifying smile. It was hard to believe this was the same terrifying creature I had seen a moment ago.

"Well, when most men talk about another man as a partner, it means they're gay. Which I have no problem with, just for the record."

He sat down on the couch again and laughed. "I am not sure what is more absurd: the thought of anyone actually loving Hades or the thought of Hades being capable of love."

"I don't mean to be rude. It's been a long day. I didn't sleep well. I'm not up for company. Is there a reason you're here?" I threw a little giggle in at the end, so he wouldn't get mad again.

The grin fell off his face as he took on a detached professional demeanor. "Yes. The fire. I was checking to see how you survived this time."

I should have known. "You did that, didn't you? Made me nearly set the house on fire while I suffocated." What a dick.

"No, this time, I did not facilitate the, uh, incident. In fact, I had commitments in Germany and Africa, which is why I missed your rescue. And yet, you did not succumb? How?"

Death had not set me up. My own stupidity had nearly killed me. I felt a little guilty for accusing him. "I don't know. The reporters must have seen the smoke and called 911. I woke up outside with Matt and some firemen looking over me."

"Oh, him again. I see. He has certainly proven useful to your rescue time and again. How felicitous for you." The disdain in his voice was obvious, but he confused me. Was it the fact that I kept getting saved that bothered him or that Matt was my rescuer?

"Is he who you were with when I came to call last night? Perhaps there is more to this lawman than meets the eye."

I did not like Death's sudden focus on Matt. That kind of interest had nearly killed me several times now. My hand snaked up to the medallion I wore around my neck. "Leave Matt alone. He's just a cop doing his job. He isn't like a superhero or anything."

I couldn't read his expression, but I felt a chill emanating from his side of the room.

"Not a superhero, but perhaps your own personal hero. How touching."

Shit. I was just making it worse. I fluttered my hands around in a panic. "No, no, no. It isn't like that. He is like, sick of having to save me, I'm sure. It's a job, that's all. In fact, he told me he wasn't working the next few weeks because he got in trouble because of me."

Death cocked one perfectly arched eyebrow at me and said, "The man risks his job for you."

How had I not noticed his perfect little eyebrows before? They were usually covered by the sunglasses, but they looked like they were drawn on. Weird.

"I too have felt this inclination to neglect my duties to spend time with you. Your ability to see me and thwart me time and again is quite fascinating. Point of fact, Hades was quite upset with me after my last visit because it caused my untimely arrival during his plague. Not enough died. China downgraded it to a simple serious health scare."

Um, okay. Death almost sounded jealous of Matt. And was he flirting with me? Was I supposed to be flattered? My life had taken a surreal twist.

"Uh, thank you?" My voice went up at the end so it sounded like a question.

Death seemed please by my answer and smiled that creeptastic smile. "When you consider the millions of people who I must watch over, the few in your hero's jurisdiction seems trivial."

"Okkkaayy." I tried to keep a neutral expression, but my tone betrayed me.

The smile left Death's face. My relief at not having to see its horrible perfection was short lived though.

"Not the kind of hero your Matt is perhaps. He is a worthy adversary. Yes, a very mortal foe, indeed." He stood and nodded his head at me and disappeared before my next pounding heartbeat.

Adversary? Mortal? Goosebumps had once again broken out all over my body. I didn't just send a jealous Death after the one man in my life who had saved me every time I needed him.

I scrambled for my phone. What the hell was I going to tell him? It wasn't like I could say, "Hey Matt, Death has fixated on me and you keep getting in the way of him killing me. Plus he seems to be a little jealous of you, so be careful." He'd probably block my number.

"Don't tell me you're having another near-death experience so soon. Your house is kinda far from mine."

"What? How did you know about him? I mean, um, no. I just, uh, wanted to make sure you were okay. I had this, uh, weird feeling, a sense of doom about you like something bad was gonna happen." I babbled like a lunatic. "I just, you know, wanted to make sure you're okay."

Oh, my God. I sounded like a crazy stalker or an obsessive girlfriend. There was a silence that seemed to last forever before Matt cleared his throat.

"Um, yeah. Thanks for your concern, but I'm doing fine."

I nodded my head, though he couldn't see me. "Well, good. You should just try to take it easy the next few days. You know, don't do anything dangerous. Stay safe."

Could I sound any more like an idiot?

"Yeah, well the most dangerous thing I have planned is letting Haley pick the pizza and maybe having a beer or two. I'll be sure to be careful when opening the bottles though." He tried to make a joke out of it, but I could practically read his thoughts through the phone. He thought I was a nut bag.

I said goodbye and hung up. That went well. I opened the front door, stomped out into my yard, and yelled out into the sky, "Leave him alone, Death. You hear me? Don't go near him."

I startled some of my neighbors who were out front power walking. They stopped mid-stride and gawked at me for a moment before whispering to each other. They both looked back at me and I couldn't resist.

"Boo!" I yelled at them and had the satisfaction of

watching them jump before they scurried away. I laughed like a maniac and then went back into the house, slamming the door behind me.

I glanced around my home and tried to conjure up some good memories. Instead all I saw were flashbacks of bad times. The entry table where I would throw the mail and my purse and David would have a fit because it was messy. The kitchen where I read the text and confirmed what I already knew in my heart was true about his infidelity. The study where I found out that little slut would get some of David's life insurance money. The couch where Death had sat and made himself at home.

My eyes fell on the banister, and I smiled. One good memory came to mind and it was of me sliding down and Matt helping me up. Matt. He was right. It was time to move out of this damned house and leave all these ghosts behind. Maybe I could escape Death's watchful eye in a new place.

# CHAPTER FOURTEEN

*Off with Their Heads!*

Ah, Tuesday morning back at the office. The frosty reception from my co-workers who had to work late through the weekend made it feel like I was working at the North Pole. Geez, you'd think I'd put them on the naughty list the way some of them glared at me. I guess that made me Scrooge or maybe The Grinch. Calling in sick on Monday hadn't helped things.

Conveniently, they forgot all the times I had covered for them so they could go to their kid's play or go on that romantic getaway. Screw 'em.

I grabbed my coffee and booted up the computer. It took me almost an hour to sort out the mess they'd made of my accounts. By lunch time, I had managed to balance all of the general ledger accounts. The financial reports were on the printer when the sickly sweet smell of Colleen's perfume announced her arrival.

I handed them to her, stood and pulled my purse out of my desk.

"Where are you going?" she asked.

"Lunch. I have some errands to run."

"But you usually work through lunch. There are still some reports and audits that need to be finished before we can file."

"Sorry, imperative things to do. Be back in an hour. Ciao!" I waived while I walked out the door. I used to be intimidated by her and would do whatever she said. Funny how facing down Death himself had made me a stronger person, or maybe it was the pending insurance money.

I relished the look on her face when she sputtered in irritation. A girl could get used to this. Before, I would work through lunch eating a salad or some other diet food. Today I was getting a burger and going house hunting.

While cleaning up my co-workers' mess this morning, I had decided it would be the last time I would bend over for anyone again. Well, unless it was something I wanted to do. An image of Matt dressed in fatigues all sweaty from combat flashed in my mind.

Oh, yeah, I was a single, smart woman with a pending settlement. I would do whatever and whomever I wanted. Time to take care of my needs now, and the most pressing one was lunch.

I drove back to the office an hour later with a full belly, taking the long route past the old Bella Vista building I had always loved. They had turned it into condos but kept the weathered brick that showcased old world architecture. I had wanted to move there when we first moved to Arizona. But David had shot that idea down fast. It was so close to work, I could ride a bike. Not that I owned a bike, or the desire to actually ride one.

There was a "Condos available now" sign out front with a real estate agent's name and number. I pulled over to write down his information before I made the quick drive back to work, ten minutes late.

Colleen drummed her nails so hard on my desk that I was surprised she hadn't chipped her French manicure. She must have been waiting a while for me. "There you are! I have been trying to reach you for half an hour. We're going to have to scramble to meet our deadline now."

By 'we' she usually meant 'me', but not today. "Oh, shoot. I have to balance the bank recs. Why don't you get started on the other reports and I will pitch in when I'm finished."

I didn't wait for her reply, just walked away to the file room to grab the bank statements. She didn't follow me inside, so I loitered in the room for a few minutes. I opened the door, clutching the bank reconciliation file to my chest while I walked back to my desk and sat down. No sign of Colleen. Whew.

The contents of the file made good camouflage spread out all over my desk along with the opened spreadsheet on my computer. After a quick glance around to make sure no one was watching, I opened a browser window and typed in the website address I had jotted down. Cheesy music played from my speakers and I fumbled with the mute button then clicked on the spreadsheet tab. My head darted to either side to see if anyone noticed.

Time for diversionary tactics. I shuffled through the paperwork in front of me and even added up some random numbers on the calculator for good measure. When I felt enough time had passed, I clicked back to the website. A picture of Rick Webber, a Realtor with a big cheesy grin, filled up half my computer screen. He had sandy-blond hair and piercing blue eyes. He looked like he should be surfing waves, not selling real-estate.

I found the link for listings at Bella Vista and had two choices, one for the penthouse on the top floor and one of the standard lofts.

Why not start at the top first? I clicked on the link and viewed the slideshow. This place was beautiful. Hardwood floors, arched doorways and a giant Jacuzzi bathtub. It even had a balcony. I could imagine having tea out there while doing the crossword puzzle on a Sunday morning. Okay, more like coffee and a trashy novel in the late afternoon. It would be awesome.

I hit the back button and clicked on the other link for the standard place. It was half the size of the penthouse. Same old carpet and tile you see in most houses. Ho hum bathroom. No closet space. Definitely a huge step down from the first.

Of course, the price tag reflected the difference. The penthouse was almost double the price of the standard. The standard loft was about the same price as my own home, but half the size. If I bought the penthouse, I would have more room, but would be spending most of my insurance check. How would I pay off the credit card debts David had racked up? Would I be stuck in this higher paying, more stressful job forever if I bought this place?

It was crazy. I already owned a nice house. Sure it was way out in BFE and it reeked of smoke, but this was a bad market to sell anything. My imagination tortured me with an image of David and Mandi 'christening' each room while I was at work busting my ass to pay for it. Screw him. I never signed for those credit cards so I wasn't paying for them. Besides bad house trumped bad job.

I filled out the online form to let the Realtor know I was interested and listed my contact information. I had just hit send and closed the webpage when I heard the click of stiletto heels tapping down the hallway and felt a presence lurking behind me. Colleen was back.

Dun. Dun. Dun.

"Are you finished with the bank recs yet? I need some help auditing the expenses and payables." She was standing with her hands on her hips, not even trying to hide that she was looking over my shoulder at my monitor to check up on me.

"There are some charges that aren't accounted for. I'm going to have go through the hard copies of the receipts." I smiled at her and opened my eyes as wide as I could, trying to look like an innocent child. Judging by the look on her face, I probably looked more like one of those creepy dolls with the big heavily made-up eyes and fat heads.

She gave a nervous laugh, a first from her, and crossed her arms in front of herself. "Well, okay then. As soon as you finish, let me know. We might have to stay late tonight to complete the reports."

I was spared having to come up with an excuse for not staying by my ringing phone. "Oh, I gotta take this. Been waiting for this call all morning. Very important."

I turned my back to her and answered the phone. It was Rick, the Realtor, calling about my interest in the condo. Guy must sit on his email waiting for prospects. Gotta love people who worked on commission.

"Would you mind holding for a moment?" I asked him but didn't wait for his agreement before hitting the hold button.

Colleen was still standing behind me. She was trying to eavesdrop on my call. *Bitch.* "You know, I might be a while. I'll talk to you later?"

In case my dismissive tone didn't do the trick, I stared a hole right in the middle of her forehead without blinking. At first, she tried to stare me down, but please. I learned that move from my witch of an aunt, who was convinced she could glare the sin out of me. I channeled Auntie Dearest, and Colleen didn't stand a chance.

Colleen blinked first and mumbled something as she walked away. I kept my eyes on her until she clip-clopped away from my desk and down the hall to her office.

Victory!

Riding my high, I went back to Rick on the phone. "Thanks for holding. I'm interested in the penthouse condo at Bella Vista."

"Oh, yes, Bella Vista is a great location. It's a historic building with only nine stories and sixty units. There is an onsite gym and an Olympic sized pool on the ground floor as well as concierge services. Oh, and kids just love the train rides and water features of the park right across the street. It's *the* spot for kids' birthday parties."

He was selling his little heart out, but he didn't have to bother. I was sold from the video tour on his website. "No kids for me. It sounds great though. When can I see it?"

I heard him clicking away on a computer, then a moment of silence, followed by furious typing. "Oh, my apologies, looks like this unit has an offer pending. But don't worry, Mrs. Reynolds. I have four similar properties available nearby that I can show you at your convenience."

I didn't want a similar location; I wanted *that* condo in *that* building. Now that I had imagined David and his little slut having sex in every room, I couldn't stand to live in my house another moment. "It's Miss Reynolds now, actually. And I will make you an offer today. Twenty- thousand over the listed price."

This was crazy. I hadn't even seen the place in person. Didn't even have the check from the insurance company. It was so unlike me to do something so impulsive.

Damn, it felt good.

The Realtor took in a sharp breath. "Well, Miss Reynolds, I can certainly present your offer to the seller. We don't actually have a contract from the other interested party. Can you have your Realtor fax over a contract today?"

The Realtor who sold us our house was not my favorite person. He talked over me, speaking directly to David, even when I was the one asking questions. I wanted to fire him, but David insisted we use him.

"Um, I don't have one. Can't you represent both of us?" Again, I knew it wasn't the wisest decision, but I didn't care. From the first click, I knew this was my new home and nothing was going to stop me from buying it.

"Certainly. When can we meet to draw up the paperwork? If you give me some information, I can get it started for you." He was practically drooling over the phone. The thought of not splitting the commission on a half-a-million dollars would do that to anyone.

I glanced at the clock. It was almost two. Technically, I should be off in two and a half more hours, assuming I could avoid running into Colleen who would probably demand I stay the extra ten minutes I took at lunch. Having an unbreakable appointment gave me a good excuse to leave a little early. I grinned.

"Let's make it for four-thirty."

He gave me the address and directions to his office. It wasn't too far away. I would be able to make it with time to spare, as long as I left on time. The main obstacle to that happening was making a beeline for my desk.

"I hope you cleared everything up and are ready to tackle the audit. I'll order up some salads for us so we can work through dinner. I'll use my card. Don't worry about paying me back until tomorrow."

Oh, yes, nothing entices a girl to work her ass off more than diet food. And I knew the card she was using would be the company one and she would expense the whole thing and then pocket the cash I gave her. "Oh, I can't. That was my doctor. He made an appointment for me today so I need to leave a little early. He said it was urgent. You know, since I was so sick yesterday."

Her mouth puckered up like she had one of those Super Sonic sour candies. "But who is going to help me close the month?"

I would have felt guilty if I hadn't been the one doing it every single month, while she took all the credit. It was her job after all. I was just a little cog in the wheel. "The doctor said it was urgent and since the appointment is on my own time, I didn't think it would be a problem. I have so much time off accrued."

Her eyes narrowed, and I knew she was dying to rip me a new one. But she couldn't. How could she complain about me not staying late to do her job without exposing how little of her own work she actually had done all these years?

"I guess I will have to find someone who is willing to be a team player. I'll remember who was willing to help at review time." She stormed off toward one of my co-worker's cubicles.

Had she really thought I would be intimidated with her threat of giving me a bad review? She had never given me a good review because she didn't want me to get promoted. This bitch couldn't intimidate me. I'd faced down cheating, vampire David, a werewolf, and Death himself. A pissed-off controller was nothing.

I wasn't going to win any popularity contests around here, but I could live with that. The rest of the day, I was left blissfully alone. My lips should have turned blue from the chill radiating from my colleagues, but I didn't mind the silent treatment.

If they thought that was a punishment, they were sadly mistaken. Without their constant complaining and gossiping I was able to finish all of my work before three. As a reward I decided to quit a little early.

It was tempting to shut down my computer and waltz brazenly out the door, but I didn't have the balls to do it. Instead I went back online and looked at pictures of my new condo. The listed price made my stomach flip. This place was so much more expensive than the house I had bought with David. Was I insane?

Before I could panic too much and cancel my appointment, I shut everything down and speed walked to the door for my escape. I held my breath the whole walk to my car, but no one tried to stop me. The Realtor's office was only twenty minutes from my office.

A Mustang drove past me on the way reminding me of David's baby. Huh, where was his car? It was probably still in the parking garage of the hotel where he was having his liaison with his toothy friend. He loved that car, detailed it every weekend.

An evil grin swept my lips. He had never let me drive it. He said I drove too fast and it wasn't good for the car. It was a muscle car, for the love of Pete! He said he couldn't show up at client meetings in a POS car. He would never make a sale.

Meanwhile, I was stuck with my slow old Toyota with the broken CD player and the lukewarm A/C. I bet Matt could find out where the vehicle was located before the hotel had it towed. I shot him a text asking him to help me find it. Oh, man, I couldn't wait to set that horsepower free.

This was the best day ever! I had slain Colleen, the Dragon Lady, found my new castle, and would soon rescue a noble steed. Who needed to be saved by a prince or a white knight? Not this chick. Long live the Queen!

# CHAPTER FIFTEEN

*Location, Location, Location*

Rick wasn't what I expected from the cheesy photo on the website and business card. His dress shirt was tight around his muscles, but not in a gross, gym-rat kind of way. He was a good-looking guy and younger than me. His personality filled the room and he had a smile that lit up his face.

"Can I get you something to drink?" he asked.

I shook my head and followed him to his office.

"Okay, since I am representing both of you, I have to advise you that offering twenty thousand over the asking price is not a good idea. This is just the initial offer. If they don't like it, we'll counter with more," Rick said.

Huh. An honest salesman? He could teach the sharks at David's office a thing or two. "Okay, sounds good. How long do you think this will take to close?"

"Depends on your financing. The sellers are pretty motivated. Ugly divorce. Husband cheated on her with his secretary. How cliché, right?"

Must be an epidemic of adulterers in this town. Was it that hard to stay faithful?

"Have you been pre-qualified? Do you have another home to sell first?"

"No and yes, well kind of. I don't have to wait to sell my old house before buying the new one. I really want to get out of there as soon as possible."

Rick arched a brow at me and said, "Sounds intriguing.

May I ask why?"

He looked at me with genuine interest. He really wanted to hear my answer. Poor guy.

I didn't realize how desperate I was to tell someone my whole horrible story, minus the parts with Death. Since my life had destructed, Matt was the only friendly person I'd had contact with, well, besides that one barista at Starbucks. The people in line got so damned impatient, but hey, the guy asked me how I was doing. I didn't even get through half my story before they started honking.

Rick, bless his heart, listened to my whole sordid tale with the appropriate amount of disgust, terror, and awe. "Oh, honey, you are so better off without that loser. That dog deserved to get bitten and turned into a vampire. Talk about karma biting you in the ass. That man does not deserve another tear from you."

He stood up and walked over to hug me and handed me a tissue. When did I start crying? I wiped my face and decided that would be the last tear I would shed for a man who had never really loved me. "You're the first person who, after hearing about my husband turned vampire, didn't look at me like I had two heads. You don't think I'm crazy?"

Rick sat down on the edge of the table and leaned over to me and said, "My husband works at the hospital. He has told me stories that make me want to throw on some cammo, get a gun, and become a prepper. The government can deny the existence of monsters and try to blame it on some new drug, but girl, I know better."

Having someone else know what was going on made me feel so much better. I pushed all thoughts of David out of my mind and asked, "Do you think you can sell my old house as soon as possible?"

Rick turned to his computer and asked me for the address. He typed it in and clicked for a few minutes. "I've pulled up some comps. There's quite a few houses for sale out there. But I'm sure we can get it sold."

He printed up a listing price and I realized I would be lucky if I broke even on the sale, if I were even able to sell the damned thing. Could I stand to live there until it sold? "If I pay cash for the condo, can I move in right away?"

"Certainly. If you have that much cash available, an early close shouldn't be a problem and will make your offer even stronger to the seller. I just need a bank statement or some other proof of funds before submitting the contract."

Oh, shit. I didn't have any proof unless you counted Steve's promise of a check within a week. "I have to wait for a check from the insurance company. Who knows how long that can take considering the shady circumstances? Maybe I should look at the cheaper one and try to get a mortgage."

Rick reached out and put his hand on my arm. "Let me get this straight, Presidential's employee, the same one who was having an affair with your husband, forged your signature on the policy, and they are paying her part of the settlement so she doesn't ruffle feathers?"

"Yeah, fucked up, huh?"

"I can think of another F word that fits. Fraud. As in insurance fraud. For a company whose motto is 'Insurance with integrity' this would destroy them in this God- fearing town. They should be tripping over themselves to give you money to shut you up. Girl, call them. Now. Demand that check."

I hadn't really thought about it that way. I had been happy just to be getting such a large settlement. He was right. They owed me. Rick was holding up my cellphone in front of me. I grabbed it and dialed Steve's number on speaker phone.

"Steve Michaels," he answered in his radio personality voice.

"Hello, Steve, this is Sara Reynolds."

"Sara. How are you doing?" he dialed it down and spoke in a hushed tone.

"Fine, thanks. I was calling to see if I could pick up my check for David's life insurance. I have expenses that I need to pay. Funeral costs are expensive. You know how it is."

Funeral costs. Ha. I had no plans on having a funeral or any kind of memorial for David. He was a foster kid with no family that I knew of, and his few friends were a bunch of assholes I had refused to have any contact with years ago. His girlfriend might have wanted the spectacle so she could play the weeping widow, but I hadn't even bothered to watch when the crime scene guys swept his ashes into an evidence bag.

He cleared his throat. "I can only imagine how hard this is for you. Accounting needs executive approval for bank drafts of that size. It's standard procedure. We can send an ACH directly to your bank, if you'd like. It shouldn't take more than a week or so."

"A week or so?" I repeated. Rick shook his head vigorously at me. "No, you said that last time, and I haven't heard back from you. I need this money. I can pick up a check… today?" The last word was more of a question aimed at Rick.

He nodded his head.

"I see. Well, perhaps we can cut you a check for a partial payment and then send the balance of the funds in a certified check to your bank once the claim has been processed. That should help ease some of your worries."

Rick shook his head no adamantly. He mouthed the word "scandal".

"You know, the more I think about this, the more I wonder if I should be reporting this to the police or the state's Department of Insurance. I mean, Mandi committed fraud against both of us, right? Isn't the right thing to make sure the guilty party is punished?"

Steve sputtered. "Well, let's not be too hasty. She's been fired and we've taken steps to ensure it can never happen again. Why go through a long drawn out trial? I would hate to drag you through that given all you've already suffered. I'll have accounting get a certified check from the bank in the morning. You can pick it up tomorrow."

"Cut me a company check for the whole thing; doesn't have to be certified. I know you're good for it, Steve. Integrity is your motto, right? We both want to put this incident behind us with the least amount of public humiliation, for both of us. I can be there in half an hour." My stomach was clenched so tight, my ab muscles hurt.

"Fine. You'll have to sign a non-disclosure agreement before you can get the check. Good day." Steve hung up and Rick grabbed me in a hug.

"Good job. I knew you could do it. Now, let's write up this contract and I will send it while you get your check. You can run by the bank to deposit it. Just remember I need a ten-thousand dollar cashier's check for an earnest money deposit, which will go toward your down payment. Make it out to this title company." He handed me a card with the amount circled in red pen.

I signed my name and initials over and over in a daze.

All my life I had bitten my tongue, never standing up to myself. Now, in one day, I had done it twice. It felt good. Rick promised to call the sellers while I picked up my check.

Presidential Insurance had a fancy office in a building not too far away. I checked in at the receptionist's desk. It wasn't long before Dan, David's supervisor, showed up. "Ah, Sara. I just need you to sign a few forms before we can give you the check."

In one hand he had a stack of paperwork, in the other an envelope that presumably had my check.

"Let me just take a peek to make sure it's correct," I said before I reached for the envelope. Eight hundred, fifty thousand dollars. My heart sped up while I stared at the check. My hand shook so much I could barely read my name on it.

Holy shit. Holy shit. Look at all those zeros! This day rocked, and me, I was a rock star. A rich one.

"Ahem. The forms?" Dan interrupted my moment.

Asshole.

Just to piss him off, I took my time reading every single form before I signed them. When I finished signing the last form, I smiled brightly at Dan. I got what I wanted. I could be nice now.

"All done. Take care of yourself, Dan."

"Sara, we took the liberty of packing up David's personal things in his office." He nodded at the receptionist who pulled a storage box out from beside her desk.

A quick inventory of the items showed the usual stuff people keep in their desks. I dug through looking to see if he had any pictures of me. Nope, just some snacks, soda, little trinkets he had gotten from God knows where and... *was that? No fucking way.*

Sure as shit, it was a little foil condom packet. I dropped it in disgust.

"Burn it," I said to Dan. He looked scandalized when he saw what I'd dropped. I shoved the box back on the desk and walked out the door. Why couldn't David be alive so I could kill him right now? I should send Death a thank you card.

No. Not gonna think about him any more. He was not going to ruin my good day. I stopped at the bank to deposit the money and get a cashier's check for the ten-thousand dollars. The teller had to call the manager, who tried to talk me into opening a different account. Yes, I knew the whole amount would not be guaranteed by the FDIC, but I would take the risk the bank wouldn't go bankrupt overnight. I was a rebel, baby. They also let me know there would be a ten-day hold on my big, fat check, so that ten-thousand dollar one would wipe out everything in my savings and checking and I would have to dip into my credit line a little.

Gulp.

I walked into the real estate office with two celebration lattes. A grateful Rick took a sip of his and said, "Guess who is the proud owner of a new penthouse condo in beautiful Bella Vista?"

"Yes! Oh, my God, I'm so happy!" I danced around in front of his desk and he got up to join me, before turning serious once again.

"You're happy? I just made a thirty-eight thousand dollar commission," he flashed his infectious smile and said, "You have to let me take you out to dinner tonight! The Suns are playing LA. It's a pre-season game but we're big Suns fans. Do you like basketball? We go to this sports bar with great food and watch the games. Come with us."

Let's see, go home to a smelly, empty house full of bad memories or go out to eat with my new friend and his husband. It was an easy choice.

Brandon was a hilarious, bald, and green-eyed man who greeted me like I was family. When he heard about David, Brandon tried to set me up with hot men at the bar, and when I told him I wasn't interested in another man, he pointed out some women. All of his choices were way out of my league though, but it felt damn good to have someone think I was attractive enough to land one of them.

"Here, darling, next week, you and I are meeting for lunch. Can you believe, I'm the doctor, yet this guy is always too busy to have lunch with me?"

"Hello? You don't get paid on commission and you only have to leave your cushy office to do rounds at the hospital during business hours. I gotta make the dough, can't have you looking for a new sugar daddy." Rick shoved him playfully.

Brandon handed me a card with his contact info on it, along with his cheesy picture which was an exact replica of Rick's picture, complete with matching outfits.

I tried to compose my face into something pleasant and noticed both men had gone silent. I looked up and they both had their hands over their mouths holding back laughter.

"It's hideous, isn't it?" Brandon asked.

"Thanks a lot. It isn't that bad," Rick countered. He tried to appear pissed off, but blew it by laughing.

They got matching cards? I wasn't getting the joke and started to feel left out. Brandon came to my rescue. "Tell me what you thought the first time you saw that picture of him. Cheesearific! Right? So awful."

"Then why did you use them, Rick? And why did you get ones that were just as bad, Brandon?"

Rick jumped in, "Because they were mandatory at the real estate office. The broker's wife fancies herself a photographer. So we all had to get them to put on our cards and websites. Hu.mil.i.ating. But this big lug," he put his head on Brandon's shoulder and Brandon kissed his forehead. "He contacted her and got pictures taken to match so I wouldn't be embarrassed alone."

"Your husband is supposed to carry half your burdens. And honey, that picture was a burden!"

They laughed and I wondered if anyone would ever love me like that.

"Take it to the hole!" Screamed Brandon at the TV.

I was so startled, that I knocked my empty glass over. The crowd was getting loud so I figured it was a good time to leave.

We hugged our goodbyes. I made the long drive home, thinking about what a wonderful day I'd had and the two new friends I'd made.

I wasn't surprised to see Death waiting at my door. I was so rarely happy in my life, the universe was bound to step in and put me back in my miserable place.

## CHAPTER SIXTEEN

*Death at my Door...Again*

I parked the car in the garage and went inside. He waited for me at the kitchen table. He wore the black jeans again, but this time, he sported a tight black t-shirt that showed off his pecs. Not as muscled as Rick, but still impressive. Death must work out.

The first few visits I had been too flustered to do anything but answer his questions, but this time I was going to do the asking. "So, isn't someone dying every second? How can you be here and still take care of business, so to speak?"

He flashed his pearly-whites in his creeptastic smile. Thank God he wore sunglasses. The combination of his soul-sucking, pitch-black eyes and overly-perfect smile would have stopped my heart right then and there.

"Surely, you don't think I collect everyone for their final journey? It would be impossible for one being to do. There are others who do my bidding as well."

Death had minions? I pictured those little yellow guys from that cartoon dressed in black hoods and carrying scythes. I smiled and sat at the table with him.

"Are you one of those humans that believe in a fat, jolly man dressed in red who delivers presents to all the children of the world in one night too?" he inquired.

"No, I know Santa Claus isn't real."

"Oh, no, he was real. An agent of Hades, that one was. But he didn't give presents to good little girls and boys so much as kidnap them from their beds and disembowel them as sacrifices in his quest for immortality. Which is why his clothes were stained red."

A shiver ran down my spine. The line from the Christmas carol, "He sees you when you're sleeping" took on a whole different meaning. The holidays would never be the same.

I shook off the disturbing images. "You almost sound disgusted by him. Thought you would like him since you're on the same team."

Death stopped smiling and cocked his head to the side like he did when he was trying to understand me. "My team? You think because I ride with Hades, I am evil?"

"Well, duh. You kill people."

He sat back and brought his hands to the table. I never really noticed before, but Death's hands were small, almost dainty. "Is it evil to relieve the suffering of the sick? Should I ignore the cries begging for me? The elderly who greet me as an old friend when they are too weak to carry on?"

I fidgeted with my car keys, not knowing what to say. He was right. In those cases, death can be a mercy. "Okay, but what you're doing now with the vampires, werewolves and other monsters to bring about the apocalypse isn't a good thing. Everyone is going to die. You're trying to end the world, for God's sake."

He flinched at my use of the Big Guy's name. Was it the word itself or my using it in vain that bugged him?

"You have read The Book of Revelations, then and understand what is going on? Good. Then you must also know that it is the lamb who broke the seals and put me on this path. If I am doing God's will, how can I be evil?"

It was strange to think of Death as a good guy. I had hated him, and blamed him all these years for my miserable life. Was everything that happened to me all just part of God's plan? "If you're just doing your job, why do you keep visiting me? Why do you keep trying to kill me?"

"I find you fascinating. Aside from the fact that you can see me and know who I am, you don't fear me. You are alive, yet you don't really live your life. You wish you had not survived the car crash, yet you have escaped me time and again. I don't think I have met a human quite so contrary."

Was Death able to read my thoughts? There were many times since losing my family that I wished I'd died. Except for a few brief moments, in the beginning with David, I had been just going through the motions, just surviving for so many years. I hated that he could see that in me.

"I was surprised not to find you home when I arrived. You weren't with that police officer, I know; I checked."

Matt! Oh God. No. "What did you do? Is he okay?"

Without waiting for an answer I dumped my purse out on the table to get my cellphone. I looked up Matt's number and hit send. Come on, come on. Pick up. It went to voicemail. Shit. "Matt, it's Sara. Call me when you get this, okay? Doesn't matter how late it is."

"Do not worry. I did not collect him tonight."

I dropped my phone on the table and ran my shaky hands through my hair. "Oh, thank God."

"You care about this man." He said it in a flat voice.

"He's a nice guy and doesn't deserve to die simply because he knows me. Just leave him alone. Please." The please came out a little more forceful than I intended.

Death stood, but before he could respond, my cellphone rang. We both looked down at it as my ring tone, the music from the Buffy intro, played.

"There is your police officer now. I shall leave you to your conversation." I didn't even blink this time. He just disappeared before my eyes.

"Hello." I knew it was him but didn't want to sound like I was staring at the phone waiting for his call.

"Hey, it's Matt. I got your message. Everything all right? You sounded kind of frantic." He talked fast, like he didn't feel like talking, but didn't want to be rude and not return my call.

"Oh, not frantic, just excited. I wanted to tell you my good news. I bought a new place." I was trying to think of how I could ask him if he had any near-death experiences today, courtesy of my new stalker, Death. But I couldn't think of any way to phrase it without sounding like a total whack job.

"Hey, that's great. Congratulations. When do you move in?"

Rick had put a two week closing date on my offer and we both prayed the hold on the check would be released by then. "Two weeks."

"Wow, that's fast. You'll be packing like a madwoman. Two weeks, huh? I should be healed by then, so give me a call and I can help you move."

Healed? What the hell did Death to him? "What do you mean you should be healed by then? Healed from what?"

"Oh, well, it's stupid you know. I had the truck up on the jack while I was doing some work on it, and it fell somehow. Damned lucky I had the jack stands under it or

I'd be toast. I cracked my head on the engine block when I tried to sit up. That's me, a real Einstein, jumping toward the truck coming down on me."

Holy shit! Death had dropped a truck on Matt just because he thought I was interested in him. That was insane. "Oh, my God! Are you sure you're all right? I told you not to do anything dangerous. Remember that feeling I had?"

"Hey, I listened. I couldn't find the stands at first and was just gonna risk working on it without them, but I remembered your warning and kept looking for them. Don't know how they ended up in the spare bedroom."

I bet I knew. Death, that asshole, had hidden them there on purpose to make Matt risk his life. He said he couldn't make anyone do anything, but he could do whatever he thought would make that person take the risk.

"I survived a war in Iraq and a couple of shoot outs on the force only to almost die in my own garage by my own damned truck. Man, that would have been messed up. Guess you never know when your time's up."

Except it hadn't been his time to go until I had put him in Death's crosshairs.

"You know," he continued, "it's been a long day. I'm gonna pop some Tylenol and go to bed. Congratulations on the new place. Oh, I'll send you a text tomorrow to let you know where the car is at. Talk to you later."

I said goodbye and hung up. Exhaustion hit me. The adrenaline surge I'd felt when Death had mentioned Matt was starting to fade. Matt. What was I going to do? It was bad enough Death was fixated on me. I couldn't let him focus on Matt. He had a kid.

I would have to just cut my ties with him. His offer to help me move was great, but I had to hire movers. I looked around the room at the ten-year-old furniture that smelled like it had been sitting around a campfire.

On second thought, I wouldn't bother to move anything. New place, new stuff. No memories of unhappy times.

# CHAPTER SEVENTEEN

*Stains, Planes and Automobiles*

The week seemed to creep by. I gave in and stayed late the rest of the week, not because I wanted to help Colleen, but because I didn't want to go home to my empty house. I decided to work on my good karma and do everyone's filing.

There were no windows in the file room, so I lost track of time. When I finally emerged with a growling belly and several paper cuts, it was dark. I was supposed to call security to walk me to my car, but Ernie was working tonight. His arthritic knees made him move as slow as that last bit of ketchup stuck in the bottom of the bottle.

Ketchup. Food. My stomach growled again, telling me I would probably starve to death before making it to my car if I waited for Ernie.

I would be fine. It wasn't a bad neighborhood or anything. And Death had left me alone all week. Just in case, I took out my cellphone so I could call 911 and held my keys in my other hand with the points sticking out between my fingers like a set of brass knuckles.

It was quiet, not a soul in sight. David's car was parked in my space and for a second I was confused. Duh! It wasn't his car any more. It was mine. A few feet from the car, I stopped to put my keys away and dig out his from the depths of my purse. The purse fumbled out of my hands and the contents scattered on the ground.

It was the fumble that saved me.

As I knelt on the ground, trying to catch an errant lip balm that had rolled part-way under my passenger door, I saw feet on the other side. Someone was hiding there, waiting for me.

I turned and ran back to the building, but I had left my keys on the ground, and I couldn't get back inside. I heard swearing before the slap-slap of shoes hitting the pavement got closer to me.

Uselessly, I yanked on the door and then turned to see what kind of a monster was attacking me now. It was a human, just one scraggly human dressed like a bum. I looked at what he held in his hand.

A human with a switchblade.

Screaming as loud as I could, I ran toward the other end of the building. The scrawny guy had long legs and managed to get way too close to me while I ran. I jumped into the wall of hedges that blocked the sidewalk, and expected to feel the knife slice my back open any minute.

I barreled through the bushes, heedless of the thorns, then jumped over the small wall and made it to the sidewalk on the other side. Thank God it was casual Friday, and I was wearing jeans and sneakers. Those bushes would have ripped my legs up if I were in a dress, and I would have probably twisted my ankle jumping in heels. I stopped to take a breath to see if I lost the guy.

"Ouch. Fuck." My pursuer cussed while he stumbled through the bushes not far behind me.

Dammit, no time to catch my breath. *Run!*

My feet started moving and so did my brain. My phone.

I'd shoved it into my pocket when I dropped my purse. Ever try to yank something out of your pocket when you're running? It's worse if your jeans are a little too tight from eating Chinese loaded with sodium every night. Damned MSG! After I nearly tripped over my- own legs, I managed to extract my phone and dialed 911.

Cutting off the 911 operator, I screamed for help and gave my location. The dispatcher was asking me questions, but it was too hard to catch my breath while running to answer.

Behind me, my pursuer burst out of the bushes behind me head first. He must have not seen the wall and tripped over it. He rolled on the ground, clutched his stomach and screamed, "Shit. You fucking bitch."

I was half-way down the sidewalk when Ernie started shuffle toward me from around the back of the building.

"Miss, are you okay? I thought I heard some noise out here."

Noise? The guy was yelling obscenities at the top of his breath, and I had been screaming bloody murder the last five minutes while he chased me. Was the old guy deaf as well as lame?

"Help me! I'm being chased. He's got a knife." I screamed at him while pointing behind me.

The security guard looked at where I pointed. The guy had just stood, but was hunched over holding his stomach. He weaved uncertainly for a few seconds, and then ran back into the bushes.

"Hey, you, stop! Stop right there!" Ernie shouted. He pulled his mace out, but his hands shook so badly I was afraid he would spray me by mistake.

"No, Ernie. He's leaving. Let him go." The adrenaline

made my hand shake as much as Ernie's when I reached out to lower his hand.

I was safe.

I tried to catch my breath while Ernie and I walked slowly back to the parking lot. We stopped where the attacker had fallen and saw a dark stain of blood. No way. Did the guy fall on his knife and stab himself? Maybe I finally have a guardian angel looking out for me. His wings must be pretty tired by now.

The blue and red flashing lights pulled in to the parking lot about the same time we turned the corner. A uniformed officer jumped out and asked, "Ma'am. Are you okay? Are you the one who called 911?"

"Yes. The guy had a knife. He ran back through the bushes over there." I pointed them out and added, "Not sure where he went. I think he might have injured himself when he fell."

"Stay here next to my car. I'll be back."

Ernie sat on the back bumper of the cop car, rubbing his knees as though they hurt. I was too amped up to sit, so I paced.

A few minutes later, we heard rustling in the bushes on the other side of us, and Ernie, bless his heart, stood between me and it. No boogie man jumped out. It was the police officer checking to see if anyone was hiding in the thicket. "All clear now. You say you saw a knife? Can you describe the guy?"

"He definitely had a knife. He was kind of skinny, with long legs, wearing jeans and a black hoodie, but he had his hood up so I didn't see his face. He might have been Hispanic, or maybe a white guy with a tan or dirty maybe? His skin was a little brown. I'm not good with height, maybe a little shorter than you? It happened so fast."

I was the worst eye witness ever.

The cop pulled out a notepad and nodded at Ernie, "You?"

"Well, I heard the lady screaming, so I hustled around the building. I weren't wearing my glasses, so I didn't get a good look. I saw something get up off the sidewalk and run back into the bushes. Coulda been a man."

Make that the second worst eye witness ever.

He took our statements, but since nothing was stolen—my purse and its contents were still laying on the ground by the car—and with our stellar descriptions, there wasn't much he could do.

"He was probably just some druggie, looking to get some money for his next fix. Next time, call security to walk you to your car if you're working late," he admonished.

I grabbed my purse and shoveled everything back inside it. "I will. Thank you, officer, and you too, Ernie. I don't think I could have run any farther when you showed up and saved me. You arrived in the nick of time."

Ernie puffed up proudly and said, "That's what I'm here for."

He tried to act like it was no big deal, but his hands shook when he tried to button up the mace back in its holster. Heck. Mine were shaking so much it was hard to get the key in the ignition.

I managed to start the car and back out on the street on auto pilot. This wasn't just a random mugging. I had dropped my purse. If all he'd wanted was money, then he wouldn't have chased after me. Death did this, that homicidal bastard. I nearly swerved the car into a lamp post when Death appeared in my passenger seat. "Sweet Baby

Jesus! You scared the shit out of me."

I veered back off the sidewalk and into my lane while I waited to see if my heart was going to explode out of my chest. Gulping air, I looked over to see Death watching me intently. "Quit watching to see if I'm going to have a heart attack, asshole!"

His booming laughter was like a herd of cats banging around in a dryer. It assaulted my ears. I didn't think any of this was funny.

"I knew it. You sent that guy to kill me. What the fuck is wrong with you?"

Death controlled his laughter and said, "I thought if you weren't faced with a supernatural foe you might not survive. Perhaps you would let your guard down. And yet, despite not having the aid of your police friend, you live. Interesting."

Police friend. I had half expected Matt to show up, like my own personal guardian. But after Death mentioned him again, I was glad he hadn't. I couldn't risk his life any more.

I was sick of this crap. Sick of being Death's sock puppet. Like I was here for his amusement. "Get out. Get out of my car, and get out of my life. I am done with you. Go, leave me alone!"

I screamed the last part and the car swerved erratically between the two lanes as I lost my mind. There was a whoop of a siren and then blue and red flashing lights in my rear view mirror. I looked over and Death had gone.

It was the same cop who had shown up at the office. "Ma'am, are you okay? I spotted your weaving taillights and thought you might be drunk, until I recognized your vehicle. Did you hit your head or anything when that guy chased you?"

I covered my eyes from the glare of his headlights reflecting in my side mirror. "No, officer. Sorry. I was just a little upset. I'm fine now."

He looked at me for a few beats and said, "Okay, well, maybe you can call someone to give you a ride. You really shouldn't be driving if you're that upset."

Who could I possibly call that would drive downtown on a Friday night to pick me up? "No, really officer. I can drive. I swear. It was just a momentary lapse. I'll be fine."

He nodded his head and walked back to his car. He followed me home, and I made sure to keep it right at the speed limit and right in the middle of the lane. I breathed a sigh of relief when he made a left and stopped following right before my subdivision.

I had pulled up to the gate and was punching in my code when Death appeared again in my passenger seat. My foot slipped off the brake and my bumper kissed the gate while it was opening. "Son of a bitch, will you knock that off?"

He ignored me and didn't budge from the seat.

"Why do you disappear when someone else shows up?"

He played with the visor before answering. "No normal human has ever been able to see me. Until I figure out how you are able, steps must be taken to ensure no one else inherits your ability. I must make sure it doesn't spread from you like a contagion."

Did he just call me a germ? Didn't matter. His answer revealed what I had already suspected, that if I weren't alone, he wouldn't show up. "Maybe I should get a roommate."

He ignored my remark and continued. "Besides, you would not be able to speak with me while someone is with you, and I find the thought of being ignored distasteful."

Hmmm, Death didn't want to be ignored. It gave me an idea. "Where did you go? Hello?"

It was childish, I know. I continued to pretend Death was invisible while he followed me into the house. He got mad and stepped in front of me when I walked into the kitchen. I pulled up short and then tried to play it off like I was trying to think of something. An obvious ploy, but Death got my message.

"Your immature games are rude. I have always treated you with the utmost respect, never seeking you in private places, never intruding on your thoughts."

Private places? My thoughts? A chill crept down my back at the thought of Death appearing while I was taking a bath, or worse, running through the thoughts in my head. "Oh, my God. Leave me alone, would you? What? Do you have nothing better to do than harass me? Isn't there a plague somewhere you should be attending? Or a plane crash? Don't you have a life?"

"Several actually, and I shall leave you to yours. I have business elsewhere." He disappeared without another word.

I sucked in a deep breath of relief that he was gone, and smelled BO. My clothes were still a little damp from my stress and running induced sweat. Shower first, then dinner.

A short time later, I was dressed in my favorite old nightgown standing in the kitchen while I nuked some leftover egg foo young. While the microwaved hummed, I filled a glass with ice and poured a diet soda. Voices came from the living room. The TV was on? Did I leave it on last night? The microwave beeped, so I grabbed my plate and glass and headed into the living room. Not really paying attention to what was on the screen, I eased down into my favorite recliner and balanced my plate on my lap.

*Capital Airlines Flight 693 to Lake Tahoe has crashed. Survivors unknown.*

A plane crash? I remembered what I had yelled at Death. No. It was a coincidence. I put the plate with my uneaten dinner on the end table and scooted to the edge of my seat. I leaned toward the screen, but there were no updates, just those same damn words running over and over in a loop. After a few minutes, I stood to go check online.

Then the banner changed: *Capital Airlines Flight 693 has crashed into the Sara Nevada Mountains. Rescuers are on route to search for survivors.*

What the hell? Did that read Sara Nevada Mountains? It ran once more before the words were blanked out and corrected to read *Sierra Nevada Mountains*.

I fell back into the seat. Sierra, Sara. No way. He wasn't sending me a message. Death couldn't have done this to send me a message. It was just a typo.

A somber newscaster appeared on the screen. "Officials have confirmed that Capital Airlines Flight number 693 has crashed into the Sierra Nevada Mountains. First responders are rushing to the crash site now. It is unknown if there are any survivors."

I thought he was going to just repeat what they had already announced, until a shaky video clip aired.

"Eye in the Sky News has obtained an amateur video from a witness who had been hiking nearby. I must warn you this footage may be disturbing to watch. On this video, you can see what appears to be an explosion before the flight plummeted into the mountains."

I sat transfixed and watched the footage while it replayed over and over, until the newscaster appeared again. "Hard to imagine there are any survivors. Our hearts and prayers go out to those affected by this great tragedy."

This was my fault. I had made Death mad and he had lashed out. Soda spilled down my chin when my trembling hand brought my glass to my mouth. I sipped it and shut off the TV.

Two hundred and three people.

This was what Death meant when he said he had many lives and business elsewhere.

Two hundred and three souls.

He'd already planned on doing it. It had nothing to do with me. Right? I headed for the fridge to grab the wine. Until now, Death's visits hadn't terrified me, because he seemed like a normal guy who had a little crush on me.

How stupid could I be? Death wasn't a normal guy. Death wasn't a guy at all. He was evil, despite his claims to the contrary. He had just killed hundreds in a temper-tantrum. Sure, he would claim they made the choice to get on that plane and risk dying. But I knew better. He was angry I had refused to play his little games. I had taunted him.

And hundreds had died. He had come after me in my home and now at work. Where could I hide from Death without him destroying mankind in retaliation?

# CHAPTER EIGHTEEN

*Don't Blink*

By working late and staying out in public places, I'd managed to avoid both Death and Matt for the last week, though I couldn't stop myself from watching the news every night in bed. Hearing about all the innocents killed in crazy mass shootings, monster attacks, and even freak acts of nature made it hard to sleep. Was Death still mad? Was this his way of getting my attention? Like killing a bunch of people would impress me. What did he even want from me?

My thoughts raced and my stomach did little flip-flops while I waited for Rick to meet me in the lobby of my new home. The home inspector was meeting us that morning, and Rick had insisted on being there to give me the grand tour on my first visit.

I wiped my sweaty palms on my jeans. What if I hated the place? Sure, I saw the tour on the website, but what if it was all Photoshopped or tricks of the lighting? I could have spent everything I had on a dump.

Before I could spiral down into a wave of despair, Rick appeared and gave me a hug. "Hello, darling. Are you ready to see your gorgeous new home? You are going to love it to death! Want a coffee first?"

I flinched at the mention of death. Since Death's tantrum, things had been quiet. A little too quiet. Waiting for

Death's next attempt on my life had made me so jumpy, I'd nearly screamed when Colleen banged the bathroom stall door into the wall on Friday. Good thing I was already sitting down or I would have peed myself.

Rick must have taken my silence as a no and hustled me onto the elevator. The smell of the coffee cart followed us the whole ride up.

"Hello? Could you at least pretend to be excited about seeing your new *casa*? It's *muy bueno*. You're going to love it." Rick grabbed my hand and coaxed me out of the elevator.

He was right. This place, my new place, was amazing. The kitchen had a six-burner professional range, a sub-zero refrigerator and a walk-in pantry.

"Check out this island. This quartz is gorgeous. Granite is so last season. Will you adopt me so I can live here too?"

I couldn't help but laugh. I'd never met someone as fun and free-spirited as Rick. "You and Brandon are welcome anytime," I told him.

He grew serious for a moment and said, "Thank you. Brandon was worried you didn't like him when you didn't call or text to meet for lunch. I told him to just call you, but he didn't want to be pushy. He's a little insecure about making friends. Growing up gay in a Podunk town in the Midwest will do that to you."

"Oh, no. I didn't mean to hurt his feelings. I loved him. I've just been so busy at work and now with the move. I'll call him, I swear."

It was only partially a lie. I had been busy, but the real reason I hadn't called was fear. When I didn't have anyone I cared about in my life, Death hadn't been as frightening. Now that I started to care about people, he could take them away from me and leave me all alone again.

The thought left me in a funk that even touring the rest of my new house couldn't dispel. I tried to fake enthusiasm, but the only thing that made me smile was the enormous bathtub with jets. The home inspector arrived before Rick figured out I was acting more interested than I felt.

I told Rick I wasn't feeling well and let him deal with the guy, while I slipped out. Instead of heading back toward my car, I wandered aimlessly down the sidewalk in front of the condo.

A train whistle caught my attention, and I looked at the decorative gates of the park across the street. Rick was right when he'd said it was the spot for kids' birthday parties. Red, pink and blue balloons danced in the breeze while tied up all around the ramadas. The tables were decorated in 'Happy Birthday' tablecloths and were covered with cakes and brightly wrapped presents. Kids ran around playing games and laughing. It looked so inviting, I found myself crossing the street to get a closer look.

I eased down on one of the benches and watched some children and their parents ride a serpentine path around the park in primary-colored railcars while the conductor sat in the engine tooting the whistle every few minutes. The cacophony of the train and their squeals of delight soothed my trouble mind.

My eyes closed and I took a few deep breaths to try to relax. I was finding my Zen until I heard the clomping of a hoof and the whinny of a horse behind me.

I jumped off the bench and staggered backward toward the entrance of the park. Not here. Oh, God, I'd brought Death to their Eden. What if he hurt the kids? I turned to flee and collided with someone holding a brightly wrapped package.

Large arms grabbed me and kept me from falling. "Easy there. Is everything all right, ma'am?" He paused for a moment then said, "Sara?"

"He followed me here. I've gotta go so he doesn't hurt the kids," I stammered at Matt while I tried to yank him toward the gates.

Matt dropped the present and swooped up a little brown-haired girl who squealed in protest. He grabbed my arm, pulling me out of the park.

"Daddy, stop it. I'm gonna be late for Katie's party." The little girl wriggled in Matt's arms until he let her down.

"Stay here with Haley," he said to me. He turned to her and said, "You hear me Haley? You stay here."

He pulled out his gun and raced back into the garden with no idea of the danger he faced.

My heart pounded like the beat of a heavy-metal drummer playing a solo. I shouldn't stay here. I should try to draw Death away. But I couldn't leave Haley alone.

Haley reached out, clutched my hand, and said, "Don't worry. My Daddy will get the bad guy. He'll keep you safe. He's a policeman."

The surety in her voice was absolute, not a tear in those big brown eyes. I couldn't remember ever feeling that way about someone. I should be comforting her, not the other way around.

After a few moments, Matt appeared at the gates with his gun holstered. He held the slightly scuffed birthday present in one hand.

"Daddy!" yelled Haley. She dropped my hand and ran to her father who scooped her up in a hug.

"It's okay, baby. Nothing to worry about. I think the nice

lady just got scared of the horse. Why don't you go and give that to your friend." He handed her the package

Before she ran off to play with her friends, she stopped to smile at me and said, "Don't feel bad, I'm scared of spiders." She waved goodbye to me.

I waved back and walked over to where Matt stood. A police officer, who sat astride a horse, rode up next to him. The officer nodded his head at me and blood rushed to my face. Death had been nowhere around. I had freaked out like some damsel in distress. How weak could I be?

"Sorry, ma'am, didn't mean to frighten you. But trust me; this old girl's pretty gentle. Unless you're a criminal." The officer winked at me.

"It's me. I've been really jumpy lately. Sorry about that," I replied. I added, "Keep up the good work, officer."

I gave an awkward laugh and then turned to make a beeline for the park entrance. I'd hoped Matt wouldn't follow. I should have known better.

"Sara, wait. Johnson said he saw you bolt but didn't see anyone threatening around. Why are you so scared? Are you okay?"

I felt like such a dumbass.

"Yeah. I'm fine. The horse just startled me." It was lame. I knew it, but I couldn't think of another way to explain.

He gave me a dubious look and said, "The horse? But you said 'he followed you here' and you were afraid someone was going to hurt the kids."

I tucked my shaky hands into my jean pockets and shook my head, "Nah, just got a little freaked. I'm fine. Scary horse, ha ha." I gave another high-pitched giggle. What was wrong with me?

"Are you sure? I heard someone attacked you the other

night at work. Is someone harassing you? Talk to me, Sara. I can help you."

He would help too. Help himself right into a grave and leave his daughter without a father. I pictured her big brown eyes filled with tears. No way.

"I'm fine. Thanks, Matt." I straightened my shoulders and walked back toward my condo.

He wasn't buying it. He followed me and grabbed my arm. "What's going on? You seemed really scared, like more scared than you were when you nearly died, uh, both times."

I gently pulled my arm from his, "Seriously, I'm good."

He opened his mouth to say something but was cut off when Rick called out from the front of the building. "Sara, there you are, honey. I was afraid something had happened to you."

We walked toward Rick, who reached up to protectively put his arm around me when we caught up to him. He asked, "Who's your friend?"

Matt glared at Rick's arm and took a step back. "Well, looks like you're fine now. I better get back to the birthday party. Haley's waiting. I'll see ya around."

He turned and left before I could stop him.

"Who was that tall drink of sangria?"

"That's Matt. He's the officer who saved my life, among other things."

"Oh, all that Latino goodness and he's heroic? Be still my heart. Why were you trying to get away from him? I noticed you trying to ditch him and channeled my inner butch to give off jealous boyfriend vibes. You did want him to go away, right? Or am I wrong?"

Was he wrong? No. I was trying to get away from Matt for his own sake, but I didn't actually want him to leave.

When did I turn into a lovesick teenager? "It's for the best."

Rick gave me a dubious look and pulled me toward the building. "Straight people. I just don't understand your relationships." He shrugged and said, "Come on, I have a surprise for you. I talked to the owners, and they said you can move in as soon as you sign the paperwork at the title company as long as your insurance policy is in place. Since we're going there this afternoon, I don't think anyone would know if I forgot to put the key back in the lockbox and gave it to you instead."

He slipped the key into my hand when we reached the door, but didn't enter because his cellphone buzzed. "Duty calls, love. There's the key, and if you decide to call that hot cop back and christen the new digs, it'll be our little secret. Don't forget to meet me at the title company at noon."

He rattled off amenities of a house he was selling into his phone while he walked away and left me a little shell shocked. I looked at the key in my hand and couldn't believe this was my new home.

"Ahem."

Someone cleared his throat, and I realized the doorman was standing there, holding the door open for me while I gaped like a dork. "Sorry. Um, thanks."

I walked through the doorway and headed for the coffee cart. Armed with a double cappuccino, I was ready to be in my new home all alone for the first time. The smell of my coffee filled the elevator, making me feel warm and happy. My front door opened smoothly without even a squeak in the hinges. I got that tickling feeling in my stomach, like when I was a child and would go really high on the swings.

Mine. This beautiful place was all mine. The sound of my footsteps echoed off the walls of the empty condo while I walked around each room and grinned from ear to ear. I set my coffee down on the counter and did a little tap dance right there in the kitchen. I doubt anyone would have paid for the performance, but I thought I sounded quite impressive as the sound bounced off the tile. I went into the bathroom and sang "Take, take me home." It was a little off-key, but the acoustics rocked.

Coffee back in hand, I headed outside to check out the view on my balcony. The streets were laid out in a grid, and my place was in the center. I took a few sips while I gazed out over the city. When I turned to leave, I smacked face to chest with a large, shirtless man.

I dropped my cappuccino and shrieked while I backed up against the railing. My eyes darted around the empty balcony, looking for a weapon, but stopped to settle on him while a pair of blindingly white wings protruded from his back.

He was a beautiful horror. His wings looked as delicate as they did deadly. I forced myself to look at his face and a scream tore from my throat. My vision went fuzzy like the little pearly feathers that covered his back.

# CHAPTER NINETEEN
*Earth Angel*

I jerked awake and sat up. I had face-planted right into the now cold puddle of spilled coffee. Luckily, I had asked the barista to put a few pieces of ice in my cappuccino to make it safe to drink without peeling off a layer of my tongue, so my face wasn't burned.

Low blood sugar. Yeah. Had to be. I hadn't eaten and must have hallucinated. I'd thought about a guardian angel when I got attacked at work, so my mind created an angel. I gave a shaky laugh and picked up my coffee cup before I stood.

The balcony didn't seem like a great place to hang out while feeling woozy. I went inside and turned to lock the balcony doors. All the hair on my arms stood up and I felt a presence behind me. "Holy—"

Don't swear at the angel, idiot. Oh, my God. Oh, shit.

Was it taking the Lord's name in vain if I didn't say it out loud?

There was an angel in my living room. A shirtless angel with amazingly sculpted abs and arms and no chest hair. Oh, crap, I was checking out an angel. That had to be a sin.

After crossing myself quickly, I dropped to my knees in front of him. "I'm sorry, uh, sir. Um, your holiness?"

What do you call an angel when you don't know their

name? I should have paid more attention when I was in church with my aunt.

"Rise. You may call me Uriel." He folded his wings back into his sides and stared down at me with his arms crossed.

"Uriel? As in the Archangel who stands at the throne of God?" I raised my head to look at his face but remained on the floor. He was blond, and his eyes were almost pure white, with a pale blue pupil. He was painfully gorgeous, like one of those creepy computer generated images you see in movies. I shuddered and looked away.

"Yes. I am here with a warning. Death stalks you. You must not die. Stay with Mateo. He shall protect you."

Death stalks me. Yeah, tell me something I don't know. Like why was an angel, especially one this important worried about me? And couldn't he just get Death to back off?

"What? Matt? He's supposed to protect me from Death? He's just a mortal. Why can't you stop him?"

His wings unfurled and my heart skipped a beat when the crushing weight of his anger threatened to smother me. "Do you question the will of your Lord? Obey."

My body started shaking. Thankfully, I was already kneeling on the floor, because my legs turned to rubber. I had never been so terrified in my life.

White light radiated from him, blinding me. I ducked my head covering my already shut eyes to try to block it out. Then he was gone. I sneaked a peek and could still see the after images of the angel's wings glowing in the air like a reminder.

Or a threat.

The pressure of his anger lifted off my chest and I gasped for air. I wasn't sure if it was my imagination or if the air really tasted like burnt brimstone. I collapsed on the floor and blinked my eyes to try to get my vision back. It was like I had been staring into the sun and the image, his image, was burned into the center of my corneas.

After several minutes, or it could have been days for all my scrambled brain knew, I crawled to the fridge and fumbled to yank open the door. Rick had stocked it with sodas for the movers. I grabbed the first one and popped it open hoping to get the burnt taste out of my mouth. The flavor of the soda didn't even register, but the sugar helped me to control my shaking. I leaned against the open fridge, my head blasted by the cold air while I gulped down the drink. When I was finished, I grabbed another can. When that too was empty, I crawled to lean against the island, using my foot to kick the fridge door shut.

I sat there and took deep breaths, which helped my head stop spinning. My pulse finally started to calm down. My cellphone rang from inside my purse on the kitchen counter. The mundane sound gave me strength. I decided to attempt to stand up. Wobbly legs led me to my phone. I answered hoarsely, "Hello?"

"Sara, where the heck are you? We're all waiting for you at the title company. Remember, you have to sign the papers before I can give you the keys." Rick was talking quietly into the phone, like he didn't want others to hear.

"Huh? But that isn't until noon." I leaned against the counter and focused on making my hands stop shaking.

"Honey, it's twelve-thirty. You're late. You need to get here pronto because they close at one today. If this doesn't happen now, you'll have to wait until Monday to *get the keys*."

He punctuated the last three words. How long had I

been knocked out? It had taken me a while to recover, too. Poor Rick had stuck his neck out for me by giving me the keys before he was supposed to, and I screwed it up by being late.

"I'm sorry. I'll be there in fifteen minutes," I told him. The adrenaline gave me a boost and cleared the last of the angel fog from my head while I ran for the door.

I drove like a bat out of Hell. Luckily, there weren't a lot of cars around so I made it to the title company in ten minutes. Rick was pacing out front.

"Finally. I told them you were having car trouble. They close at one so we have to hurry. Go. Go. Go." He softened his words with a smile and squeezed my hand while he guided me into the office.

By the time I'd finished signing my name a million times, it was after two, and I was exhausted. Rick gave me a hug and said, "Give Brandon a call if you want help decorating it. The man eats and breathes every design show on that home network. Gotta run, sweetie. Saturdays are primo Realtor days. Call me."

He ran to his car, and I waived at his retreating back. My car was parked crooked since I'd been in such a hurry to get inside. Some asshole had parked next to me so close I couldn't get my door open. Great. Now what? I could squeeze through on the passenger side. Knowing me, I'd probably get a cramp half-way over and get stuck.

I looked around and saw a little deli nearby. My stomach growled, reminding me I hadn't eaten anything all day. Food first, and then I could think about my celestial visitor.

After I ordered at the counter, I sat in a window seat that faced my car so I could see when the douche next to it moved out of the way. So many questions ran through my mind that I should have asked the angel. Why me? Why was Death stalking me and why should Uriel care? Easy to question from the safety of the deli, but when faced with the angel, I had just wanted him to go away. Engrossed in my thoughts, I jumped when the waitress walked up with my food.

"Philly with peppers and a side of onion rings with ranch. Want a refill on your soda?"

"Yes, thank you. Diet Coke, please."

Her eyes darted down to the calorie-palooza in front of me, but she smiled politely and grabbed my cup.

What can I say? I'd rather eat my calories than drink them. Plus I skipped breakfast so this was like two meals. My inner voice agreed and I shoved an onion ring into my mouth.

Hot! So hot! Molten oil shot out from the onion ring as soon as I bit down. The batter on the outside hid the lava-like temperature of the onion on the inside. I looked around for a napkin and realized I didn't have any on the table. Just as I was ready to spit it out in my hand, the server set my drink down on the table.

When I snatched it up to get some relief for my blistered tongue, I ended up spilling it all over myself. The shock of the ice cold drink in my lap made me jump up out of my seat knocking it backward.

Luckily it was after the lunch rush, so I had only a few spectators to my klutzfest. The stupid onion ring bested me while I tried to chew it, pushing it from side to side with my tongue to keep it from scorching any one spot in my mouth. Screw it. I swallowed it mostly whole and took some shallow breaths to cool off my mouth. I pealed my cold, wet shirt away from my stomach and tried to squeeze some of the soda out.

Another customer handed me some napkins, but they weren't going to cut it.

"I'm so sorry," I told the server as I made a dash for the bathroom and hoped they had one of those air dryers in there.

The door to the bathroom had just closed when I heard a loud screech, the sounds of glass breaking, and people screaming. I ran back out the door and skidded to a halt, staring in shock.

Steam rose from a car that had crashed right where I had been sitting. The entire front of the restaurant, including the window I had been staring out moments ago, was in a pile of rubble on the linoleum floor.

"Oh, my God! I was just there cleaning up your soda. I could have been killed. We both would have been killed by that car. It just came out of nowhere. There wasn't even anyone driving it." The server gripped my arm in her horror.

I gaped at the wreckage. If I hadn't spilled my soda and run for the bathroom, I would have been under that car. I backed away and my thighs hit the front of a seat. Without bothering to look, I sat down on it before my shaky legs could give out. My heart thundered in my chest and I worried the strain of everything that had happened to me all in one day would be too much for it.

"Here, drink this," the gentleman whose table I had plopped down at must have jumped up off the seat with his glass in hand before the table toppled over. He handed me his water while staring at the rubble.

"Thanks," I mumbled before taking a sip. The ice cubes tinkled in the glass as my trembling hand brought it to my mouth. My eyes never left the car. Something clicked in my head and I realized it was the same car that had parked so close to mine that I couldn't leave. No way was that a coincidence.

Since I wasn't in the room when the accident had happened, I didn't have to stay to give my statement to the cops. One of them was nice enough to dig out my purse from under the rubble so I could leave.

I slowly backed out of the parking lot and headed home. I drove carefully, obeyed the speed limit and double checked that no one was coming at every intersection.

How many times was that fucker going to try to kill me?

After I arrived safely home, I walked in from the garage and was greeted by an angry angel whose wings spread the length of my kitchen. You would think there would be no more adrenaline left in my body, but I apparently had plenty in reserve. My heart leapt into my throat. I dropped to my knees.

This time he didn't tell me to stand. "You were told to go to Matteo so he can protect you. I cannot keep interfering with Death. You are not the only mortal I protect."

The questions I'd thought of before lunch bubbled up in my head. I stood up and asked, "You saved me? Why? Why, keep interfering? How many times have you stopped Death?"

Uriel's gaze felt like a wall of concrete pressing down on me and I fought the urge to drop to my knees again. Seconds passed like hours just when I was sure he wasn't going to answer, he said, "What does it matter if I sent the Samaritan to save you from the accident when you were a child? Or made David forget his phone so you would read the text message and not succumb to your husband's pleas? The end result is the same, whether I helped or not."

My mouth fell open. All the times I'd thought I survived on my own, by my own dumb luck, was it Uriel who had saved me or had I save myself? Was I just a pathetic damsel in distress?

No. He didn't make me run from that mugger. I did that on my own. When the werewolf attacked, I didn't just scream and trip while I was running away. No. I ran and hid in that SUV until Matt showed up. And today, even if I hadn't spilled my drink, I was facing that window. I would have seen that car coming and would have gotten out of the way. I didn't need to be rescued. Some of my fear of the dreaded angel left me and was replaced by confusion. "You never answered. Why did you save me?"

"It is not for you to question my ways. I cannot interfere any more. You will contact Mateo to protect you until Death runs out of the time he has to turn you into his sacrificial lamb." Uriel wrapped his horrifically beautiful wings around his body. The breeze blew across my skin like a thousand little shards of glass.

"Obey," he said and disappeared without another word.

I wasn't sure what bothered me more, that Death wanted to kill me as some sort of sacrifice, being bossed around like I was child, or Uriel designating Matt as my babysitter.

I'd lived my life being the good little niece, wifey and employee, always bending to the will of others, and look where it'd got me. No, I was done following orders and doing what was expected of me. Now I could do what I wanted. Feeling empowered, I straightened my shoulders and raised my chin up, until a thought crept in that made me slump back against the counter.

Before I could live my life the way I wanted, I would have to find a way to survive Death's interest.

## CHAPTER TWENTY

*The De Luxe Apartment in the Sky*

A quick glance at my phone let me know I had another text from Matt. I stuffed it back into my purse, but not fast enough to hide it from eagle-eyed Rick.

"It's him, isn't it? That sexy cop from last week? Stop ignoring the hottie." Rick gave me a knowing look.

I stuck my tongue out at him, and he laughed. Brandon turned around from the imported leather couch he was inspecting and asked, "Are you two even paying attention here? It's all in the stitching. Hand tooled is so much better than mass produced. You don't want an off-the-rack decor, do you?"

I chewed on my thumbnail before I confessed, "I don't like leather. My thighs stick to it when I get hot and then it makes fart-like noises when I move."

Rick covered his mouth, but you could see the guffaws struggling to escape from the confines of his clamped hand.

Brandon looked as if I'd suggested making the couch out of Spam.

"Just no. No. I didn't hear that," he said in a sing-song voice before continuing, "Suede it is then. Come, come." He marched toward another living room set while Rick and I obediently followed our beswatched, benevolent commander.

I had taken Rick at his word and called Brandon to see if he could recommend a place to get some furniture. One simple phone call had unleashed a shopping whirling dervish. Brandon insisted Rick and I go shop that day because his schedule at the hospital had gotten crazy, and he needed a break. I was surprised Rick wanted to accompany us, but now I suspect he was there to help shield me from Brandon's zeal.

Brandon came dressed for battle, in a Suns shirt, jeans, and sneakers armed with color swatches. Rick, also dressed in Suns gear, grabbed my arm and pulled me along.

I hadn't slept much the night before, since Uriel was on my mind, so I'd made some of my infamous Devilishly Chocolate Angel Food Cakes. I had wrapped one up in plastic wrap and put a pretty bow on it, before I slipped it into a gift bag.

I tried to fend him off with the cake at the last store, but after a few bites he was back focused on his mission.

We'd looked at couches. We'd looked at loveseats. We'd even looked at mythical part-chair part-couch creatures known as the chair-and-a-half.

A month ago, heck, a week ago, it would have bored me to tears. Funny how being stalked by Death and terrorized by an angel makes you welcome mundane into your life.

I heard Uriel's voice loud and clear in my head. "Contact Mateo to protect you."

At least I thought it was in my head. For a second I wasn't sure if Uriel's command was just a memory or if he'd shouted the order in the middle of the showroom floor. I looked at Brandon and Rick, but they hadn't flinched while they looked at the couch right next to me. Yup, just my head messing with me. Uriel didn't seem the kind of guy, uh, angel, to care about being incognito. He would have appeared right there on the coffee table if he wanted to command me.

Defying an angel was not a good idea. Look what had happened to Lot's wife when she defied one. No matter how much I wanted to, I couldn't risk Matt's life. I would not call him, even if I ended up a pillar of salt.

Matt had texted me twice during our shopping trip. Each time my text notification went off, Rick shot me a knowing look. He didn't understand. Matt was hard to resist. I knew if I talked to him, I might be selfish and give in to my desire to spend more time with him. Being with me would put a big target on his back.

A clean break. It was for the best. I sneaked a peek at my phone and saw that he had sent an image. I clicked to open it. A bark of laughter escaped before I could smother it.

"Finally, a heartfelt opinion! I think this couch is hideous as well. The beige suede is the one. You can accessorize it with so many colors. Now, let's move to the boudoir." Brandon headed off to the bedroom furniture while Rick followed.

I glanced at the picture on my phone of a horse making a goofy face with the caption, 'Run for your life!' Matt was such a smart-ass.

"There you are. Okay now you have to lie down on the bed to really know if you like it." Brandon instructed Rick to lay beside me.

Now this kind of shopping wasn't so bad. We tested out several mattresses before finding one I refused to get off. Rick agreed with me, so Brandon plopped down on my other side and we all lay there in the enormous bed. It was heaven.

The salesperson cleared his throat and I realized we must look kind of strange, two guys and a girl piled on to one bed. Sounded like a TV show. "You know, my fantasy about being in bed with two men seemed to go much differently."

Rick was quick to reply, "Honey, this is not my ideal threesome either."

We all laughed and even the sales guy smiled when I said I would take the bed. "Can you have it delivered today?"

Now that I had tried it out, I didn't want to spend another night in my crappy David and Mandi cootie-infested old one.

"Same day delivery is possible, but there's a surcharge."

Before I could agree, Brandon interrupted, "A surcharge if she was just buying the bed, however since she is furnishing several rooms, I'm sure you can waive the fee and include free set up."

I didn't even think about having to put stuff together. David had paid to have all our furniture assembled, though I thought we could have done it on our own and saved the money. If they were going to do it for free, why not? It was nice to have Brandon there to negotiate for me.

"The bedroom suite we can deliver today, but some of the custom pieces will have to wait for a week. Let me call scheduling to find out what appointment times they have available." He wrote down the address and walked away to make some calls.

"Thank you so much for your help. No way would I have been able to do all this in one day. Heck, I would probably be sitting on cardboard boxes for months."

Brandon covered his mouth in mock horror before he

said, "So, tell me about the hot police officer you have been avoiding all day."

I gave Rick a dirty look, but he rolled his eyes at me. "I didn't have to tell him a thing. You were pretty obvious every time you checked your phone. Your face would light up like you were getting a new puppy, then you would drop the smile like it peed on your rug before putting your phone away. What is going on?"

What was going on? I should be running to Matt with open arms. He was a good-looking guy who cared about me, was funny, and smart. An angel had even ordered me to do it. Talk about a match made in Heaven, but I was worried about Matt. He had his daughter and his mother who needed him. Plus something about Uriel seemed off somehow. "I don't know. He's got a kid and all this drama with his ex. I just don't think I can deal with that right now."

Brandon and Rick traded looks that screamed, Bullshit! But they were both gentlemen enough not to call me on the carpet.

The salesman came bustling over with the phone in one hand and a tablet in the other. "I can deliver the bed by itself after four today, but the rest of the bedroom furniture will have to be delivered on Monday since it has to be brought in from New Mexico. The other items will be available by Friday."

I visualized asking Colleen for two days off this week and watching her head explode. "I guess you'll have to deliver it all on Friday. I can't take time off Monday and Friday. My boss would have a fit."

The salesperson nodded his head and started to punch in information on the tablet, until Rick stopped him. "No, no, no. You have a doorman. You don't have to wait there to let people in any more, sugar."

I hadn't really thought about it. I always thought the doorman would accept packages that wouldn't fit in the mailbox or other deliveries that he would keep at the front desk.

"Will they do that? Take people up to my place and let them in and everything?"

Brandon laughed and even the salesman smirked. Rick said, "Honey, you bought a penthouse. You have moved on up like the Jeffersons. They'd probably order up hookers for you if you asked."

Huh. I hadn't really thought about it. I'd been middle class all my life, and lower middle class at that. Now I was getting treated like royalty. Yes!

"There is one room you forgot about: the dining room. We have some hand-crafted mahogany tables that would look lovely next to the living room furniture. You can keep the same delivery date. Don't you think she would regret not having a new dining table?" The salesman gave Brandon a seductive smile, hoping for an ally.

Brandon waved a hand at the table the guy had indicated and shook his head. "No, we were looking for something less heavy. I think she's good."

The salesman looked down at his tablet to schedule my deliveries, and handed me the receipt to sign. I gasped at the total. Holy crap! I'd never spent this much money in my life. My debit card seemed to fight me when I tried to pull it out of my wallet, or maybe that was just my imagination. I handed it over and the guy scurried off to run it.

"Thanks, Rick. Asking for time off for one day was going to be traumatic enough. It would have been full-on drama asking for two. God, I hate that job. My boss is such a bitch.

At least the new place is so much closer. I can sleep in a little more. Of course, if she finds out where I live, she'll be calling me in every weekend."

Rick gave me a puzzled look after my whinefest. "Then, honey, why are you working? You've still got some money left from that big fat check, and you don't have a mortgage. You can afford to quit that job."

Yes, I did have about three-hundred thousand left in the bank, but I still owed almost as much on my current house, plus David's car and the credit cards in our name needed to be paid off. "I've got another house to pay for, remember? Who knows how long it could take to sell it."

Rick stepped away and put a hand up to his chest in mock indignation. "Hello? I *am* the best realtor in town. I *will* sell your house, don't you worry your pretty head about that. Quit and find a career that makes you happy."

Brandon chimed in with, "Life's just too short to stay with a job-or a man-that makes you unhappy. Trust me, something better is out there. And once you find the one that makes your heart sing," he paused and kissed Rick's hand tenderly before continuing, "Your life will overflow with happiness."

I could feel the little green-eyed monster rising up inside me. No one had ever loved me like that, and if Death got his way, no one ever would. Matt flitted briefly through my thoughts, but I clamped down on them. It's easier to have nothing to lose, that way when you're left alone, it doesn't hurt so bad. Those idiots who say it is better to have loved and lost are freaking nuts.

Rick turned and put his arm around my shoulder. "I can read your thoughts. They are all over your face. Just because your ex was an ass, don't give up on love. You'll find it. In the meantime, we will help you find your calling in life, 'cause I can tell you it ain't accounting." Before he could say more, his cellphone rang, and he walked away to get it.

Brandon said, "Oh, no. No looking necessary. I'm telling you, that cake you made was like crack. I wanted to stuff my face with it even though I knew I would have to spend hours at the gym working it off. You should sell those!"

Maybe he was right. I'd gone into accounting because it was all I knew. Even in my old job, I had loved my boss but hated the actual work. When we had moved here, I toyed with the idea of opening my own business. I wasn't much of a cook, but I could bake better than anyone.

I could hear David's voice in my head. "How could we afford to take such a risky financial step? Too many small businesses go bankrupt."

I shook my head to clear it. Why was I even thinking about what my cheating bastard of a dead husband would have said? This was the same tool who said he was afraid the temptation of being surrounded by all those carbs would be too hard for me to resist, and I would gain a bunch of weight. Since he'd worked hard to stay in shape for me, it was only fair I stayed in shape for him.

He was a mistake better left in my past. Why should I stay at some job I hated to pay for bills he made without my knowledge? Before I could think more about it, the salesman was back. He handed me some paperwork and my bank card.

"Thank you for shopping with us. You have exquisite taste." The last he said to Brandon.

He pulled out a business card and slipped it into Brandon's hand before saying, "Call me if there is anything I can do for you."

I wanted to kick the guy. Brandon immediately handed me the card and said, "Thanks, will do."

He turned and walked away without so much as a glance at the guy, who was kind of hot. Brandon, who only had eyes for Rick, didn't even seem tempted. Amazing.

We met Rick outside while he was finishing up his phone call. "Sorry. These people can't seem to understand boundaries. Hello? Sundays I'm off. The game is going to start soon, you ready?"

My face split into a giant grin, and I giggled. "I have decided I'm going to give notice tomorrow. I'm going to start a bakery. It'll take some time to get the supplies and equipment though. Then I have to find customers. Shit." I stopped smiling. "Maybe I should wait to give notice?"

"No. You are going to give notice tomorrow. Don't worry about customers. Hell, I can guarantee the office will buy those little cakes to give to clients. Wrap them up in fancier paper and we will give them away to new homeowners every time we close a deal. Customers will be beating down your door!"

"And I am placing an order as soon as you can make it for my staff. I've been so busy at the hospital. This mysterious illness that's cropped up out of nowhere is like the plague. I've been neglecting my office staff. They stampede over anything chocolate." Brandon added.

Oh, my God! I was going to open my own business. I would be my own boss. Even better, the only company books I would have to close again were my own, and I already had clients lined up. Tomorrow would be a new life for me, but with Rick and Brandon by my side, I wouldn't have to start that life all alone.

We said goodbye and I hummed to myself while I

walked to my car. I even tried to skip but tripped over a bench at a bus stop. There was a "friends don't let friends drive drunk" sign on it with a cartoon picture of death hovering over the words friends.

What if Death got mad at me again and went after Brandon and Rick? The grin fell off my face and tears sprang to my eyes. For just a brief moment, I had hoped that I wouldn't be alone any more. I should have known better. Friendship and love had always been illusions for me. When I get too close to either, bad things happen. How could I embrace their friendship when it put their lives at risk? No more socializing with them. I would keep it strictly business. It wasn't a big deal, I'd been alone all my life. At least once I quit, I would be working at a job that made me happy.

# CHAPTER TWENTY-ONE

*Fore!*

Was it the bed, my new home, or my plan to quit my job that gave me the best night of sleep in my life? I woke Monday morning before my alarm. While I showered and got ready for work, one of my favorite songs played on the radio. I couldn't quite hit the high notes, but it didn't stop me from belting out, "Don't Stop... Believing".

There were a few salted caramel muffins left from the previous night's bake fest, so I ate one and brought one with me to work.

I actually made it in to the office before Colleen, the perfect time to type up my letter of resignation. My fingers flew over the keyboard while I typed, pausing only at the effective date of my resignation. My heart screamed at me to type in today's date, but my head said no, to give at least two weeks' notice.

While I debated, Colleen arrived and walked by my cube. "Aren't we here nice and early this morning for a change, and you're working like a busy little beaver. Good for you. Channel your grief into work. It'll help you heal."

My hands gripped the arms of my chair. Losing my husband was a way to increase my productivity? Who says things like that?

Before I could make a sarcastic response, she stopped

me by saying, "And if you do get lonely, you can always take up golf. There are these three widows Phil and I always see playing at the club. You could join and make it a widow foursome. We might be able to get you a guest pass. If you like playing, maybe you can find a municipal course you can afford." She patted my arm before walking away to the break room.

She made a dig on my being alone and being poor?

Bitch wants to be like that, let's see how she likes doing my job as well as her own.

My head agreed with my heart this time. I typed in today's date into the letter and hit print. On the way back from the printer, I grabbed an empty box, and then pulled things out of my desk and started packing. My co-workers were shuffling in by this time. They eyed me and whispered to each other. When I started humming they must have gotten nervous, because they all disappeared into the break room.

I heard whispering then Colleen headed toward me.

"What's going on? You doing some spring cleaning?"

I ignored her and kept packing. When finished, I sat down, pulled up my emails and started deleting them page by page.

"Is everything all right, Sara? Do you want some coffee?" This from the same woman who would fill her cup of coffee and put the pot back, even if you were standing right beside her, your cup mere inches away from hers, waiting to get some.

Delete. Delete. Delete. I ignored her while I deleted everything personal from my computer, not that there was much, and then stood up. I noticed my gawking co-workers had returned to their desks. The few people in the office I was friendly with weren't in yet.

I turned back to the computer and typed a quick goodbye email to them before shutting it off. Only then did I acknowledge Colleen with a smile. "Nope, I will pick up a latte on the way home. Here ya go. This is for you. You can just mail me my last check. Bye, everyone."

I threw my purse over my shoulder and grabbed the box.

"What? You can't do this. We need at least a month's notice. You can't just leave," she sputtered.

I turned and set the box back down on the desk. "You know, you're right, Colleen. What was I thinking?"

She breathed a sigh of relief and folded up my resignation letter. Ha. Gotcha, bitch.

"I need to give you my keys and badge. Here you go." I dumped them into her hand, grabbed my box and walked out without giving anyone a second look. I stopped at the security desk and asked for Ernie. He shuffled up and I gave him a hug and my extra muffin.

"You take care, miss," he called after me.

I made it home and stripped out of my work clothes before I curled up on the bed, but I wasn't sleepy. Boxes were stacked up along the walls. There was no furniture but the bed. I hadn't hooked up the TV yet or the wifi and had no idea where my books were in this mess.

A responsible adult would unpack. A glance at the nearest box quieted that thought. Who wants to be responsible, or even an adult, for that matter? I noticed David's golf bag next to the hall closet. The movers must have brought it by mistake. It reminded me of what Colleen said about golfing.

I threw on some clothes, grabbed his bag and decided to

donate the clubs to charity. Maybe some poor kid will learn how to play and show up at her precious golf club and beat the pants off of her.

The golf bag hung awkwardly over my shoulder while I struggled to the elevator. I hit the lobby button and recognized some '80s hair band's song playing in Muzak form. Was that Guns and Roses?

I dumped the heavy bag off my shoulder and rested it on the closed door. Maybe Colleen was right, and I should give golf a try? People usually network at golf courses. It could be good for business.

*Ding!*

"Leggo my package. They're my earrings. Mine! Gimme it, loser."

I was blasted by a woman's yell as soon as the elevator doors opened. No. Couldn't be. No freaking way.

First floor: Street entrance, mailboxes, coffee cart with a dead and fairly chewed up barista beside it and my husband's former girlfriend, who apparently was fighting with the doorman. No wait, judging by his glazed over eyes and the violet color of his hands, the doorman was a zombie. I wasn't sure what bothered me more, Mandi, the coffee-guy's corpse, or the zombie doorman.

"Don't touch my boobies! Ish sexual harassment. I'll shoo!" Mandi's slurred words indicated she was drunk, but was she really so wasted she didn't notice the horror around her? Mandi answered my question when she yanked on the brown package the doorman clutched in his hand.

The poor bastard must have died while holding the package and for some reason couldn't release his death grip on it. The side of the box facing the elevator and away from Mandi was stained with blood and some nasty looking pink globs that did not go well with the smiley face logo on the box.

God, was that a chunk of scalp with hair attached stuck on the corner of the box? Probably from the poor barista whose face was thankfully turned the other way, otherwise I would be replaying the gore in my head every time I closed my eyes to go to sleep.

I jabbed the CLOSE button several times. Come on stupid thing, shut before they notice me. The metal doors started their slow crawl toward each other and then bounced back open. Why wouldn't the damn thing close? It was then that I noticed the golf bag had fallen over and one of the clubs was blocking the door. "Fuck!"

The zombie doorman turned my way. Bet he thought I would be a heartier meal than tiny Mandi. I pawed at the club with my left hand to get it away from the door, while my right never stopped hitting that CLOSE button. He took a shuffling step toward me, but Mandi yanked the box, and the attached zombie, toward her.

"Gimme, now. I'll call the cops."

No way. She was so loaded, I was gonna have to save her stupid ass again. The doors started to close, so I put a hand out to stop them. "Look at him, you twit. He's a zombie. Run!"

That got her attention. She let go of the box, screamed and ran towards me, holding her hands up like her manicure was wet and she was trying to make her nails dry faster.

"Eww, eww, ewww! I touched him, and he's dead. I think I'm going to be sick." She tripped over the golf bag and landed in the back of the elevator just as the doors started to close again.

The zombie shambled toward us. The doors finally

closed shut. I breathed a sigh of relief that was short lived when I heard a ding and the doors slid open again. Oh, shit. I had forgotten to push the floor number.

The finger on my left hand hit a random floor while my right held down the button to close the door. Each agonizingly slow step brought him closer to the elevator. Could these doors move any slower? There was less than a foot between them, when he reached his hand-the one holding the box- toward us.

The damned door bounced on his hand, dinged, and popped back open. Fuck! Trapped in a metal box like some kind of zombie Happy Meal. I scrambled to the back kicking the golf bag out of my way.

Mandi screamed her head off while she cowered in a corner. Maybe while the zombie ate her I could make a run for it? I wanted to yell "Eat her, not me. She's younger, more tender" but even though it was Mandi, I just couldn't do it.

Besides, no way would he even hear me over Mandi's caterwauling. She wouldn't be any help at all. Not even as bait.

Something tangled around my foot, and I'm not ashamed to admit I outdid Mandi with my shriek. But rather than a zombie hand, it was a golf club. What was the really big one called? I shook off the random thought and remembered watching that zombie TV show where the guy killed a bunch of them with a golf club. Piece of cake, I thought before I snatched up the club and whacked at the zombie's head as hard as I could.

# CHAPTER TWENTY-TWO

*You Ought to be in Pictures*

The club made a thunking sound like someone tapping on a watermelon when it made contact with the zombie's head. He stumbled back a bit but was otherwise intact. I swung the club back to take another swing and the head of the golf club went flying off and hit the back of the elevator, shattering the mirror. Mandi curled up into a ball to protect her face and screamed again.

What the hell? This didn't happen to the guy on the show. I used the shaft to shove the zombie back so I could reach down and grab another club. I found a metal one that seemed sturdier and took another swing at the zombie.

The club made contact with his eye and sank into the socket with a wet slurping noise. I tried not to puke. It seemed to bother me more than the zombie. He kept shambling toward me. I yanked the club out and swung for the side of his head.

His eye flew to my left and blood splattered the front of the elevator. He fell back into the lobby, but his feet still blocked the door. He sat up and reached forward for me as though I hadn't just gone all Tiger Woods on his head. I raised the club, and hit him again in the same spot.

This blow knocked off the left side of his skull but the damn thing still reached for me. I stepped out of the elevator, a foot on either side of his legs, and beat the golf club into his exposed brain like I was squashing a spider that had strayed into my shower.

The silly thought snapped me out of mindless smashing. I noticed a pale horse standing outside on the street by the front door. I couldn't see Death's full body, only his black-clad legs, but who else would be riding that beast? I shook the golf club over my head. "Mother fucker. Leave me alone!"

Even though I yelled, I knew he couldn't hear me over Mandi. She sounded like a British police siren, Aaaaahh, ahhhh, Aaaaaahhh, ahhhhh, low pitch to high pitch over and over.

I turned to her while she cowered in the elevator. "Shut the fuck up! I have several more clubs in there that I will beat you to death with if you don't stop screaming right now."

She stopped screaming and started whimpering. Who wouldn't when faced with a crazy woman waving a bloody, brain encrusted golf club in the air? I probably looked as bad as Mandi who resembled a deranged clown with mascara running under her eyes and her lipstick smeared down to her chin.

"Police! Drop the club. Put your hands on your head and get down on your knees." Two uniformed police officers had entered the building with their guns drawn.

I dropped the club, put my hands on my head, but took one look at the blood- covered floor and said, "No fucking way I am kneeling in zombie brain soup."

One of the cops looked like he was going to protest, then he turned and puked right on the floor by the front doors. The sound, or maybe the smell made the other cop turn green, but he managed to hold it together. He put his gun in the holster and called for backup on his radio before telling me, "Park it somewhere. Don't touch anything. CSU will be here shortly. As well as a HazMat unit."

I looked around for a place I could sit as far from the mess as possible. I ended up back in the elevator on the floor next to a cried-out Mandi. She clutched my arm in a daze, like how the zombie had clutched her package. "So, ordered something from Amazon, huh? Did you get free shipping with that?"

Mentioning the package snapped her out of her fugue state. "He wouldn't leggo of my diamond earrings. Bad things keep happening to me. They were mine. He was trying to steal them."

She punctuated her statement with a hiccup. I guess her fear hadn't burned through her buzz yet. She must have been really wasted. It explained how she didn't notice the carnage when she came in. Even she wouldn't be that self-absorbed. "Probably was the first time a man wanted you for your brains, I bet. Ha, I guess these would be considered blood diamonds now. Get it?"

I laughed so hard I snorted. She didn't get it. She dropped my arm and leaned into the corner of the elevator away from me. Okay, maybe I was in shock and a bit hysterical. It was then that I noticed the doors closing. The cop who had puked, yelled when he heard the *ding* of the elevator, but it was too late. We were already moving up.

The look on the cop's face started me on a new fit of giggles and this time Mandi joined in. We rode up to the fifth floor which was the button I must have been desperately pushing. I stood up, stumbled over a golf ball and hit the lobby button. I bent down to pick up the bag, clubs, and all the other scattered golf crap.

The doors opened while I was trying to jam the clubs back into the bag. My ass was in the air when I heard, for the second time in my life, "Freeze. Drop the club."

This time I recognized the voice. "Hi, Matt."

I waived a hand in the air behind me, while shoving the club down with the other, not bothering to turn around.

"I should have known," Matt said. In the reflection of the shattered mirrored back of the elevator, several Matts turned to the twitchy cops who had aimed their weapons at me when the door opened. "Put the guns down. She's probably the victim here. Go see if the other one is okay."

What did he just call me?

I straightened and turned to face him. "I am not a victim. She," I waved my hand at Mandi, who was basking in the attention of the police officers helping her stand up, "is your victim. Me, I just was going to play a little golf, but I should've just played on through."

I collapsed into a fit of giggles again as my shaky legs gave out on me. When I looked at Matt, his hand was up rubbing his head, as I knew it would be. Just seeing him there pushed back some of the hysteria. I felt a sudden need to dump everything into his lap and ask him to make Death and Uriel go away. So much for my empowerment moment. Come on, Sara. Grow a pair.

"I think you're going to need a new driver first."

Driver! That was the big one I'd used. I could never remember all the names of the different kinds of clubs.

"Course, if you ask me, I'd say you should stick with that iron." Matt gave me his smart-ass grin before walking over to give me a hand up and pull me out of the way of the cops guiding Mandi out of the elevator. "You're not gonna get all hysterical and pass out on me now are you?"

Was I? I looked around at the mess and the golf club still embedded into the zombie's brain. "I'm fine. Maybe I should try hockey instead of golf. At least the hockey sticks would make better weapons because they're bigger."

"Yeah, plus you got all that padding."

Gotta love a man who could keep up with my sarcasm.

"What are you doing here? Why haven't you called me back? How come you're not at work?" His questions came rapid fire while he frowned down at me.

I answered the easiest one first. "I live here now, remember? And I quit my job today." I skipped over why I hadn't called him.

We both looked over when Mandi started whimpering again. One policeman put his arm around her. The other swiped some napkins and a water bottle from the coffee cart and brought it over to her. He wet the napkins and wiped off her face like she was a little kid.

After her face was clear, Matt did a double take. "Is that...?"

He didn't need to finish his sentence. The look he gave me said it all.

"Yes, that's my deceased husband's girlfriend. Well, one of them anyway. I was in the elevator and heard her screaming. She was fighting with the doorman for a package when the doors opened. I have no idea why she is here. Why are you here?"

Mandi raised her chin and said, "I live here. But thanks to you getting me fired, I'm probably going to have to sell my home now and rent somewhere."

You almost have to respect someone who is able to twist every situation so it is never her fault. Almost, but not quite.

"You're lucky losing your job was all that happened to you. You got your pay day for screwing my husband. Stop bitching before I break a golf club off on your ass."

One of the cops pushed her behind him and said, "Watch out, she's getting violent again. She's probably on that Draino stuff. I saw her with that bloody club beating that poor guy to death. Cuff her before she flips out and attacks us." He advanced toward me as though he were going to try to cuff me himself.

Matt rubbed his head again and mumbled, "Rookies. Always stuck with the rookies." He reached a hand up to gently push the other cop back and said, "As I told you when I arrived on scene, one look at his hands and you can tell the guy was a zombie. Most healthy people don't have all their blood pooling in their fingers. They should have covered that in training."

Matt must have checked out the bodies while we were taking our ride up to the fifth floor.

"It's pretty clear, it was self-defense, but we need to wait for CSU and the coroner to check it out first. I'll keep the witnesses with me until we confirm. Who's the idiot who puked in the middle of our crime scene?"

The poor guy blushed red and held his hand up. Matt gave him a withering look.

"Next time, step outside first. You can stay here and keep people away from the area. McPearson, right?" he asked the other cop who nodded.

"Go track down the security guard, wherever he's at, and get the security tape from those cameras up there, so we can see what happened."

The other two split off, obviously relieved to have someone else in charge. Mandi pouted when they left but didn't try to stop them. We waited in the lobby for the rest of the cops to come and put up the police tape to keep the gawkers out. The coroner arrived shortly before McPearson had tracked down the security guard.

"Where were you during the attack?" Matt asked the guard.

"I was patrolling the parking garage. I saw the flashing lights and ran down here, but the cops wouldn't let me back into the building."

"Can he get the tape?" Matt asked McPearson.

The cop cleared his throat and wiped his palms down his pant legs. "No, they don't use tapes any more. It's all digital now."

I couldn't help it. A hiccup-like guffaw slipped out of my mouth. "I think he's saying your age is showing there, Matt. See if they have it on Betamax or laser disc."

He gave me a dirty look and pointed to his handcuffs, "Want me to put these on you?"

"Not without buying me dinner first, big boy."

That comment made him smile. I liked when he smiled. It softened up his whole face from the military-like scowl he usually wore.

"I should make you wait here with the rookie to give your statement, but it might be helpful for you to give us the play-by-play as we watch it."

Did Matt really want my commentary, or was he making an excuse because he wanted to be around me? David was my first and only relationship, so I never became fluent in the art of flirtation.

"I get to go too then, I was a witness too." Mandi chimed in before I could think of a flirty response.

Oh, sure. Now she sobers up and notices what was

going on around her. It was just as well, I probably would have said something really lame.

"Yeah, you can come too."

McPearson lead the way. While we followed him, I wondered what it meant that Matt had let Mandi come. Did it mean he wasn't giving me special treatment because he liked me? Or maybe he was but had no choice but to let her come too? He couldn't be interested in her, could he?

I was so distracted by my crazy thoughts, I almost ran into Matt's back when we stopped outside the security office while the guard unlocked the doors. Matt told him, "Let's see what you got."

One monitor showed the area outside the front door. The next featured the lobby with the doorman on duty and the barista with his face whole and body intact. The third had a view of an empty elevator.

Wow, didn't realize they had cameras in there. I made a mental note, no picking of anything, when I rode on them.

The coffee dude walked to the front desk to say something to the doorman. I imagine it must have been something like: Watch my cart; I have to hit the bathroom. He walked toward the lobby bathroom while the doorman went over and opened the decorative umbrella on one end of the coffee cart.

The doorman played around with things on the coffee cart, stacking them up on top of each other. I was focused on the weird behavior of the doorman, until I saw a familiar face appear dressed in a black trench coat in the middle of the lobby.

It was Death caught on video. I raised my finger to point him out but realized no one else saw him. Damn. Even big as day on the screen, I was the only one who could see him.

# CHAPTER TWENTY-THREE

*Ho in One*

"You see something?" Matt asked me when he noticed my hand raised toward the screen. He stood up to lean closer as if he'd missed something.

"Nope, thought I did. But I was wrong."

Matt gave me a doubtful look. He turned so he could see the screen and keep an eye on me at the same time. "You sure?"

I nodded and he turned back to watch the action. Death was on screen walking toward the coffee cart. He touched a few of the pastries on a plate that were for sale, before he whispered something into the doorman's ear. Death then stepped toward the door, pausing to turn to look right at the camera. He held his finger up to his lips as if he were shushing me.

I jumped back and his eyes seemed to follow me. Goosebumps broke out all over my arms. That couldn't be possible. Even if Death could see me through the camera somehow, it was a recording not a live feed. I moved over to the right and Death turned his head with my movements, smiled, and winked at me. The light gleamed off his perfectly straight teeth and completely black eyes. I held my breath until he turned and walked out the door.

"What's he doing?" Matt asked.

Finally, someone else saw him! I looked at where Matt pointed and realized he wasn't talking about Death. He was talking about the doorman. The guy's hand reached in, quick as a mouse, and snatched a bear claw. He wrapped it in a napkin and shoved it into his pocket, and then moved the other pastries around so it wouldn't be obvious it was missing.

About a minute later, the coffee guy came back into the frame and the doorman went back to the front desk. The barista shook his head and laughed when he saw the creamer, napkins and sugar stacked haphazardly on the cart.

A delivery van parked out front and the doorman walked outside to meet the delivery guy. Once out of the barista's sight, he crammed the pilfered pastry into his mouth, before he signed for the package.

The barista, unaware of the theft, straightened up his cart. He was closing the umbrella the doorman had left opened when the doorman burst back inside pale, gagging, and clutching the package. He collapsed on the floor before the coffee guy could catch him.

"Did anyone see why the guy turned? He wasn't attacked." Matt asked.

We all shook our heads. No one but me knew that Death had done something to that pastry to poison the poor doorman and turn him into a zombie.

The barista looked panicked, and he put his head on the doorman's chest, probably to check for a heartbeat. He sat up and fumbled in his pockets for a few seconds before he ran to the coffee cart and threw open drawers.

He was frantically searching, which was why he missed the doorman slowly sitting up. It was like watching a horror movie. I wanted to yell at the screen, "Turn around you idiot!"

The barista found his phone about the same time the doorman was within reach. It looked like he managed to dial the number, because he started speaking, right before the doorman took a large bite out of his neck.

We all jerked back away from the screen while we watched the blood spray like a broken water fountain. The barista dropped the phone and grabbed his neck, falling to the floor. He crawled toward his cart, as thought it would give him some protection against the zombie that hungrily chased after him. The poor man lay beside the cart, while the zombie lapped his blood like an ice cream cone.

Mandi made her stumbling grand entrance then. She shuffled to the mailbox, weaving slightly while she walked. Too wrapped up on her cell to notice the carnage, she finished her call and put her phone in her purse, and then she fished out her keys to open her mailbox.

"How long have you lived here?" I asked her.

"Ten years."

Ten years. No wonder David was dead set against us moving here. Imagine the awkward elevator rides. "You lived here ten years and didn't notice something was wrong in the lobby?"

"It's not my fault for not noticing him. They were behind the cart and I was on the phone."

"The guy's covered in blood. How could you not notice that?" Matt asked her.

"His uniform is maroon like the carpet. It blended in, plus these meds I'm on are really strong. They make my head all woozy. They said not to drink alcohol with it, but I thought they meant the hard stuff, not wine." She paused, took a step closer to the screens and said, "Wow, my ass looks big on camera. I don't really look like that, do I?"

I just shook my head disgustedly. I looked at Matt, and he rolled his eyes. We both turned back to the Mandi on the screen. At least we couldn't hear that one.

She had trouble getting the key in the lock and fought with it while the doorman continued to eat his first victim. How could anyone be so oblivious? The doorman stopped chewing the barista's face off and moved toward Mandi.

He made it half-way to her by the time she closed the mailbox door. She was struggling now to get the key out of the lock. The key must have gotten unstuck suddenly because her hand flew back away from the mailbox in an arc behind her. Her elbow hit the package the doorman extended toward her as he tried to grab her. She turned and said something to him without ever actually looking his way.

She yanked on the box and the zombie's left arm pulled closer to her. Mandi put one hand on her hip and her head bounced around like a bobble-head doll.

"Here comes the funny part," I said to Matt before turning to Mandi, "Did you threaten to have him fired first or is this were you claim sexual harassment because you thought he touched your boob?"

Mandi gave me an evil glare. Matt snorted and the other cop couldn't hide his smirk. The security guard kept a sober expression, probably through years of practicing discretion while working here.

"He did touch my boob. I didn't know he was a zombie. I thought he was trying to steal my package and was copping a feel. How was I supposed to know?"

"How? The corpse in the corner wasn't a clue? Or the

glazed look on the zombie's face as he shambled toward you and the way his hands were all discolored?"

"I thought he was wearing gloves. I told you, I couldn't see the coffee guy. I had no idea he was dead. I don't even drink coffee. It's these meds. They make me confused sometimes." She got up from her seat in front of the monitor and blocked the screen while she defended herself.

"All right, miss, you can go and wait in the lobby until we get your statement," Matt told her in a cold voice while he reached around her to hit the pause button.

"Oh, I'm so sorry. Matt, was it? I didn't mean to be a distraction. Can't I stay here with you?" Mandi stuck her chest out and smiled coyly. She leaned her shoulders back against the monitors. I felt the urge to rip her face off like the zombie almost did earlier.

"It's Officer Espinoza, ma'am. Do I need to have Officer McPearson show you the way back or can you find it yourself?" Matt tipped his head toward the door.

Mandi let out her breath in a huff. She stood up and flounced toward the door, flipping her hair over her shoulder. She checked to make sure Matt was watching.

He wasn't. Good ole Matt was watching the screen, ignoring her antics. Yes! I'd found a man immune to her charms. She slammed the door behind her, and I laughed. "Guess she isn't used to men rejecting her."

"Not really my type. I prefer my women to have more brains than boobs." Matt looked at me, and I felt my mouth twitch like it does when I get really nervous.

My hand snaked up to my face, to cover my spasmodic smile. Luckily, before Matt thought I was having a seizure, the security guy drew the attention away from me by asking, "Should I continue with the playback?"

The third monitor showed my not so grand entrance on the surveillance video. McPearson gave me a thumbs up when I whacked the doorman in the head. Even the haughty security guy gave me an approving nod.

Matt raised an eyebrow at me and said, "Your backswing could use a little work, but it's pretty obvious it was self-defense. I don't think we need you to come down to the station or anything. I'll type up your statement and maybe I can bring it by later to avoid the press. The jackals will be foaming at the mouth when they hear you're involved with another supernatural attack."

Matt was coming back to see me. It was my chance to tell him what was going on. If he didn't lock me up in a psycho ward somewhere, maybe he could help me.

"Sure. Why don't you bring dinner? This time, try not to squash the pizza."

Matt laughed and turned to the head of security, "Can you burn a copy of this for our records?"

The security guard nodded and started rifling through the desk, presumably for a disc. Matt jerked his head at the door and told McPearson, "Go out and get the blonde's statement after he makes our copy."

"Yes, sir. Should I bring her down to the station?"

"God, no. I don't want to have to hear her jabbering on and on while I'm trying to type up the reports. Just make sure she corroborates what we saw and then have her come down in the morning-when I'm gone-to sign off on them."

The security guard handed the disc to McPearson. The officer nodded in thanks and left to question Mandi.

Matt walked me back to the elevator and picked up my golf bag, which someone had used to prop open the elevator doors. "You want me to help you carry these up? I can probably get that club back for you tomorrow if you want it."

"Toss 'em. They were David's and I was just going to get rid of them. You want them?"

Matt smirked and shook his head. "My ex-brother-in-law took me a few times. Not really my thing. You would hate it. They wouldn't have even let you in wearing that shirt."

I looked down at my favorite t-shirt that read, "Normal is so over-rated."

What was wrong with my outfit? There weren't any holes or swear words or anything.

Before I could ask, Matt said, "You have to have a collared shirt to play. But even still, not your style. They're stuffy and boring. If you're looking for a new hobby, go to the Indian casinos. A lot more fun, plus no dress code, cheap food, and free booze."

Free booze! Matt was a genius.

# CHAPTER TWENTY-FOUR

*Calling in the Calvary*

"Wow!" Matt returned with pizza as promised. He whistled when he walked into my new place.

I rubbed my suddenly sweaty hands down my legs before I grabbed the pizza and put it on the island counter. How could I feel so comfortable with a guy some of the time and then as awkward as a teenager with a crush the next? "Let me give you the grand tour."

He oohed and aahed while he walked around, but he liked the balcony the best. "Too bad you don't have a patio table. We could eat out here." He paused to look around my empty living room, "So, where do you eat?"

I didn't want to admit that dinner last night was cereal straight out of the box in bed. "I've been eating out. My furniture is being delivered on Friday."

Matt shrugged and pulled two big cardboard boxes marked "books" up to the counter then gestured with a flourish. "Your table awaits, Madame."

"Wow, it took two movers to bring those heavy boxes up, I'm impressed. You've earned the good china." I grabbed some paper plates and napkins and sat on the box next to him. He opened the pizza box and offered me the first slice. What a gentleman.

I was almost too nervous to eat. I had made up my mind

to talk to him about Death and Uriel but didn't know where to start.

Alcohol. Yes, that was the answer. "Want a beer? I got the good stuff."

He hesitated, so I added, "Come on. You have to celebrate with me."

Nodding his head, he waved his hand around, "Yeah, I can see why you are celebrating. This place is real nice."

I cocked my head to the side and said, "Thanks, but I was talking about quitting my job and starting a new business. I'm going to sell baked goods." Saying it out loud made it real.

"Baked goods?"

"Um, yeah. Like cakes and brownies and stuff." When Brandon had made the suggestion, it sounded like a great idea. Now I sounded like a little kid wanting to set up a lemonade stand.

"Oh, you're opening a bakery?"

After I'd considered it, opening a bakery sounded like a lot more work than what I was interested in doing. I stalled by going to the fridge to get some beers. Handing a bottle to him, I said, "No, um, more like making stuff to order. Maybe sell in farmers markets and bookstores? Stuff like that."

I sounded like a total idiot.

"Cool. Cheers," he said and clinked his beer to mine before taking a drink. I almost spit my beer out when he added, "Can't wait to taste your goodies."

My eyes darted to his, and I saw the mischief in them. I punched him on the arm and he laughed. "You call that a punch? I need take you to the gym and teach you to box."

An image of Matt in boxing shorts and little else, all sweaty with his arms around me, flashed before my eyes.

Bad mind, bad mind. Can't go there. I drank a big gulp of my beer and snagged another slice of pizza.

We ate and joked around until the pizza was almost gone. I'd finished before Matt and jumped up to grab a cupcake for him. It was a new flavor I was trying out. A butter cupcake with a maple infused frosting and some chocolate covered bacon pieces sprinkled on top. I was curious to get his reaction.

"Oh, man, this is good! This is really good. Oh yeah, you definitely can sell these." He spoke around mouthfuls of cupcake. It disappeared in a few bites and I caught him looking around the kitchen for more.

Score!

"I have a few more. Remind me to give you some to take home. Maybe your daughter would like them."

He made a face. "My ex extended her vacation so I won't see her for another week." He crumpled up the cupcake wrapper into a tiny ball and put it on his empty plate.

I took it from him and threw it into the grocery bag I was using for trash.

Matt wandered into the living room and noticed the TV sitting in the middle of the floor, wires hanging out forlornly.

"You want me to hook this up for you? Not saying you can't do it yourself and need a man to hook it up. Just, you know, trying to help. When my friends move I'm the one who always sets up the entertainment system."

It suddenly occurred to me, self-assured Matt was acting a little awkward with me. Maybe he really did like me. I grinned a goofy grin and noticed Matt was rubbing his chin again.

"That would be great. Thanks."

He ducked behind the TV, popping out only to rearrange the DVD player, DVR box and the sound bar. I grabbed us some more beers and played assistant.

"You want me to hook these up too?" He pointed to David's game consoles. I'd never had time to play them before so I hadn't given them much thought. But some of those graphics looked pretty cool. Why not?

"If you feel like it."

"Man, you must be a hard core gamer. You have every system." Matt whistled in appreciation at David's collection of games.

"I never really learned how to play. David didn't like to share his toys. Funny, considering that he shared himself with all his other girlfriends." Except it wasn't funny at all.

Matt didn't comment on the dickishness that was my late husband and said, "What? Oh, no, you've got to play Apocamania. You've gotta survive the zombie apocalypse until the military can rescue you. Hell, you've already got experience. You should kick ass at it."

He set up the game, handed me a controller and started it up. Like a couple of college kids, we sat on the floor, drank beer, and played video games. I had no idea how much time had passed when Matt yelled, "Grab that pipe and smash his brains in. Oh, no, look out. Run!"

A grim reaper flashed and the words "You died" appeared on the screen. That character looked nothing like Death. I stood up and cracked my back. Man, I was too old to sit on the floor for this long.

Matt was still alive so I went to the fridge for more beers. When I walked by the microwave, I glanced at the clock. Holy shit! We had been playing for hours. He would probably be leaving soon, and I hadn't even broached the subject of Death and Uriel.

I decided to ease in to it while he played the game. I fingered the Saint George charm he had given me. "So, Matt. You must be a religious guy, right? Since you wear this." I tapped his necklace gently.

It distracted him from the game and he died. An angel appeared on the screen.

"Oh, shit. I'm so sorry. I'll leave you alone." David would have been so pissed if I made him die in his game. I'd learned to hide out in the bedroom when he played so he couldn't blame me for making too much noise and distracting him.

"No biggie. It's not as much fun saving the world on your own. What were you saying?" He turned the game off and gave me his full attention.

Wiping my now sweating palms off on my lap, I pointed toward the tv and said, "I was just asking if you were a religious man." He nodded his head so I continued, "So you believe in angels, God and the Devil."

He leaned back away from me and said slowly, "Yeah, I guess. Why?"

"Do you believe in Death? As in the Fourth Rider of the Apocalypse?"

He looked away from me and fiddled with his beer.

"Um, that's what I was always taught in church. You're not going to try to convert me are you? I'm pretty solid in my Catholic faith. My *abuela*, God rest her soul, would kick my ass from Heaven if I even thought about changing. You're not one of those doomsday believers, are you?" He laughed, so I knew he was joking.

"No, no. Nothing like that. I just wanted to know if you believe in the end times and all that stuff about angels bringing on the rapture."

Matt stood up and gathered our empty beer bottles from the floor. He seemed to be considering what I was saying, rather than just brushing me off.

"Yeah, I do believe in it. Why? You seeing angels?"

It was now or never. I took a deep breath and said, "Yeah, actually… I have. Well one angel, Uriel."

The empty beer bottles fell into the bag with a loud clank. "Maybe we should switch to water."

I shook my head and walked toward him. "No, I'm not drunk, and I am not crazy. He was here, in my living room. I've seen Death too. He keeps trying to kill me."

I'll give Matt credit. Most men would have already headed for the door by now, but he stood his ground. "I don't get it. Is this a joke?"

I threw my hands up in the air and walked away. "No, I'm not joking. I knew you would think I'm crazy."

Matt walked over to me and reached out to turn me around. "I don't think you're crazy. I've seen vampires, zombies and werewolves. I've seen men do shit you wouldn't believe when I was in the Corps. Hell, my wife screwed another cop and then took my kid and screwed with my career when I caught her. Evil's there. Why would angels and devils be that far off?"

I let go of the breath I didn't realize I'd been holding. He believed me. I had someone else to talk to about this craziness.

"You're saying you saw the angel, Uriel. And Death?"

"Death was the one who turned David into a vampire to kill me. And he was responsible for all the other times I nearly died. Uriel was here to warn me about him."

"How do you know they're the real thing and not two

psychos messing with you? Maybe they're just playing a sick game."

Dammit, he didn't believe me after all. "You didn't see them, Matt. Death just appeared in my house, several times and then disappeared. He even showed up in my car after I was attacked at work. And Uriel," I paused to rub the goose bumps that covered my arms at the thought of seeing Uriel again, "he had wings coming out of his back and, he made you feel like he could capture your soul with a single breath."

Matt must have thought I was being overdramatic, but I couldn't think of a better way to describe that dread Uriel made you feel in his presence. "That airplane crash in Nevada was my fault because I yelled at Death. I thought if I moved to a new house I could hide from him and he would leave me alone. He's been stalking me."

"Wait, why would you think the airplane crash is your fault? What does that have to do with you?"

"I taunted him. I wanted him to leave me alone and asked if there wasn't a plane crash or something going on. That same night he killed all those people because of me. He made sure I knew it was my fault by making the TV say Sara Nevada mountains, instead of Sierra. I'm not crazy. I saw him on the security monitor tonight."

"Aha! I knew it. I knew you saw something. You're a terrible liar." Matt smiled for a few seconds before the smile disappeared off his face, "What did you see him do?"

"He touched the pastry the doorman ate that turned him into a zombie. He also somehow knew I would be watching because he turned to the camera and winked at me. It was like he could see me watching."

"That is screwed up. Why is Death stalking you? What

was the Angel doing here?"

For some reason I was embarrassed to tell Matt I thought Death was interested in me. It sounded so ludicrous. "I don't know. Uriel said something about Death's quest to make me his sacrificial lamb?"

I left out the part where Uriel ordered me to run to Matt for protection.

"Okay, I'm still trying to wrap my head around this. Why you? Why do they both care so much about you that they would both visit you?"

A good question I wished I had the answer to, but I didn't. Why was Death so fixated on me? "I don't know why. I'm nothing special or anything."

"No, you *are* special," Matt said with annoyed look on his face. Before I could react he went on, "So Death keeps trying to kill you, and you don't know why. Do you know why Uriel would be trying to save you? From what I remember from my Bible studies, Uriel is like way up there in angel rank."

I shivered at the thought of trying to get some answers from Uriel. "He got upset when I questioned him and told me to do as I'm told. He was kind of Old Testament, if you know what I mean."

"What did he tell you to do?"

Uriel had ordered me to go to Matt to have him protect me from Death, but that made me sound pathetic. "He said something about Death running out of time for his quest to kill me and that I needed to stay alive." The words sounded lame coming out of my mouth. I can only imagine how they sounded to him.

Matt rubbed his head, lost in thought. "Nah, something's not right. Why would Death want to kill you so bad? And why hasn't he done it already? He's Death, right? So he should be able to snap his fingers and take you. And why does it matter to Uriel if you live? We're missing something."

"Maybe I can ask Death the next time I see him," I said off-handedly. "He likes to pop in to chat sometimes."

He gave me a thoughtful look and said, "It might be a good idea, if you see him again."

Death had answered my other questions, so it might work. "He won't come if you're here. I have to be alone." I was torn between wanting him to refuse to leave so he could protect me, and trying to get some answers from Death.

"I don't like the idea of leaving you alone. But after watching you take out that zombie, I guess you can handle yourself. I've got a buddy who has some contacts in intelligence. If anyone has heard about angels or Death sightings, he would. I'll give him a call when I get home. I need to get some Zzzs before work tomorrow. That'll give Death a chance to talk to you."

That was the plan? Asking old Marine buddies for help and me quizzing Death on why he wanted to kill me? I handed him the container with the rest of the cupcakes.

"I'll be back in the morning, after I do some research on Uriel. Hey," he put the cupcakes down on the counter and slipped his hand under my chin. With one finger tip, he lifted my face up so I was looking at him, just inches away, "don't worry. We'll figure this out. I'm not going to let anything happen to you."

My stomach did cartwheels while he stared a beat too long. Oh, my God. I had beer and pizza breath. My mints mocked me silently from my purse not a foot away.

He leaned in, and I sucked in a breath, and then his phone rang. We both froze while a familiar song played. It was his ex. I deflated, and he stepped away from me. "Sorry, I better take this in case something's wrong with Haley. Goodnight."

He walked out before answering his phone. I closed the door, and then walked over to the island and sat on a cardboard box. I knew it was stupid, but I thought telling Matt would be the hardest part. I'd followed Uriel's orders. Following holy guidance had to be a good thing, right? Then again, the Bible wasn't known for its fun times. Look at what happened to Jesus.

# CHAPTER TWENTY-FIVE

*Saints and Sinners*

"A bit forward of him, you being the grieving widow and all."

I yelped and scrambled to stand.

Death appeared out of the shadows on my balcony.

"What are you doing here? Have you been out there all night?"

Death walked through the open balcony doors. He paused to sniff the air like a dog does when you walk by with food. He looked around before settling his eyes on me.

Dressed in a dark pin-striped suit, he reminded me of the CFO from my job, super intimidating. He wasn't wearing the sunglasses so the full weight of those dark orbs pressed down on me like a vice. I couldn't catch my breath or even turn away.

"Aside from your officer friend, you have had another visitor, but not one of this world."

My mouth opened and closed but nothing came out. Death turned away from me to lock the doors. I gulped a few deep breaths.

"You should keep these locked. Who knows what sort of unsavory characters might intrude." He must have realized why I was gaping. When he looked at me again, he was wearing his sunglasses.

"Ah, Uriel, I do believe. Tell me, why did my old friend visit you?"

Not for one second did I consider lying. "He said you were trying to kill me, and it wasn't my time, so he had to save me a bunch of times, and I needed to stay alive to stop your quest."

The words spilled out of me in one breath. There was a half-empty bottle of beer on the counter. I had no idea if it was mine or Matt's, but I didn't care. I snatched it up and took a few gulps.

"Interesting." Death would make an excellent poker player. I had no idea if my news made him angry or not. He smiled at me, which with most people would mean he was happy, but Death's smile felt like a threat.

"You are honored. Very few mortals ever get to see Uriel, much less speak to him. Very few."

I didn't feel privileged at all. Meeting Uriel filled me with mind-numbing terror, even more so than meeting Death. It must have shown all over my face.

Death laughed and said, "Ah, yes, I imagine Uriel would be upsetting to most humans. He disdains to conform to the mortal world, unlike myself."

I clamped my lips together, but a small stream of beer made it past my lips and down my chin as I choked on his words. 'Conforming' is not how I would have described Death. Compared to Uriel though, he was the guy next door. I wiped my chin before Death noticed my beer drool.

"You could say that again. I thought angels were supposed to be sweet and comforting." I walked over to throw the now empty bottle into the trash.

"This is something that has always confused me about

humans. Why do you portray angels as gentle and good? Angels punish the wicked. They do not follow mortals around to save them, despite your tales to the contrary."

I hadn't really thought about it much, but he was right. I swept crumbs into the empty pizza box. "What about the angel that stopped Abraham from sacrificing his son, Isaac, to God?"

"Was it not the angel himself who told Abraham to make the sacrifice in the first place? The same angel, in fact, that visited you today. Uriel, the Voice of God. But never forget, he is also the hand, or most often, the Fist of God."

Death walked over to me. I stopped cleaning and froze. He reached for my chin, and I flinched away.

"What are you doing?" My voice was so high and shaky, I sounded like a little old lady. I backed up until my butt hit the counter.

"I will not hurt you. Your mention of a sacrificial lamb and Abraham has provided me an idea as to why Uriel might be interfering, but I need to check to see if you carry the mark." He reached for me again.

I tried not to flinch when the cold hand of Death gripped my chin and turned my head to the left. With a surprisingly gentle touch, he lifted my hair away from my neck. I felt one soft finger run over the birthmark that ran behind my ear.

When Death let go of my hair, it tickled my neck and gave me goose bumps. I let out the breath I didn't realize I'd been holding when he stepped away. "So?"

You know what was worse than when Death smiled? When he grew serious. It was like all the life in the room was being snuffed out. "Yes. You are a daughter of Isaac."

I walked out of my kitchen so the island was between us. "No, I am the daughter of Ben."

Death ignored me and said, almost to himself, "I had no idea of your lineage, would not have even suspected it, if not for Uriel's interference. I understand why he would want to save a daughter of Isaac, especially one that was sacrificed by her own father."

"No. I told you, my dad's name was Ben. And my father didn't sacrifice me. Hello, alive here." I waved my fingers at him and he focused on me. Oh, bad idea, idiot.

"You do not remember the accident do you?" Death asked.

Was he serious? Like I would forget the thing that changed my whole life. No, ruined my whole life. The sound of metal grinding against the guard rails and glass shattering flashed through my memories. "Of course I do."

"Your father Ben was driving," Death prompted.

At least he got my dad's name right this time. I tried to block the memories but felt like I was trying to swim in a tidal wave and was drowning in the deluge. I remembered how pretty the sparks looked when the car slid along the guardrail, and the acrid smell of burnt rubber from the tires when they rubbed against the metal.

Rachel had screamed but my mom was strangely silent. I looked up at her face and had seen the terror there, but she wasn't looking at the sheer drop just beyond the flimsy rail. She had been trying to grab hold of the steering wheel, while dad shoved her away with one hand.

"No. Stop it. You're doing this. You're making me remember. I don't want to remember." Every memory was so real, but I'd only seen this part in the nightmares I'd had afterward. This couldn't have happened. Death had to be doing this to me.

"You must remember. It is time for you to see what

really happened and not the version your mind created to spare you." He placed a hand on my head and the memories played as though someone had unpaused them with a remote control.

I closed my eyes to face my worst nightmares.

Dad's other hand gripped the wheel. I'd always thought his eyes were closed in fear but realized now they had been closed in prayer. His lips murmured a litany about God and faith. He wasn't fighting to stop the car from going over the side. He was struggling to pull it right toward the drop.

"No! My dad wasn't a monster. He didn't do that." Flashes of Mom and Dad fighting went through my brain. Dad happy one minute, then screaming or worse, crying the next. Having to move constantly because Dad had lost his job or gotten into a fight with the neighbors. My mom begging him to get help. Death looked blurry through my sheen of tears.

"I am sorry, Sara." He actually sounded contrite, even gently patted my back while I sobbed.

"Why? Why did you make me go through that again? Just leave me alone!" I screamed at him before I sunk to the floor.

Death let me drop but hovered over me. "You have to know. To understand. This is why Uriel saved you. You were to be sacrificed by your father. Uriel could not allow that."

His words bludgeoned me, and I stopped weeping as anger flooded my head. "Why not? Why would he care? Thousands of people are killed every day. Some by their parents. So why me? Why couldn't he just let me die with them?"

Death reached a hand out to me to lift me up off the

ground. When I stood, he didn't let go and gently pulled me toward my room. Alarm bells should have been clanging in my head at the thought of Death leading me to my bedroom, but I was too numb to care.

He eased me toward the bed and then let go, walking back to stand by the door. "You mentioned the story of Abraham and Isaac, but do you also know that Uriel made a promise to Abraham?"

I nodded, though I didn't have any idea what he was talking about. I just wanted him to finish what he was saying and go away.

Death must not have been convinced because he continued. "When Uriel stopped Abraham from killing Isaac, he told him that because of his faith, he would be granted a fruitful line. He then went to touch his sword to the top of Isaac's head to bless him, but Isaac cowered and turned his head to the right, so the tip of the sword touched him here." He touched the back of his neck in the exact same spot my birthmark was in.

He couldn't be saying...No. That was crazy. "Are you saying Isaac was my great, great- however many greats-grandfather?"

Death nodded. "You carry his mark. It is not an uncommon thing. Uriel was true to his word and made sure Abraham's line grew strong and plentiful. But there was a darkness in Isaac that was created that day."

Yeah, I bet there would be some lingering psychological issues after your father hauled you up a hill as a sacrifice because a voice in his head he claimed was God told him to do it. That story in the Bible always bothered me. How could a parent murder their own kid?

"His seed multiplied and spread throughout the world

like a weed. Many were depressed or violent."

Like my father, though until that night he hadn't been physically violent to any of us. He never once raised a hand to my mother. Had he? How could I trust my own lying memories?

"You still haven't said why me."

"The lamb sacrificed in place of Isaac, served by the Lord's side. Did you know the lamb is the one to break the seals signaling The End of Times?"

"Yes, The Book of Revelations was my aunt's favorite part of the Bible. I heard it so often, I memorized it. That's how I knew who you were when I saw you on your pale horse."

Death nodded and continued, "What the Book does not tell you is that the scrolls can be resealed."

Okay, weird. "Why wasn't that in the Bible?"

"Who wrote the Book?"

"Disciples and holy men. But it's supposed to be the Word of God."

His eerie smile was back, and I shivered. "Yes, His Word, as told through others. Spoken to mankind by Uriel himself. Who else but an Archangel would dare to make edits?"

"Why would Uriel leave that out? I don't understand. And what does that have to do with me? There have been plenty of sacrifices throughout the years."

"A mere sacrifice isn't enough. Heaven is filled with martyrs. To seal the scrolls, one must be the original sacrifice that was spared, or one of his lineage. One whose blood was spilled by her own parent in God's name. A true martyr."

"So you're saying he would have saved any descendent of Isaac if their parents tried to kill them?"

Death nodded. "He has intervened for others, but I think my curiosity sharpened his focus on you. He must have thought I was trying to bring you before the throne where the scrolls are kept to be judged."

Too much beer, exhaustion, and grief made me want to lay down on the bed and go to sleep, but I needed to know what was going on. "Judged?"

"Suicides are not allowed into Heaven. Sacrificing yourself to save another is the one exception. In those cases you appear before the throne. If you are worthy you are allowed into Heaven. Her blood is the only thing that can seal the scrolls. So she must be a martyr."

I didn't like the way he kept saying she and you. I had a nasty feeling this martyr he mentioned was me. He expected me to volunteer to die to save the world like some kind of saint. Boy was he in for a rude awakening. I'd always been more sinner than saint.

## CHAPTER TWENTY-SIX

*Taking One for the Team*

"It's me, isn't it? You're saying the martyr needs to be me? That's why you keep trying to kill me."

I gave Death the stink eye, and he had the grace to look uncomfortable.

"No. Until today I did not realize your lineage. I kept trying to kill you because you kept escaping. It was fascinating."

I didn't know if I should have felt relieved that Death had only been trying to kill me for the fun of it or worried that he now had additional incentive for murder. Instead I got pissed. "Fuck the world and fuck you for asking me to martyr myself. This world has given me nothing but heartbreak. Why should I save it?"

"Uriel would have guessed that to be your answer. By picking you, he has... what do you humans call it?" He paused a moment before adding, "Hedged his bets? But what about your officer? Or his child? Are they not worth saving?"

"You fight dirty. Why do you even care?"

Death paused as though deep in thought. He blew out a breath and even from across the room its icy fingers reached for me. I shivered and grabbed my blanket.

"I had thought the end was inevitable. I had fulfilled my

duties and was doomed to the Pit. You offer salvation for the world, and myself, by becoming a martyr."

So he did have a personal stake in my dying. How could I trust anything he told me? "Okay, so now I know why you are trying to save the world. Explain to me why Uriel keeps saving me. Are you telling me he wants the world to end? He's an angel, for God's sake."

Death shook his head from side to side and let out a little laugh. "As I have told you before, humanity's idea of angels is much different than reality. They are not put on this earth to protect and guide you. They catalogue your sins and judge you. As for Uriel's motivation, it is quite simple. Once humans are extinguished, angels are given the earth."

Holy shit. Uriel wanted to wipe out humanity so he can upgrade his home? That was crazy.

"Understand, you will die no matter which choice you make. Choose to die now, and you spare humanity. If not, you will die after suffering the rapture alongside them. You must make the choice. I shall leave you to consider and will come back for your answer."

Just like that, he was gone.

My death was humanity's only salvation, but no pressure or anything. Shit. My choices were to die now to save the world, or die later during a biblical apocalypse. It wasn't fair.

Exhaustion hit me and I fell back against the pillows and curled up to go to sleep. I'd quit my job, killed a zombie, saved the ho, bared my soul to Matt, and had a scary conversation with Death. I couldn't process another thing tonight. I hoped the answer would come to me in the morning.

You know how sometimes when you have a problem and go to sleep your unconscious mind will work on it and you'll wake up and know the solution?

Didn't happen.

Maybe the answers were about to be revealed in my dreams, but the ringing of my cellphone over and over at nine o'clock woke me up before I could find out.

"'Lo?" I mumbled into the phone.

"Sara? Are you okay? You're late."

I must be still dreaming. It couldn't be Colleen on the phone. "What?"

"It's Colleen. Sweetie, I know you weren't feeling well yesterday, and wanted to call and check on you."

I shook my head to clear it and said again, "What?"

I was never much for conversation before my morning coffee.

"Because you're late. It's past eight o'clock. Don't worry about it, just get down here as soon as you can and you can just work through lunch to make up for it."

I stopped myself from uttering "what" for the third time, but just barely. Surely even Colleen wasn't this delusional.

"Sara, are you there?" Colleen asked.

Yup, she really was that delusional. Time to pop that bubble. "Colleen, I quit yesterday, remember? The letter, my personal items being carried out in a box, is it coming back to you now?"

"But you can't quit. You were just being emotional. No one's going to hold that against you, just get in here before the CFO comes in and asks for the financials." Her last sentence took on a pleading tone. I remembered how Death, dressed in his suit and tie, had reminded me of the CFO last night and shivered. Oh, poor Colleen. My heart would be breaking for her, if she hadn't kept me under her thumb for ten years.

"Uh, yes. I can, and did, quit. I don't care about the financials. Lose my number."

"No, you aren't thinking clearly. Your husband just died, Sara. You need your job. How are you going to pay your bills? What about healthcare? Stop being so irrational and get in here."

Now that sounded more like the Colleen I knew and despised. "You're right, Colleen. I will have to get healthcare. I'll put that on my checklist once I get my new business started. As for bills, they're covered thanks to David's life insurance. I don't need that job, and I don't have to deal with you for one second longer. Do your own work for once."

Though it pained me to miss out on her shocked reaction, I hung up on her.

Well, crap. Since I was awake now, I might as well get up and make some coffee. I stumbled into the kitchen and ignored the stack of boxes I needed to unpack later, if I was still in this world later. I flashed back to Death's conversation the night before and nearly tripped over a box in the hallway. I tried to tell myself it was the near wipe-out that caused my heart to race and my hands to shake, but I knew it was a lie.

I had to die. If I didn't, everyone else in the world would suffer and be slaughtered. Oh, God. I thought I didn't care about my life, but now, faced with my own mortality I realized I wanted to live.

No. Not now. Don't think about it now. Coffee first. I opened the boxes marked "kitchen" and searched for my coffee maker. Where the hell was it? Could it have been mislabeled? I thought of the coffee cart downstairs, but then remembered the poor barista had been eaten. I doubt they had reopened it so soon. Before I could tear into the box marked 'misc', my phone rang again.

"I told you to lose my number, bitch!" I yelled without looking at the Caller ID.

"Not a morning person, I see," Matt answered.

I set down the scissors I had been using to open boxes and ran my hands through my hair to straighten it out. "Oh, hi, Matt. Sorry, thought you were my boss, well, ex-boss now, I suppose."

Matt chuckled, "I hope you wouldn't be calling your current boss a bitch."

There was an awkward moment of silence until Matt cleared his throat, "So anyway, I was calling to check on you, make sure you're okay."

"I'm fine, though my coffeemaker is MIA. Figured I would face unpacking a little today."

A thought came to me, maybe if I had some company it would help keep my mind off of my impending doom.

"All this unpacking is kind of daunting all by myself." I had no shame and used a pathetic tone on him.

He laughed at me. "Good luck with that. My ex took almost everything, so didn't take me long to unpack. I hear it sucks."

"Well, I better get to all this unpacking, all on my lonesome. Yup. Solo. Just me in my lonely condo with no one to talk too."

"Fine, I'll try to stop by later to help. Man," his voice rose to a falsetto, "help me unpack. Save me from a werewolf and a zombie," his voice went back to normal and he added, "You are so high maintenance."

"I do not sound like that, jerk face. I saved myself from the zombie, thank you very much. Just for that, I'm going to eat the rest of the cupcakes you left behind last night." I laughed so he knew I was kidding.

He gave an exaggerated gasp. "You wound me, milady. Lemme take care of some things, and then I'll stop by. Don't you dare eat my cupcakes!"

A smile broke out on my face after I hung up. Matt would probably make unpacking fun. I gave up on trying to find my coffee pot and ran to take a shower and make myself look half-way human for him.

Just when I had finished dressing, there was a knock on the door. A peek out the peephole revealed it was Matt holding coffee. I opened my door slowly. "Thought you were coming by later."

He waved the coffee under my nose and cocked an eyebrow. "I happened to be nearby when you called. Besides, unpacking with caffeine deprivation is a recipe for disaster."

I grab***bed the coffee greedily and walked back toward the kitchen. "Coffee in twenty minutes or less? You should open a delivery business." I took a sip and added, "You try to act tough, but you're really a nice guy."

Matt made a face and said, "Nice? No. I am not nice. I'm using you for your cupcakes, only."

I snorted and handed him a cupcake. He took a bite and looked around. "Wow, I see you've made tons of progress since last night. Lots of boxes opened, but you know you have to remove the stuff inside for it to be considered actually unpacking."

"Well, I had a rough night. Death popped in for a visit after you left."

Matt set the cupcake down and walked over to me. He put one hand on my arm and the other on my face. "Are you okay? Did he hurt you?"

My stomach did little flip flops from being this close to him. I shook my head, and he stepped back and took a seat on one of the boxes. Telling him I wasn't hurt meant he would let go of me? Wait a minute, I wanted to change my answer, but it was too late.

"What did he say? What happened?"

I plopped down on the box next to Matt and tried to take deep breaths to calm my heart without Matt seeing. "Fine, I'll tell you, but it'll cost you half that cupcake."

It was supposed to be a joke, but Matt wasn't laughing. He pushed the cupcake in my direction and said, "Spill."

"Well, I know now why Uriel and Death are so interested in me, and it isn't my baking skills." I took a big gulp of my coffee and proceeded to tell him everything, well almost everything. Death's comments about Matt almost kissing me weren't important. A girl's got to have some secrets.

## CHAPTER TWENTY-SEVEN

*Whisky a Go Go*

"No. No way. Are you crazy? Absolutely not!" Matt stood up and paced around the island. Just when I thought he might wear a groove in the floor, he stopped and grabbed my shoulders and added, "Don't even think about martyring yourself. You hear me?"

Matt's reaction wasn't unexpected. Talking about killing yourself, even to save the world, would be upsetting to hear from anyone. It must be worse to hear it from the chick you almost died saving.

"We are talking Revelations here. Hell on earth. Demons rising up and slaughtering humanity. How can one person's life be more important than everyone else's'?"

I sounded like I was ready to drink the Kool-aid.

"It just is. You shouldn't have to die. This isn't right. I think Death and Uriel are a couple of sociopaths messing with your head, and none of this is real."

I put a gentle hand on his chest. "Matt, the evidence is staring at you right in the face. Come on, you've known about these monster attacks for how long? The only reason the world has even heard of them is because the government couldn't keep it hushed up any more. Something has got to be triggering them, making them worse. This is it. This is the reason. The End of Days is here."

"Do you hear yourself? End of Days. Do you really think the whole world is going to end and you are the only one who can stop it? You really think God would do that?"

"I don't know. When I get up there, I'll be sure to ask him."

"Not funny." He crossed his arms, a fierce look crossed his face. I bet he intimidated many a criminal with that look.

"I'm sorry. I was just trying to lighten things up a bit. I'm not saying I'm on board with the plan, but I can't dismiss it outright. You didn't see them. No way were they human. Think about Haley. What if I can save her? Or would you rather she face the apocalypse?"

Matt jumped up as though I had slapped him. "How can you say that to me? I'm trying to keep you alive, and you say some shit like that to me!"

I reached for him, but he backed out of the way. "Don't be like this! I don't want to die. If you can think of any way to save me, I'll take it. But if there's not, shouldn't I try to save your life and Haley's life?"

He rubbed the side of his head so hard and fast it sounded like he was scrubbing his skin with a wire brush. "I'll find a way. I'm not going to sit back and let you die."

Well, at least he'd stopped yelling, though the way his fists clenched and unclenched, he looked on the verge of losing it again.

"You don't have to *let* me do anything. This is between me and Death."

He turned and punched the wall.

I reached up and grabbed his hand, rubbing my fingers softly over his red knuckles. "Matt, I'm sorry. You've been amazing to me. No one has ever cared for me like you have.

You mean a lot to me." I knew if I said another word, I would burst into tears.

I expected him to yell or beat on the wall again. What I didn't expect was for him to wrap his arms around me and hold me so tight I could barely breathe. The last time I'd cried in front of someone was right after my parents had died when I was a little girl.

The tears flowed down my cheeks unchecked. In Matt's embrace, I almost felt like he could save me from Death's clutches himself. Abruptly, he let go, and I hung my head down so he wouldn't see my tear-swollen eyes.

"No, I refuse to accept this. I've saved you before; I'll save you again. Just, give me a day. I'll call some old contacts I had in the service. They owe me. And I'll call my priest. He's a good guy and won't think I'm crazy. We'll figure out another way. Promise me you won't do anything for at least a day or two."

What else could I say? If I didn't agree he would stay glued to my side. "Okay. I promise."

He smiled and pulled my chin up and then used his thumb to wipe away my tears. "I'll be back, okay. Give me one day."

I nodded again and let my head drop. He kissed the top of my head softly and then turned and left.

Great. Nothing got unpacked, my nose was all runny from crying and I was depressed. Yay. At least he left me the coffee. I sipped it and munched on the cupcake he had left behind. *Tears are not allowed when eating chocolate*. I let a few more fall and then wiped my face. I squeezed my hand into a fist until my fingernails made little indentations into my palms.

Stop crying! I told myself. A few deep breaths and

several sips of coffee later, I got myself together. No more crying. As soon as I finished eating, I was going to get up and unpack. Life was too short to feel sorry for myself.

Especially my life.

Hell. Why should I bother unpacking if I was gonna die anyway?

The cupcake turned to sawdust in my mouth. I took a big gulp of coffee to wash it down.

Because, it was still my life. Mine.

I might not have any control over when I died, or how I died, but I could control what I left behind. Someone wasn't just going to go through my place and cart off boxes so easily after I died. They were going to have to go through my things and know that I had a life. That I lived here. I was a person, not just a bunch of boxes full of crap.

I stood up and attacked the first box I saw. It was the kitchen stuff. Several sweaty hours later, I had unpacked my entire kitchen, hung up all my clothes, and unpacked my precious books. My coffee pot was still MIA, but I had managed to hang a few new pictures I'd bought. My old friend, the big iron cross I'd used to fight off my vampire husband, and almost used to kill Mandi, was the only decoration I had brought from the old house. Such good memories.

Totally spent and mostly unpacked, I collapsed on the bed. I did a double-take when I looked at the clock. It was four in the afternoon. No wonder I was so tired. My stomach growled making sure I didn't forget it needed attention too. Starving to death in my own bed would hardly earn me martyr status.

Crawl into bed or get something to eat? Oooo, maybe some wine and a hot bath. Shit, the movers hadn't brought the wine fridge like I had told them. I could order food and actually get it delivered here. It was nice to live in the middle of town. Wonder if they would stop and get me some wine if I tipped extra? But it would be my luck that the delivery guy wouldn't even be old enough to buy alcohol.

Damn the movers for leaving my coffee pot and wine fridge behind!

There was stuff in the bathroom and the laundry room I'd left behind anyway. Plus I needed to throw out the stuff in the fridge and put the garbage out so it didn't stink up the house. If I ever wanted to sell the thing, I would have to make it look nice, a happy place...a place Death, vampires, and werewolves would never visit.

Eh, maybe I should just settle on it not stinking.

After making up my mind to leave, it still took me another ten minutes to move. Somehow, I managed the Herculean task of putting one weary foot in front of the other until I made it to the elevator. Once inside, I decided to stand off to the side in front of the panel, in case I was greeted with another zombie, or worse, Mandi.

When the doors opened I peeked out and saw both a security guard and a doorman at the front desk. The coffee cart had been removed from the lobby. They must have been here all night cleaning the place. If I hadn't been there to see the gruesome scene, I wouldn't have had any clue about the horrors of the previous day.

I made it to the parking lot without incident and looked for my Toyota before I remembered I was driving David's car now. I pushed the remote door unlock button and it chirped. Nice. One good thing about the long drive to my middle-of-nowhere house, lots of open road to see how this baby drove. With the radio cranked up and my foot heavy on the gas, I made it to my old house in record time.

Awww, home bitter home.

The lights from my car highlighted several envelopes jammed into the door frame of the front door while I pulled into the garage. I had sealed the mail slot shut when I left in case vandals, or asshole neighbors, tried to put the hose in it to flood the place while I was gone. I walked around to the front entry see what they were. Some were junk mail, but one stood out. Ah, the HOA had sent me another missive that read:

*Dear Homeowner,*

*Your lawn has been reported as being non-compliant with our covenant, codes and restrictions. Landscaping not properly maintained can bring down the home values for the entire community. You have ten days to replace or repair any damaged sections or you will be fined.*

Aren't there more important things they should be worried about, like the werewolf and vampire attack right there in their precious gated community? These idiots probably believed the party line about them just being normal humans on drugs, rather than the monsters they actually were. Come on, I've been attacked and nearly killed ad nauseam for the last several weeks. I even have police reports to back me up. I'd been visited by not one, but two mythical beings, both of whom expected me to follow their agenda for the way I would die. My marriage, job and house had fallen to ashes, the last almost literally. And these assholes wanted to fine me?

"Can't you cut me a break from this petty bullshit?" I screamed at the sky, not really sure if I was talking to Uriel, Death, or God Himself.

Fuck the HOA. They can fine me all they want. Good luck trying to collect it from a corpse. In fact, I had a little message of my own that would tell them what I thought of their precious property values.

I stomped into the garage and yanked the weed killer off the shelf. I used the whole bottle, but the grass looked the same. If we had some gasoline, that would have been perfect, but since we were trying to save our planet by cutting back on fossil fuels, we only had an electric lawnmower.

Damn. I could try some wine, but I hated to waste it. Oh, wait a minute. My eyes landed on David's precious single-malt Scottish whisky. He had bought a bottle every year on our anniversary, but we were never allowed to drink them. I was never a big whisky fan myself, so I didn't care. He would have been livid if he had known what I planned on doing with it.

Perfect.

I grabbed a couple of bottles and marched back out to the lawn. You couldn't even tell where I had sprayed the weed killer. That wouldn't do at all. I broke the first bottle open on a nearby rock and pronounced, "This one's for my homies."

The burnt toast and molasses smell I always associated with whisky reminded me of David. I poured it out, carefully making a big F on the grass. It took a couple of trips, and almost all of his stash, but I finally finished all of my letters.

Now for the finale. I lit a match and threw it on the whisky soaked grass. I expected a dramatic whoosh as the flames shot up to spell FU HOA across the lawn. Nothing. I lit the rest of the matches but it wouldn't burn.

Geez! I lived in a desert. Shouldn't it be easier to set my lawn on fire?

I went back into the garage and found the weed burner David used to burn out the weeds growing in the rocks. Once I opened the propane tank, the flame came to life with a few clicks of a button. I held the flame to the letters until the grass burned on its own.

Wonder if I have any marshmallows? I was trying to remember if there were any left in the kitchen when my cellphone rang. I answered asking, "Is this Sparky the fire bear?"

"Sara? Are you drunk? Where are you? I've been calling you for the last half hour." It was Matt.

"Oh, sorry. I had the radio cranked up, plus the Mustang's engine can be a little loud when you let it rip."

He blew out a breath in frustration. "Don't you think it'd be safer to stay home? Driving in this city is dangerous enough without Death and angels gunning for you."

"I just needed to get some things at the house. And light a little fire."

"Damn, woman. Tell me you aren't trying to burn something else inside the house."

"Well, no, not exactly inside the house, more like on the grass."

"The grass? Put it out now before the fire department shows up."

He wouldn't let me hang up because he wanted to make sure I didn't pass out from the smoke. Which I thought was totally unfair. What are the odds of that happening to me, again? I turned the sprinklers on and the fire went out.

"I wasn't going to let it burn much longer anyway or else it would mess up my letters."

"What letters?" he asked.

"I burned a message to the HOA on the grass using David's fancy Scottish whisky."

Matt sucked in a breath. "Are you crazy? Good whisky costs hundreds of dollars per bottle. Just don't burn anything else. Get your stuff and then go home and stay there. I'm waiting for that Marine friend of mine to get back to me. It should be soon. Remember your promise."

"I know. It's not like I planned to stick around here anyway. I'll talk to you later." I hung up without saying goodbye, annoyed at the way he had ordered me around. Did he think he was the boss of me now? He'd saved my life, so now it was his?

Then again, given what I'd told him about sacrificing myself, I should probably cut him some slack. He cared about me and was trying to protect me and to thank him I acted like a bitch. Nice. No wonder I ended up married to a guy like David. I looked at the bottle of whisky I held in my hand and had an idea. They rest of the bottles would make a good apology gift to Matt.

I put the last three bottles into the car and tried to decide what else I should bring to my new home. Did I really need to fill up the car with a bunch of stuff I would have to lug up into the condo? Why bother if I was going to die soon? On the other hand, those whisky bottles looked so lonely by themselves. I couldn't expect Matt to drink by himself if he came over later to get them. Since I don't like whisky, I'd drink wine.

No way could I carry the whole wine fridge to the car, so I grabbed two of my favorites and left. I was making my final trip to the car with my precious coffee maker when Death appeared out of the shadows of the garage.

"Ahhhh!" I screamed and dropped the coffee pot on the ground, "Shit. You scared the bejesus out of me."

For once Death didn't smile at me. I was used to him laughing, usually at my expense, but a somber Death? My stomach clenched.

He picked up the stainless coffee pot that had landed by his feet and set it in the open trunk, before leaning casually on the side of the car. Dressed in black slacks, a black Polo, and black loafers, he looked like an average guy from the nose down, as long as he didn't smile. He wasn't wearing his sunglasses so those soul-sucking eyes were exposed along with his weird sculpted eyebrows.

"My apologies. I did tell you I would be back for your answer."

I walked to the trunk and put the rest of the coffee maker in it, and then slammed it shut. For some reason, I didn't want to talk about it in this house. "Get in. We can talk on the drive back."

Without waiting for an answer, I sat down behind the wheel. Would Death use the door? Nah, he'd probably just appear inside the car.

As predicted, one second he was outside the car, the next he was in the passenger seat sans seatbelt. He didn't set off the seatbelt sensor. How much did Death weigh? The car gave a throaty growl when I started it up and I felt a surge of motor lust. I understood now why David hadn't let me drive it. He didn't want to share it.

As we drove past the still smoldering lawn, Death gave a weak smile. "Would it not be more efficient to use the machine to cut the grass, rather than burning a few blades at a time?"

I wasn't in the mood to explain it. "Yeah, maybe next

time. So, you want an answer right now I'm guessing."

Death didn't respond, just turned and looked at me patiently. Great, now he decides to stop being Chatty Cathy.

"I don't really have much of a choice, do I? You're just going to whack me the minute I let my guard down."

Death sighed and his cold breath fogged up my windshield. I turned off the AC and rolled down the window.

"No. This choice is entirely up to you. I spoke with Hades to see if there was another way, but there is not. You have to choose to martyr yourself by saving another. And Hades says your cause would be made stronger if the one you saved is an enemy."

"You asked Hades how to save me? Why? I thought you wanted me dead."

Death turned and gave me a puzzled look. "At first I was intrigued by your survival, but I would not have chosen this path for you. Do you think any of these events are under my control? My role was predestined, much like Jesus or Judas. God gives the orders, the lamb breaks the seals, and Uriel ensures they are enforced. I perform the tasks I am ordered to fulfill."

Death was trying to spare me? Death was the good guy while God and Uriel were the bad guys? I just couldn't wrap my head around that.

We drove in silence for a few minutes, Death patiently waited for me to gather my thoughts. "Okay, so I die. Then what? How am I supposed to know where to go or what to do?"

Death reached out and patted my hand. The first time he had touched me, I'd braced for pain that never came. You'd think his touch would be cold or painful, but it just felt like a normal hand.

"Did you think I would abandon you? I will guide you over to the other side and bring you to the chamber where the lamb sits on the throne. I cannot speak while in that room. They will know of your lineage and your sacrifice. You must ask for the scrolls. If they deem you worthy, you will be given them. Only your blood can seal them again. Once sealed, you will move on," he paused and turned his head to look out the window before adding, "without me".

The air in the car seemed to grow heavy. I was happy I still had my window rolled down. "When? I'm guessing it will need to be soon."

"When one fourth of the earth's population has been eradicated, the next two seals will be broken. The world will not recover." Death said the words softly, but I heard each distinctly.

That was it then. Attacks had only started showing up on the news this past year, but who knew how long they'd been going on before someone caught them on video and plastered it all over the internet? Matt had been trained when he was in the Marines to deal with them, so the deaths had to have been going on for a few years now in secret. Wouldn't I have noticed if a quarter of the earth's population had been annihilated? Maybe not if it was in third world countries. Even if there were time, was it right to let hundreds, possibly millions, more be slaughtered just because I wanted a few more days to live?

"Fine. Tonight's mine though. Just let me pretend I'm a normal woman and leave me alone. Deal?" I looked over and Death was gone. Guess he agreed.

What does one do on what might be their last night alive? I steered the car to the best restaurant in town. Eat, drink and be merry, for tomorrow I would die.

# CHAPTER TWENTY-EIGHT

*Liar, Liar, Pants on Fire*

You'd think finding some company on the last day of your life would be easy. I called Matt but got voicemail. I tried Rick and Brandon, but they were spending some much needed alone time together. Brandon had been working round the clock at the hospital because of this mysterious plague. I'd watched him give an interview on the news the other day, and he looked haggard.

I hadn't planned on falling asleep. I could sleep when I'm dead, right? That would come soon enough. When I arrived home everything sort of hit me at once, and I got depressed. Plus, my arms were still sore from smashing that zombie in the head with the golf club. Maybe it would become a new workout craze. I ended up crawling into a bottle of wine and sweet oblivion.

The sound of my ringing phone woke me at noon.

Before I could manage to figure out which of the three blurry talk buttons was the actual one, the call went to voicemail. A few seconds later I received a text message from Elise Travino, HOA President. It was riddled with typos that autocorrect must have gotten wrong. It said I was a 'price of shirt that I am going to get ride of'.

The HOA must have received my message and weren't happy about it. It apparently made them a little hot under the collar.

Ha! The HOA wasn't a big threat any more. I snorted to myself before texting back, "Whatevs."

Didn't take long before my phone rang again. I dropped it on my nightstand, letting it go to voicemail and stumbled into my kitchen in search of coffee. A glance at the slightly dented pot reminded me of my conversation with Death.

Today was the day. My twenty-four hour reprieve was up. No call from the Governor would save me now. Destined to die saving an enemy. But which enemy? Who would the likely candidates be? Mandi? My old boss Colleen?

I wanted to crawl back into bed and pull the covers over my head to hide from my fate, but the scent of the Columbian black magic hit my nose. My hands shook while I poured what would probably be one of my last cups of coffee. I went out to my balcony and leaned against the rail to enjoy my precious caffeinated gold without having to hear my cellphone go off.

That first cup disappeared quickly. While inside getting a refill, my cellphone chirped to remind me I had messages. I let out a deep sigh. I couldn't even relish one of the few joys in life I had left without someone demanding my attention. I went into the bedroom to see what was so important.

Holy crap! That Travino bitch had gone off the deep end. I skimmed through her texts until the phone rang in my hand. I glanced at the Caller ID before I answered it.

"Girlfriend, what did you do to that Travino chick?" Elise must have called Rick when I wouldn't answer her.

"Sorry. Bet she gave you an earful. I was pissed off and burned FUHOA in my grass last night."

"Unhinged is the word! The woman has popped her

cork. I told her not to worry, I would have a landscaper out there pronto to fix your little, uh, message. That seemed to appease the nut bag. But I would avoid her for a little while. She is dancing on the edge of complete meltdown. I heard some gossip from another realtor in the area that her husband cleaned out their account, stole the HOA money, and fled the country with his secretary."

"Yeah, but my husband cheated on me and tried to kill me. Didn't mean I acted all psycho."

"Exactly my point. I guess someone found her running in the street barefoot wearing her wedding dress and ripped nylons. Her makeup was all smeared like one of those freaky porcelain dolls. It was crazy. The neighbors had to take turns staying with her to make sure she didn't hurt herself. Stay away from her. She could be violent."

Rick knew more about my neighbors in a few days than I had in ten years. When I was attacked by a vampire and a werewolf, they were nowhere to be found, but they took turns sitting by her side? Why was I sacrificing myself for these people?

"Will do. Hey, can I give you power of attorney to sell my house in case anything happens to me? I know where I want the proceeds to go to."

I realized when I died everything would go to my aunt. No way in hell would I let that happen.

"Whoa, what's going on, Sara? You okay?"

"Yeah, just with David dying, and this talk about Elise being dangerous, I realized I need to have a will just in case something happens to me."

He paused for a moment and said, "You're okay though, right? You aren't planning on doing anything? I can come over right now if you need me."

Tears filled my eyes. It was in the middle of his work day and he was going to drop everything to save me. I lied to him, "No, silly. Things are going good in my life. No way I would off myself. You are going to be stuck with me for a very long time."

I sold the lie as best as I could, thankful he was on the phone and couldn't see my face.

"Okay. I will text you some info for an attorney we do a lot of work with. You can talk to him about setting up the will and the POA in case of death. Give him a call and let me know when I need to sign. I gotta run, sweetie. Love you."

He hung up before I could choke out an "I love you, too"

I called the attorney and for an added 'expedite fee' was able to get an appointment in a three hours. I took my time getting dressed, carefully putting on makeup and doing my hair. With two hours to kill, I decided to go across the street to the park. It was in the middle of the day, so there wouldn't be a lot of people there, but I wouldn't be all alone sitting in my condo.

Like before, I sat on the little bench and closed my eyes, enjoying the sounds of the kids playing and the birds chirping. Before long, my bangs were blown off my face by warm, putrid breath. I opened my eyes and saw the big black teeth of Death's horse.

"Back off, Trigger." I said and leaned away.

"Apologies," Death said. He backed the horse away a few feet, before he climbed off and sat down next to me.

"Don't sweat it. Halitosis is the least of my problems right now considering I am dying today." My joke fell flat and we sat in silence and watched the activity in the park.

"I wish there were another way. I am powerless to stop this." It was the first time I had seen Death so sad. Even the horse gave me a doleful look.

"So do I need sign an agreement in blood or something? Or just wait until someone comes along and offs me?"

Death smiled and shook his head. "I have to ask, of your own free will you sacrifice yourself?"

My face warmed as my heart started pumping blood furiously. I felt like a million little ants were crawling all over my skin. My ears rang. The end could come any second. No backing out of a deal with Death.

It wasn't much of a choice. Die now and have a chance to save the world, or die later when the world is overrun by the demons from Hell. The Book of Revelations made it pretty clear which was the better choice. My death could buy Matt and his daughter the chance for a long, happy life.

"Yes. I'll die to save the world." I paused and tears filled my eyes. "Is it gonna hurt? Will I suffer long?"

Before he could answer, the sound of a police siren drew our attention to the entrance of the park. Matt parked in front of my condo. He got out and marched toward the door as though he were going into battle. I ran to the park entrance and yelled, "Matt, over here."

I waved my arms wildly and yelled again. When he saw me, the tension went out of his shoulders. "Sara! Why haven't you been answering your phone?"

Death had followed me to the park entrance. I told him, "I'll be right back."

I jogged out to meet Matt.

He ran his hands up and down my body, checking for injuries, and said, "Are you okay? I saw that I missed your call, and then you didn't answer."

"I'm fine, just needed some fresh air, so I went to the park." I tried not to look at the park entrance where Death sat upon his horse like some terrifying statue.

Matt noticed my look and said, "Is he here? Is that what this is about? Sara, please. I told you, I'll find another way. I'm not going to let you die." He looked across the street and raised his voice, "You aren't taking her, asshole."

Death was off his horse and across the street in the blink of an eye. I blocked Matt with my body and pleaded with Death, "**Leave him alone. Please. He's upset. You can have me, but not him."

Matt stepped back in front of me and gave me an anguished look before he grabbed my shoulders to pull me into a bear hug. "God Sara, what have you done? No."

I peered over Matt's shoulder trying to read Death's enigmatic face.

"I would not harm him. He cares for you. Deeply. As do I. He grieves for you. Something I have experienced far more than you could comprehend. I would never begrudge one their moment of grief."

Did he mean he had experienced grief himself or had watched others go through it? The blue and red light from Matt's truck flashed over Death's face. Maybe it was a trick of the lights, but I saw sorrow there.

Before I could figure out what that meant, Matt pulled back to lower his face to mine. "Tell me you didn't do anything stupid that you can't take back, Sara. Please."

His head hovered inches from mine. He searched my face, looking for an answer I desperately wished I could give him. "Me? Do something stupid?"

He closed his eyes and shook his head, before he rested his forehead on mine. "No, don't do this." He took a wild look around and called out, "Please don't take her. She doesn't deserve this!"

Though he couldn't see him, Matt must have sensed when Death stepped beside him. He turned and looked right where Death was standing. "Take me instead."

"No! You have a child. I have no one. Don't you dare say that again." I turned Matt's face back to mine. Tears fell down my face as I forced myself to lie to him. "Okay, we'll find another way. Death's gone now. I'll be fine. Just, don't say that ever again."

Death backed away and I tried not to look at him.

"Okay," Matt breathed a sigh of relief, "Okay, good. Go inside and wait for me. I'll be off shift soon."

I forced a smile, praying he wouldn't read the deceit in it. An intense look played across his face. Oh, God, I sucked at lying. He knew the truth. I braced for him to start yelling again, but was shocked when he reached out to put an arm around my waist, pulling me close.

His lips met mine in a desperate kiss. They were surprisingly soft and warm, but before I had time to even get butterflies, his radio screeched feedback and we jumped apart.

Death's hand drop quickly to his side and knew he was responsible.

Jerk.

"Okay. Guess I better get going. Go home and stay there." He gave me one last look. Dazed from his kiss, I nodded at him and tried to smile. It must have been passable because he got back into his truck.

"Why'd you do that? You can't give me just one moment of happiness? Would a little kindness kill you?" I turned my face away from Matt so he wouldn't notice me talking.

Death walked over to stand in front of me. "Do you think your death will be easier the stronger his feelings grow? What I did was a kindness. For him."

I closed my eyes, but not before a tear managed to escape.

"He will not drive away, unless you smile and wave goodbye." Death spoke in a gentle voice.

I wiped my face, turned and smiled. Matt waved and drove off.

Holy crap. I was in love with him. How could I not have realized it until now? And I would probably never see him again. I gulped air and tried not to lose it.

Suck it up. Look at the crap that life had given me so far. Why would I think I would have a fairy-tale ending with him?

"I promise, you will not suffer for long, but I cannot prevent all the pain."

It took me a minute to register what Death said. I took a deep breath. "Let's get it over with then. I don't want to drive myself crazy trying to figure out when it's coming."

Death didn't answer. I turned, and he was gone.

What the fuck?

I looked around for him or the horse but they were nowhere in sight.

Now what?

# CHAPTER TWENTY-NINE

*All the Pretty Little Horses*

I went to the lawyer's office, signed all the paperwork, and drove back home in a numb state. I half expected to get in a horrific car accident on the way, but for once Arizona drivers weren't driving crazy. Now that should be a sign of the apocalypse. I pulled into my parking garage, sat in my car, head on the wheel, dreading seeing Matt again. The tension in my neck from all the drama in my life was giving me a headache.

How could I tell him I lied to him? That I would be dying sometime soon and there was nothing, with all his Marine training and huge heart, he could do to save me. I closed my eyes tightly to stop any tears from escaping. No time for tears. I had a world to save.

I threw open the car door and when I got out noticed the lights were out around my reserved spot. Good thing the car had a trunk light so I could go through the few items still in the car from the old house. I heard the clickity clack of high heels walking from the back of the parking garage toward me, but didn't give it much thought. Figured it was a neighbor heading for the entrance, until the sound stopped a few feet away from me. I heard a familiar voice.

Could this day get any worse?

"What are you doing in his car? It's not yours!" Mandi's

footsteps sounded like an angry typist pounding at a typewriter when she marched toward me.

I chucked the stuff back into the trunk and slammed it shut. Anger I'd held back all day spewed forth like a volcano. "What? Did you think you were going to get his car, too? Mistresses don't get anything, idiot. Only wives. Next time, get payment up front before fucking someone's husband!"

She lifted one of her bird legs and stomped the ground. "You bitch! He never loved you. He loved me! He said you tricked him into marrying you by saying you were pregnant. You don't deserve any of this!"

I dangled the Mustang's keys at her. "Oh, but I do! Look who's got a muscle car with lots of ponies under the hood. Does your ugly bug run on unicorn farts?"

I clicked the alarm button ready to walk away when the little skank threw her purse on the trunk and shoved me. She might have been taller than me, but I had a good thirty pounds on her. I shoved her right back. She landed on her ass in the middle of the lane and yelled at me, "My VW is not ugly!"

"Your taste in cars and men suck. Let me tell you about David. He asked me to marry him. I didn't want to get married, but he charmed me into it. I never said I was pregnant. He made you think he was Prince Charming, just like he did to me once. And when he was bored with you, he found another chick to string along, just like he did with me. Get over it!"

Mandi stood up and I braced for her to attack me again. But she didn't. She dissolved into a mess of tears. Why? Why couldn't she have just hit me? Mandi was in full meltdown mode in the middle of the parking garage. She was blocking the lane when a car pulled in and honked. More cars were coming up behind that one. She was causing a traffic jam.

I let out a sigh of disgust and walked over to pull her out of the way. The first car swerved around to park, as did the others. Mandi put her arms around me and sobbed unintelligible words. I looked at the ceiling and wondered how on Earth I had ended up consoling her.

Partially blinded by blonde hair, I almost didn't see the headlights of a car speeding around the corner. The driver must not have seen us standing there because of all the dark shadows around my car from the broken lights. I shoved Mandi out of the way toward my car. At the last minute, the driver slammed on the brakes.

I didn't even have time to scream before the car struck. Tires screeched, echoing off the concrete walls. I smelled burnt rubber before the pain made everything blurry, like pen marks on wet paper. I couldn't tell you what the year of the car was that smashed into me. Not even the color. But I recognized the emblem. My last crazy thought before my head slammed onto the trunk as my body flew over the car...

Huh, another Mustang.

My leg lay twisted between me and the concrete floor. My right foot was at a weird angle, pointing toward my face. I looked at it puzzled for a second, before the pain stole my breath. I could see the bone of my right leg jutting out of the skin. Blood welled up around it like a dam. Agony flooded me from all over my body, overwhelming me. Darkness filled my vision. I ached for it to remove me from the pain. The darkness solidified in the shape of a horse. The one holding its reins reached down to hold my hand.

Death gave a gentle tug and miraculously, the pain disappeared. I looked down in amazement while I was pulled from my bloody, twisted body.

I could see everything clearly, but it wasn't quite real, like I was watching everything on ultra-high definition TV. Was this what it was like for my family when they died?

The driver raced out of his car, only to puke all over Mandi's shoes when he saw my body laying broken on the ground. Any other time, I would have paid good money to see someone hurl all over her designer shoes, but I was literally de*tached from it all.

Mandi didn't seem to notice the mess at her feet. She was still on the ground, and was staring in horror at my shattered body. Her skirt was up around her waist and she was wearing, of all things, granny panties.

She scrambled over to me and screamed for help.

The driver stammered, "I didn't see her. She was in the way and it was dark."

Mandi yelled at him, "Shut up and call 911!"

She brushed my hair back from my face gently and smoothed my shirt down where it had ridden up, showing my stomach. "Help is coming. You'll be okay. Don't die. I'm sorry about what I said. You're right. You don't deserve this."

Was she… no, she couldn't be crying over me? Macabre as it was, I really wanted to see this and tried to get closer. She was! She was sobbing over me and rubbing my arm.

Time doesn't have the same meaning when you are out of your body, but it seemed like only seconds had passed before a familiar truck came roaring into the parking garage along with an ambulance.

Matt jumped out of the truck before it had fully stopped. He raced to my broken body and yelled, "Sara, no!"

He dropped to his knees near a pool of blood around my

head. Tears fell from his eyes. The paramedics had to force him out of the way to put me on a gurney.

I watched from my detached state, but my heart broke for Matt. He moved away from my body and noticed the driver. Matt grabbed the guy by the neck and threw him onto the car. "What the fuck did you do? Are you Death? I'll fucking kill you before I let you take her!"

Two squad cars pulled up.

Matt charged at the driver who had hit me. With one hit, the driver crumpled to the ground. He curled up into a ball trying to protect his face. It didn't stop Matt's rage. He would have beaten the poor guy to bloody pulp if the police hadn't pulled Matt off of him.

I yelled, "Matt, stop! It isn't his fault. I'm sorry. It's mine! Forgive me."

"He cannot hear you. All you can do is watch. I am sorry," Death said softly beside me.

They loaded me into the ambulance. Matt fought his way free of the cops and said, "I'm going with her."

No one dared to stop him when he climbed inside.

One of the cops turned to the driver and said, "Looks like you got beat up pretty bad in that accident. Why don't you let us take you to the hospital?"

The guy looked at the cop through swollen eyes and spit blood out on the ground. "Are you kidding me? That psycho needs to be arrested. He attacked me!"

The cops traded a look with each other and shrugged. He took a whiff of the guy's breath "You been drinking? Maybe I should use a breathalyzer on you, `cause I don't know what you're talking about. We didn't see any assault. Did you, ma'am?" The cop turned to Mandi who was being questioned by another officer.

Great, now the little twit would be able to get her revenge on me by getting Matt in trouble. She sniffled once and wiped her nose on the back of her hand. "All I saw was this jerk driving around the corner too fast and swerving. And, and my friend Sara got hit saving my life."

Holy crap! My mouth fell open. I stared at Mandi in surprise. She had actually done the right thing. I wanted to see what else she was going to say, but the ambulance was getting ready to leave.

Could I ride inside the ambulance with Matt and my body? I walked toward it, but my vision got cloudy. Fingers of fog encircled me. Waving one arm around, trying to the clear the air didn't help. The fog embraced me from all sides. I tried to let go of Death's hand, but he had mine in a, well, a death grip. He tugged on my hand, pulling me away from the scene. Oh, that's right, I had responsibilities elsewhere. Time to save the world.

"Where did your horse go?" I asked. Whispering seemed appropriate, given the circumstances.

"Where we go, he cannot follow. Do not fear. I will be at your side during your judgment. Remember though, I am forbidden to speak." Death was solemn. I missed his amused voice.

I couldn't tell if we were walking or flying. Was there anything beneath my feet? Which way was up or down? Didn't matter really. My world narrowed to the hand holding mine, guiding me.

The disorientation stayed until we appeared in a large room. I would have thought it was a cave, if not for its perfectly circular walls with thrones carved into them all around. I did a quick count in my head and discovered there were twenty-four of them. The two ends of the circle of thrones met at a massive throne, but this one was not carved from the cave walls. It was made of some brownish-red gemstones and had seven blazing lanterns in front of it.

*Jasper and carnelian,* a voice whispered in my head.

"Did you say that?" I asked Death

He shook his head.

I took a step forward to get a closer look at the lanterns. I would have expected them to be made of clay like they used in Jesus's time, but these were ornate bronze with glass windows. Flames danced behind the glass and for a second the flames turned a weird opalescent color.

"Tell me you saw that?" I asked Death.

He took my hand and guided me to the center of the room. The ground sloped so my head would be just below the seat of the giant throne. I bent down to get a closer look at the floor. It was a sea of glass, opaque like frosted crystal.

When I looked up, the throne was no longer empty.

## CHAPTER THIRTY

*Judgment Day*

I clutched Death's hand to my chest, as though he could help keep my heart from leaping out and fleeing in terror. His strong grip helped steady my shaky one.

It was the beast from Revelations, my aunt's favorite part of the Bible. It was once a lamb, but now it had seven horns and seven eyes and a gaping wound split him from neck to tail. Blood matted his white wool. I wanted to gag at the sight but stood transfixed.

The cloying scent of incense filled the air, reminding me of my aunt's church. I couldn't tell where it was coming from, but the smoke permeated the room.

I managed to tear my eyes away from the nightmarish lamb and realized Uriel stood beside him. Fury radiated from the angel. His wings were folded. Their ends flared behind him like armor. The feathers had changed from soft, fluffy pearlescent white to razor-sharp pieces of obsidian. Their edges looked like they would slice me into pieces with one touch. I stumbled back into Death and would have fallen if he hadn't put his arm around me.

"You are not supposed to be here. Do you think to sneak in like an intruder in the night?" The booming of Uriel's voice reverberated off the round, stone walls. My ears rang like church bells.

It took me a minute to realize it wasn't my ears ringing, but the thudding of many feet stomping on the glass floor. Twenty-four old men had appeared out of nowhere on the stone thrones. They were all dressed identically in white robes with gold crowns on their heads. Their faces a mask of anger and hatred all focused on me. Some shook their fists.

"Interloper! Trespasser!" they screamed over and over.

I covered my ears and looked at Death for help. He squeezed my shoulders, and shook his head slightly.

Oh, right, he said he wasn't allowed to speak here. I was on my own. After lowering my hands from my ears, I tried to look Uriel in the eye. My gaze stopped at his legs, unable to force my head up any higher. I spoke to them as if it were perfectly normal. "Despite your best efforts, I died, sacrificing myself to be here. To save humanity."

"Blasphemy!" screamed the old kings. Some threw their crowns, while others ripped their robes at the necklines. I wanted to back away from their rage, but it encircled me in that round room. I had nowhere to hide.

"You, who reeks of sin, think yourself worthy?"

"Unworthy!" the chorus of men chanted. Some seemed poised to jump off their seats to attack me. It reminded me of a reoccurring nightmare I had in which the neighbors and the HOA joined in a mob to attack me. Mobs freaked me out.

I lowered my eyes so I wouldn't have to see their rage, took a deep breath and whispered, "My sins were forgiven. Don't you remember? Jesus. Crucifixion. Ring a bell? I come here for final judgment and to fix the seals."

"The ruling for suicides has already been decreed. Suicides burn in the Pit." Uriel's wings spread out behind him which signaled the old men to rise from their thrones.

"The Pit!" They screamed, and they leapt up and rushed

toward me. Forty-eight hands reached out to grab me from all sides.

"I didn't commit suicide. Listen to me!" I screamed but my words had no effect on the men. I dodged the first man by moving left, but that put me right into another pair of hands. I dropped to the ground. Tears stung my eyes when they snatched at my hair. Death spread his arms around me, but even he couldn't protect me from the mob.

I'd died for nothing. I mean, I knew I wasn't worthy. This was me they were talking about after all. My aunt had told me for years how full of sin I was, but for some reason, Death seemed to think I could mend the seals and save the world. I wanted the chance to see if I could. But no, after everything I'd been through, I was going to be thrown into the Pit of Hell by a bunch of old men in white dresses to burn for eternity.

'*She has sacrificed herself to save another. She will endure the trials.*'

The words rang off the walls, and in an instant, the men were back on their thrones. I glanced at Death to see if he was the one who spoke. He nodded at the large throne.

The words seemed to have come from the lamb, though he hadn't actually spoken. I faced the monstrosity grateful for his help. Its seven eyes were all looking, not unkindly, down at me. It took me a moment to realize the lamb gazed upon me with sadness and pity.

A being this mauled and mutilated actually pitied me? That can't be good. How bad would this judgment be? What if I weren't worthy? I shook the thought away. I had no choice. I'd have to find a way.

"She was manipulated here by Death. He uses her to stop what must be." Uriel's gaze was full of scorn. He was the one responsible for my dying, not Death. He was the one who broke the seals to end the world. And now he pretended innocence? It pissed me off.

"I'm no one's puppet. I'm here of my own free will to stop what you started." My voice shook while I faced the angel, but this time I managed to look him in the face.

'*You seek to mend the seals?*' the lamb asked.

Before I could answer, Uriel flared his wings. "She has no right. This mortal cannot stand in the way of God's will."

The lamb cocked his head to the side to look at Uriel. I flinched at the crunching sound of his blood-matted wool moving. The angel seemed to deflate a little under the lamb's steady stare. Holy shit. Uriel was afraid of the lamb.

The part about the meek inheriting the Kingdom of Heaven in the Bible must be true. Bolstered by the thought, I said, "Actually, if I'm able to mend the seals, then it would be God's will. Otherwise, He wouldn't let me. Right, Cupid?"

Uriel didn't so much as twitch, but his rage was palpable. Black feathers fell from his wings like drops of ink from a quill. He didn't bother to look at me and addressed the lamb. "The mortals have had their chance. It is time for the great reaping. Death only brings her because he fears the Eternal Pit. The angels shall inherit the earth. So doth the Lord decree."

Emboldened with Death at my back, and the Lamb on my side, I challenged Uriel again. "How convenient for you. You claim to speak for the Lord, so mankind dies and you get the world as a bonus. This has nothing to do with God's will. You're ending humanity just to claim the earth."

Big mistake.

"Enough of your sacrilege! You shall burn in the Pit for

Eternity." He leapt down to where I stood, his razor sharp wings slicing through the air inches away from my face.

My legs shook so hard, my knees buckled. I dropped to the ground.

'*She has sacrificed herself willingly. A martyr for humanity. She shall not burn.*'

The lamb once again had saved me.

Uriel hovered over me, his feathers an eyelash away from my face. I watched the hatred play across his handsome features for a moment before he smiled, showing his perfect white teeth.

Angels don't eat, so why would he need teeth?

My hysterical musings were interrupted by Uriel. "Her body yet lives. Even now the mortals' machinations pull her back."

The room disappeared. Bright lights flashed in my eyes like dashes of Morse Code. Beeping noises assaulted my ears. I could hear people yelling and the sound of several pair of feet running beside me.

"She's conscious but her breathing is shallow. She's losing air. Get me a chest tube, " an unknown voice yelled.

"Sara, Sara, can you hear me? Don't die. Sara, fight." It was Matt's voice.

I tried to reach for him, but couldn't lift my arms.

"Sir, you have to move. Get out of the way so we can help her."

My lungs felt like deflated balloons unable to hold any air. The pain was a living thing, screaming in my brain. My eyes darted around looking for relief, looking for comfort.

Matt. I wanted Matt.

No.

He couldn't help me. I wasn't supposed to fight any more. Someone was trying to force my mouth open to stick a tube down my throat. I moved my head from side to side to stop her. I couldn't let her save me.

"Grab her head and hold her still," someone shouted.

The lack of oxygen was causing my vision to get black around the edges. My head grew too heavy to move from their firm grasps. I knew I just needed to stop them a few more seconds and the lack of oxygen would put me out. I locked my teeth together and closed my eyes while I felt myself drift away.

Goodbye Matt, I thought as the noises and lights faded.

I was back in front of the throne.

"She is not worthy. Look how she jealously guards her pitiful life, lusting after a man. A martyr gives themselves happily, not reluctantly." Uriel gave me a triumphant look before turning to face the lamb.

*'Yes, she covets her life, which makes her sacrifice that much more worthy. She martyrs herself freely, regretfully. Her death was not thrust upon her as mine, thus her sacrifice is greater. She is worthy to mend the seals.'*

"One of such a weak nature as this could not endure it. She is no more than clay, clay and dust. She lacks the strength, if not the conviction. It is over." Uriel flew back up to stand beside the lamb. He leaned against the side of the throne, arms crossed in front of him, wings folded. He looked away as though he were bored.

"I can do it. I will do it. I just don't know how. What do I do" I asked the lamb.

He smiled down at me, and once again I saw pity in his eyes. Why pity me now? I'd won. Hadn't I?

Uriel's evil sneer stopped my questioning thoughts. "You must endure each trial unleashed by the last broken seal. This will stop the progression to the next scroll. Then your life's blood must be spilled. Only it can seal the scrolls. There will be no release from your suffering during the trials unless you forfeit. Death cannot remove you from it until all is finished. You will suffer a lifetime of agony before the seals are repaired."

The opened scrolls appeared on the ground in front of me. I could see which one was the one on top, the fourth scroll which had unleashed Death to kill by war, famine, plague and wild beasts.

Uriel held up a sword in one hand, and I pictured him slicing me open like the Lamb. He aimed it down at me, and the scrolls disappeared. I scrambled back, still on my knees, until I hit Death's legs. I barely managed to stop myself from clinging to them to hide like a child. Uriel had said I would be tormented without even the mercy of unconsciousness or dying. Could I endure that?

Uriel reached his free hand out to me. "But I can be merciful. I can take you back to Earth now. You can live out your days in peace with those you love. Or I can usher you into Heaven to be with your family. No more pain, no more suffering."

Gone was the scorn he'd shown me before. Peace and love radiated from him. The change in his mood transformed his wings back to the stunning white they had been when I first met him. Were they mood wings?

I looked up at the beautiful angel and wanted to go with him, wanted to escape the hell that had been my life since I'd lost my family. I almost did, God help me, I almost took his hand. I wouldn't be alone any more. I could hear my sister's laugh in my head. Feel my mother's arms around me. But I looked at the Lamb sitting on the throne. His face held no fear, no wrath, just love and peace. If he could endure this suffering to open the seals, I could endure it to close them. It is what my family would have wanted.

"No. Bring on the first trial." I braced myself to feel the bite of Uriel's sword, but the blow never came. I looked up in confusion and witnessed a nightmare.

# CHAPTER THIRTY-ONE

*Hungry Like the Wolves*

The old kings were transformed into werewolves. These grotesque creatures made the one I'd faced on earth seem like a puppy. Razor sharp teeth extruded through their cheeks. Their arms were as big as my waist and ended with claws bigger than my head.

"War's first, not wild beasts!" I screamed in horror.

'*You must endure them backwards to reverse them.*' The lamb might have been trying to help, but it would have been more helpful if he had told me that in the beginning. Maybe I could have been ready. Honestly though, even if he had warned me, how could someone prepare to be surrounded by monsters slobbering for their blood?

As one, they attacked.

The first to reach me hurled me to the ground so hard I bounced. I scrambled up, knowing I had no chance on the floor. Who was I kidding? I had no chance regardless, but I wouldn't go down without a fight.

I kicked at the next beast while it slashed at me. Something snapped in its head, but it still managed to gouge me, ripping at my stomach. Wrenching myself away, I screamed in agony. I looked down, certain I would see my guts spilling out of my body like spaghetti.

Holy shit! Everything was intact. I got away from it. I

had survived. My victory was short lived. Everywhere I turned, I faced fur, fangs, and claws.

I dived under the beasts, but one caught my leg in his massive jaws. It shook its head, ripping muscle away. White hot pain sucked the breath from my lungs, and I gasped for air. A chunk of my leg tore off after it gave me a second shake. I went flying.

Despite the pain in my leg, I could still walk. After I landed in front of the large throne, I scrambled for something to use as a weapon to beat off the monsters. My fingernails collided with something that rang like a gong. It was one of the lanterns that sat in front of the Lamb's throne.

A werewolf pounced, his huge claws extended toward my face. I curled my fingers around the surprisingly cool metal and threw the lantern at it. The flame turned opalescent before it engulfed the monster.

Ha! I knew those lanterns had some mystical mojo working for them.

The creature screamed and cried pitifully. His brethren took a cautious step away from his smoldering body, keeping their eyes fixed on me.

"That's right, bitch. I will set your ass on fire!" I screamed.

One of the monsters made slow, lanky strides toward me. I grabbed another lantern and smashed it into him, breaking the glass, which crashed to the glass floor and made a clinking sound like a champagne toast.

Cheers! The explosion of flaming oil set the werewolf and the one beside him on fire.

The smell of burned fur and charred meat filled the air, masking the incense. It reminded me of a barbeque.

What kind of sides do you serve with barbequed

werewolf? Did the thought come from blood loss or had I finally gone crazy?

I focused on the now cautious monsters in front of me. Twenty-one left. There had been seven lanterns, I now had five. Five lanterns against twenty-one werewolves? Those were some fucked up odds. I didn't have enough to keep throwing them. I grabbed a lantern in each hand and used them to bash at the nearest werewolves' heads.

The lanterns were heavy bronze, but I didn't struggle to hold them. They made a solid thwack when they connected with the werewolves' heads. One monster went down, but the other just yelped and snarled its outrage at me.

I swung at it again. It caught the lantern in its jaws ripping it away and almost taking my hand with it. I scrambled back to grab one of the remaining lanterns and was almost surrounded when they rushed to attack me. I knew it was impossible. There was no way I could beat all of these monsters. But I damned well would take as many as I could with me. I threw a lantern into the middle of the mass of undulating, hairy bodies. Several animals howled while the flames leapt from one body to another.

I looked back to grab the last lantern and noticed movement. Some of the animals had circled behind me. I was surrounded. I had one lantern left. There was only one thing I could do now. I swung in a circle like a demented merry-go-round, holding on to my last lantern for dear life.

The animals stayed out of range so they couldn't attack.

It was working! But soon my arms grew tired. They shook in fatigue, and I could barely hold on to the heavy thing. I could feel the lantern slipping from my sweaty hands. I dug my fingernails into the metal frame part of the glass to keep my grip. My shredded leg threatened to give out at any time. I stumbled, and one werewolf braved the lantern, leaping at me.

I smashed it in the head, shattering the glass and spraying flaming oil all over my attacker. It stopped him, but I lost my last weapon. It didn't take long for the rest to pounce.

One hit me, knocking me down. I curled into a ball, my head tucked into my arms, until I was bitten on my side. Involuntarily, I arched my back. A furry leg was right in front of my face, so I bit it as hard as I could shaking my head back and forth like a dog with a bone. I heard a howl and thought my teeth would be ripped from my mouth as it struggled to free itself from my teeth.

That's right Cujo, I can bite too! I bit down deeper.

I had to let go when my head was engulfed in a mouth that smelled of decaying meat and digestive juices. Its jaw covered half of my face.

I felt the pop when his teeth pierced my eyeball.

Screaming, half-blind, I beat at the monster with my hands, until another started to eat my fingers. I gurgled blood bubbles when another ripped out my throat. A hellish liquid darkness enveloped me, but my ears still heard every horrid sound. The soundtrack of my own body being eaten by these monsters played over and over in my ears driving me to madness.

An eternity seemed to pass while I was eaten alive.

My world narrowed to the jerking feel of flesh being ripped off my bones, the rumbling growl of werewolves while they chomped on my body, and the metallic taste of blood.

'*Enough, she has endured the first trial. End this,*' the Lamb said.

With the sudden absence of pain, the first thing I noticed was how quiet the world had become. I opened my eyes, which were now good as new, and saw the werewolves had morphed again into sneering men who were back on their thrones. The fires had been extinguished and the lanterns had reappeared in front of the Lamb's throne, completely restored.

I curled up on the ground and wailed. "No more!"

Death reached out to help me stand. I flinched from his touch, biting at him like a cornered animal.

My mind was broken. It replayed the sound of those massive jaws crashing together through my bones, the smell of blood and bile engulfed me.

"I can end your suffering. Make you forget. Touch my hand," Uriel's said seductively, his words cutting through my crazed thoughts.

I forced my head up to look at him. He had lowered his sword to his side. Without thinking, I reached for him. Death stepped into my field of vision, a sad look on his face. I snatched back my hand.

A sob escaped my throat at the thought of continuing the trials, but if I took Uriel up on his offer, the world would end. Why was I doing this? What had this world ever done for me? I had been miserable and alone my whole life. But that had changed at the end. Matt loved me, even if he hadn't said it yet. I had friends like Rick.

"Come now. There was a reason I saved you. A hopeless, lonely soul. Let us end this charade. Grab my hand." Uriel could afford to be gracious now that he thought he'd won. He reached for me.

No.

I conjured a vision of Matt and Rick being ripped apart

and eaten alive like I had been, forcing myself to hear their shrieks and visualize their bloody and broken bodies. It gave me the strength I needed to keep fighting. I couldn't let them go through this torment. I couldn't let anyone go through it.

I turned away from him and said, "Fuck you."

# CHAPTER THIRTY-TWO

*If I Only Had a Brain*

"The first trial was far too easy. It is time to raise the stakes," Uriel said. He raised his sword and sliced through the air. I heard the fabric of reality rip like crepe paper. The Earth was on the other side, and a familiar vehicle drove down a forest road.

The scene tickled a memory. I leaned forward to get a closer look. Uriel, that bastard, shoved me into the rip in reality. Midnight sky and stars blurred by. I was falling through the air. I ended up, somehow, in the SUV and I knew why it was familiar. It was the place where my family had died.

"Ben, Ben, please. Stop it. Don't do this!" My mother was in the front seat, fighting my dad for control of the steering wheel.

No. God, no! Not this. I can't go through this again.

I heard the scrape of metal on metal as the car skidded along the guardrail. This nightmare had played out in my dreams for so many years. I knew what was coming but couldn't move or even speak.

"Ben, you're gonna kill us! Mom, make him stop!" Rachel yelled. She sat in the backseat, next to me, dressed in jeans and her favorite shirt, the black one with little pink skulls all over it.

"Though I walk through the valley of death, I shall fear no evil," my dad chanted. He was winning the fight against my mom for control of the wheel. The passenger windows exploded as the car smashed harder against the guardrail.

Shards of glass cut icy rivers of pain across my skin. My mutinous hand refused to move to wipe away the blood. For just one second, my mother let go of the wheel to protect her face. She immediately reached for it again, but it was too late. My father jerked the wheel to the right, and the car broke through the guardrail and plummeted down the embankment.

No one inside the car made a sound. We were all too terrified to even cry out. Then the world exploded. The screeches of metal as the car rolled down the hill were deafening. Clouds of dirt filled the air covering our tongues with grit and dust. An occasional branch or bush would pop up through the broken windows, only to disappear with the next revolution of the car.

When I experienced the fall the first time, I was so panicked it was over before I could scream. In the blink of an eye, my family was dead. This time, I studied my family, knowing that when we reached the bottom, they would be dead. My sister had shunned her seat belt once again. With each revolution of the car, she bounced from the ceiling to the floor like a sock in the dryer. She bit her bottom lip like she did when she was mad or upset, except this time she had bitten clean through. Blood snaked a trail across her face in zig-zags that changed direction with her falls.

I looked away, and my eyes fell on my mother. One hand still grasped the wheel, as though she thought she could somehow get control and stop our descent. Her brown ponytail whipped around like a pinwheel. Her eyes were filled with terror and tears when she looked back at Rachel and me in the backseat.

I expected my father's face to be contorted in rage or victory. Instead, he looked peaceful. He wore a small smile. The happy look, so foreign on his face, remained even as a boulder ripped through his broken window and smashed the left side of his head in.

"No!" I cried out, finally able to take control of my body. I could now feel the seat belt biting into my shoulder and chest while the car rolled. My sister and mother both screamed, as though my scream had unmuted them. I fumbled for Rachel, though I knew, like the first time, it would be useless.

My hand caught on her sleeve, a pink skull ripping free from the fabric in my fingers. In seconds she would be thrown out the window. The car would rest at the bottom, on top of her lifeless body.

No!

I was going to save her this time, even if it killed me. My hand fumbled with the release button on my seat belt. I crashed into the ceiling, knocked heads with her, and saw stars. The shock of the impact made us both gasp for breath. I wrapped my arms and legs around her. If she went out the car this time, so would I.

Abruptly, the car stopped and was quiet again. Miraculously we'd landed right-side up. I heard the creak of the car when it settled, a ticking noise from the engine and the hiss of water escaping the radiator. Rachel was unconscious but alive. Mom was... I looked over Rachel's shoulder and cried out. Mom's seatbelt had come undone, and she rested on the airbag. A tree limb had pierced her chest. Her eyes were closed, I couldn't tell if she was dead yet, but I knew, like before, she would be soon.

But Rachel was alive. Somehow I'd saved her. Was this the trial? Did I have to go through the accident again so I could save my big sister? But how did that fit in with the seal?

I sensed my audience before I saw them. I looked out the window and saw their feet. They had stepped closer to the rip in reality, like football fans crowd the TV before a big play. Death wore black boots. Uriel was barefoot.

Huh, I had never noticed his feet before. I would have thought he would wear those strappy Jesus sandals.

"Is that it? Did I pass?" I asked them, but they ignored me. My voice managed to rouse Rachel, who opened her eyes.

"Are we alive?" she asked me.

"Yes, but Mom and Dad are... hurt bad," I lied to keep her calm. "We need to focus on getting out of here. Are you hurt?"

She tried to move but her leg was stuck on something. She was pale and panting as though she'd run a race. Her hair was plastered to her head with sweat. Was she going into shock? Why didn't I ever take a first-aid class?

"I'm fine, except I can't get my leg out. How is it my foot got stuck when you're the one with ginormous feet?" She was cracking jokes to make me feel better. I couldn't help but grin.

She's alive! I didn't care how or what it meant. I saved her this time.

I leaned across her to get a better look. Her foot had gotten wedged next to the front seat, in the metal frame of the door. There was blood dripping on the floorboard.

"Lemme see if I can get my door open. Maybe I can find

something to pry your clod hopper out."

The door opened a little but not all the way. I turned and kicked it hard. It opened just enough I could get out if I sucked in my stomach. I was thankful I had my fourteen-year-old body back. My real body would never have been able to squeeze through. "Hang tight, I'll be right back."

"Like I could go anywhere. But hurry up. My head is spinning from your hard-as-a-rock head hitting mine."

I went around to her door which, like mine, would only open a little. Why couldn't it have been ripped off like the driver's side door? With both hands wrapped around the door, I pushed with my legs off the car as hard as I could. The metal screeched but finally opened enough Rachel could get out. She tried to high-five me but ended up slapping my shoulder. Her eyes were glazed. I needed to find something to pry her foot out, now.

There had been a thick branch sticking out of the back window. I pulled it out and wedged it right above her foot to push the metal frame away. I yanked as hard as I could. The car screeched like a giant rusty spring that needed to be oiled, but it was working! I'd made enough of a gap she would have been able to slide her foot out, if a piece of metal hadn't skewered her foot to the seat.

"Shit!" How can she not feel that?

"You kiss your momma with that mouth?" Rachel wisecracked. Her voice was high pitched, and she giggled.

Crap, she was definitely going into shock. I had to get help.

I looked at Death and Uriel who were watching me from the stone chamber like I was in a fishbowl. "So what? If I save my sister, it's over?"

Uriel acted as though I hadn't spoken, but Death shook

his head. More. There was something more I would have to face.

"I'm going to get help, okay? I'm coming back; I promise."

She nodded and we hugged. While I scrambled up the hill, I heard a painful moan coming from the SUV.

Rachel!

Dirt and rocks pinged off the car when I slid back down.

I ran to her open door. "Are you okay? What happened?"

Her eyes were closed, like she had nodded off. She opened them and said, "I'm fine. Thought you were gonna get help."

"I was, but I heard you moaning like you were hurt."

"Not me. Maybe you were hearing things."

A louder moan came from the front seat.

"Mom, Ben, are you awake?" She leaned forward to see them. I tried to block her view of Mom, but wasn't fast enough. "Oh, my God! Is Mom alive? Get that out of her chest!"

Mom was pinned by the tree limb. "No, I shouldn't move her. The paramedics need to stabilize her first."

Dad's body twitched. How could he have survived? The whole left side of his face had been smashed in. "Dad? Dad I'm here. Don't move. I'm gonna get help." Would I get the chance to save them all?

"Go, hurry before they die!" Rachel yelled at me. I got out of the car and limped back up the hill when I heard another groan and Rachel's wail.

Sliding back down, leaving gouges in the earth where my foot sought traction. The car shook violently. What the hell was going on?

I made it to Rachel's door and witnessed a nightmare.

My father was gnawing on the right side of my mom's face.

"No!" I dove over Rachel and pulled my dad off of my mom. He turned his head and tried to bite my hand. I snatched it back sharply. My foot slipped. I fell out of the car on my ass.

Rachel kicked my dad in the head with her free foot. Dad was trying to crawl into the back seat. I heard the wet smacking sound while he chewed on the bits of flesh he'd torn from Mom. His face was covered in blood, some from the gaping head wound on his left side, and some from my mother.

Rachel jerked on her foot like an animal caught in a snare. "What's happening? What's wrong with your dad? Help me, Sara. I can't get out!"

How could I tell her my dad had turned into a zombie? I kicked him back into the front seat. He bounced against the airbag and flung toward us again.

"It'll be okay, Rach. I won't let him hurt you. The ambulance will come soon and get you out." My voice shook. I'd fought a zombie before, but it wasn't my dad. I didn't have to kill him though, just keep from getting bitten. Rachel's eyes rolled up into her head, and she was out cold.

It was just me, my zombie father and the two spectators outside the car. Uriel had created this nightmare for me. Turning my dad into monster.

"Bastard!" I yelled at him but I don't know if he heard me.

My dad lunged for the backseat again. I kicked him as hard as I could, forgetting about his missing car door. Anger fueled my kick, and my dad bounce against the airbag and flew sideways right out of the car.

Oh, shit! I had to stop him before he got back in the car

and attacked Rachel. I crawled over her to get out, and she roused. She gripped my arm, her nails bit into my skin.

"Don't leave me, Sara!" she wailed.

"I'm not," I told her as I threw myself out the door. Rachel's nails left claw marks down my arm when she tried to stop me from leaving her.

"Please, Sara. Help me!" She didn't understand my dad wasn't in the car any more, and I didn't have time to explain it. I fell out just when my dad freed himself from the car.

Get up and run! My instincts howled at me, but like those idiot girls in horror movies who trip and fall, I froze unable to stand and run. He crawled toward me, chin covered in gore. I recoiled in horror when a flap of his scalp bounced off his shoulder from where his head was smashed in. His brain was exposed.

Brain. I picked up a rock from the ground and smashed it into his brain. I raised the pink slime covered rock again and again and didn't stop until my dad stopped moving. I wanted to run away, to dive back into the rip in reality to escape this nightmare. But I couldn't leave Rachel. I lay there on the ground and vomited.

"He's gone. He can't hurt us now," I said to Rachel, but she was out again and didn't hear me. Now what? I couldn't leave for help. She would think I'd abandoned her. If she woke up before I got back, she would freak. But what if she bled to death before help came?

I got back into the car and tried to rouse her. I leaned against the front seat and stuck my face right into hers. "Rachel? I'm here. Do you hear me?"

Wanting to shake her awake, but afraid to hurt her, I leaned back in frustration.

The dome light is still working. The random thought

made me wonder if I was going into shock, too.

It was then I heard a moan from the front seat. My mother's body jerked. No. God, no! Mom's head swiveled around to look at me. Her head rested on the airbag like it was a pillow. Her eyes were milky white, dead. Her mouth moved as though she were trying to speak.

I couldn't do it. I couldn't kill my mother. Her head was in profile so I didn't see the side of her face my father had chewed off. Except for her eyes, she looked like I remembered. Her ponytail was slightly askew but intact. She reached for me.

"Mommy," I said and clasped her grasping hand. For a second, I convinced myself she was alive. She held my hand and pulled me to her, and then she turned showing the destruction my father had done. I tried to pull my hand from hers, but she wouldn't let go.

She bit through my wrist. Blood sprayed out like a fountain. She chewed clear to the bone. I broke free from her grip and turned away. I was too late.

I could feel the virus burning its way up into my body from her bite like acid. Blood poured from my wound. I would die. Then I would turn.

I fell to the floor of the car jerking and shuddering violently. One of my legs kicked out and hit Rachel. My teeth chattered, causing a few to break and fall out. Hair dropped from my scalp in huge chunks, pieces floated around me like confetti.

The stench of my decaying body made me puke. I hacked up chunks of what may have been my lungs, along with thick green globs of mucus. Blood flooded my eyes when the vessels burst open, turning my vision red.

Mom and Dad hadn't gone through this. Why me? Mom

was almost dead when she turned, and I couldn't really die.

I wiped the red haze from my eyes, but everything still looked foggy. My body continued to jerk uncontrollably causing me to scratch my cheek. A piece of skin caught on my fingernail and ripped from my face. My brain felt numb. I hoped it meant I would disconnect from the pain, but it didn't.

I could feel my mother moving around in the front seat, trying to escape the airbag. The movement while she thrashed about woke Rachel.

"Sara," she sobbed, "you left me. How could you leave me?"

Rachel. I had to tell her I didn't leave her. She had to know. I crawled across the SUV floor to until I reached her leg.

The smell of blood from her pinned leg hit me. Eat. Must eat. Must spread.

What the hell? Where did that thought come from? I tried to let go of her leg to sit up and talk to her, but couldn't fight the compulsion shouting at me to eat. I leaned over and took a bite. My teeth sank deep into her skin. Blood squirted into my mouth hitting the back of my throat. Pink strings from her socks got caught in my teeth as I ripped the sinew from her calf.

"Sara! No! You monster. Get away!"

Her words helped me gain some control of my brain. The taste of my sister's warm blood lingered in my mouth.

I recoiled in horror and disgust, throwing up all over myself. She was right. I was a monster, and I'd just turned my sister into one too.

I got out of the car and stumbled for the rip in reality. I didn't care about the apocalypse or trying to save the world.

I just needed to get away from these horrors I'd seen and become.

Death stepped out of the tear and held his arms open for me. I dove into them and sobbed. I looked up and watched while my sister twitched and jerked in the car. She wailed in agony while the zombie virus coursed through her body. I thought going through it was hell, but I was wrong. Watching my sister go through it, because of me was worse.

I tried to turn away, but Uriel forced my head back. After her horrific transformation, she ripped her foot free, leaving part of it behind in the car. She tumbled from the car and crawled up the hill.

Finally, the horrid world I'd run from disappeared. We were back in the throne room.

Uriel lowered his sword once again and the blood, puke and gore that covered me disappeared as if nothing had happened. I still felt unclean. I'd never be clean again. I tried to fix it this time, save my sister. Instead I damned her by turning her into a monster.

"The zombie virus is a clever one. To spread, it must infect a new host. So it opens hunger receptors in your body, causing the victim to eat mindlessly, thus spreading the infection of plague proportions. Ingenious, really."

"You bastard. You bastard," was all I could say while I leaned on Death, still unable to stand on my own.

"Come now, child. Did you not want more time with your family?"

"Not like that. Not to eat them! You turned me into a monster. And for nothing. I failed." I stopped as a flash of what I'd done to my sister replayed in my brain. How could I live with those memories?

'*You stopped. You found the will to recover your humanity.*

*You are not a monster.*' The Lamb's words sounded in my head, and with them, the memories were muted. It was as though someone had taken an eraser to them. The outline of what I'd done was still there, but it wasn't as vivid as a memory.

Uriel gave the Lamb an angry look before he turned to me. "You can stop now. I can reunite you with your family and fill your time with joy. As you said, you failed. Why continue your torment? End the trials now and be done. The next will be so much worse."

Wait. If I had failed, then why was Uriel so desperate to get me to give up? "I can continue the trials and seal the scrolls?"

Uriel ignored my question. Even the Lamb didn't answer. I looked at Death. He nodded.

Uriel saw and raised his sword. "You, creature, have no voice here! Be gone before I cast you in the pit myself."

I stepped in front of Death. Uriel's sword stopped bare inches from my neck. I didn't dare to even flinch. ""He didn't speak. He didn't break any rules. Leave him alone. Bring on the next trial. It's famine, right?"

I'd been dieting for most of my life. How hard could this be?

# CHAPTER THIRTY-THREE

*Starved for Affection*

Uriel sliced his sword through the air, ripping open a passage to Earth. I didn't give him the satisfaction of shoving me through this time.

"Geronimo!" I yelled when I jumped, with no idea what was on the other side. Famine. Would I land at a Weight Watcher's meeting? A gym?

I ended up face down on a familiar couch and got a whiff of smoke. Man, despite using that ozone thing after the fireplace mishap, my old couch still reeked. This was weird. Why would Uriel send me here?

Sure, there wasn't any food, but I would hardly count that as famine. I sat up and tried to figure out what I was supposed to do. Footsteps sounded on the stairs. Someone was in my house.

Run away or confront them? Normally, I would be big on the fleeing like a chicken. But if this were my trial, I couldn't do that. How in the heck could a person be famine? It made no sense.

I stood, but only managed a step or two before he appeared.

"Hello, my love." David stood at the bottom of the stairs, wearing the power suit he'd had on the day he died.

Was this the best Uriel could come up with? This was

supposed to be so much worse than what I'd already faced? Sure, being face to face once again with my cheating husband-turned-vampire wasn't something I wanted. But there was no way it beat the nightmare of reliving the accident, becoming a zombie, and attacking my sister. David wasn't much of a threat. I'd fought him off once. I could do it again. No sweat. Just needed my handy-dandy weapon.

I took a step toward the door to remove the cross from the wall. Oh, shit. The cross was gone. I'd moved it to the new place.

David chuckled. "Lose something?"

I turned around. Light glinted off his fangs when he smiled. I backed away. He mirrored my steps, as though we were performing a dance. He moved with a grace and power he'd never possessed in life.

This wasn't David, at least not the man I had married. He wasn't even the vampire I'd seen last. The David I knew was more like a parody of vampire, a fumbling man who as a monster was pathetic.

There was nothing pathetic about the creature that stalked me now. I turned and ran into the kitchen. A few feet from the back door, he grabbed my hair. I jerked to a stop to keep from being scalped. Red faced and panting, I trembled, furious to be caught by that son of a bitch. Tears of pain and anger spilled from my eyes.

"Finally, you grieve for me. Took you long enough, Sara." After releasing my hair, he trapped me in an embrace. I felt his whiskers rub my chin when he licked my cheek, tasting my tears. His tongue felt like a putrid sponge left to dry on the sink. I jerked my head away.

This close, I smelled the familiar charred scent of the suit intermingled with the body spray he practically bathed in. It brought back the night I'd learned about Mandi. The betrayal. The anger.

"Like I'd ever grieve for you, asshole. Your death was the best thing that has ever happened to me." My cocky words couldn't hide the tremble in my voice.

David released me from his embrace and back-handed me. I crashed into the table across the room. Pain bloomed in my hip where it smashed into a chair. But at least I didn't land on the floor. I gripped the edge of the table to steady myself.

"You think being your husband made me happy? I hungered for attention, for love. It was like being married to a corpse. Now it's your turn to starve."

Starve? Was this why I faced David? Emotional famine? Uriel seriously underestimated my feelings for David if he thought this would be worse than physically starving. Shit. I'd been deprived of love most of my life.

He raised his voice into a falsetto, "Oh poor me. My family died. I'm so lonely. Pay attention to me. They probably were happy to die because you were so needy."

"At least my family loved me. They didn't dump me into foster care and split town." I hurled back at him. He'd always fought the stigma of growing up in foster care by pretending he was rich and successful. It infuriated him that he wasn't.

He tackled me. The sound of my head slamming against the table echoed in my ears as the pain exploded in my head. It left me dazed. I didn't even fight him when he bit my neck. The burn of four puncture wounds brought the fight back into me though. He lay on top of me, slithering against me. I bucked my hips to get out from under him but wasn't strong enough. He released my neck and rested his nose on mine, looking into my eyes.

"After ten years of marriage, now you show passion? Too late. Mandi satisfied all my needs since you couldn't. All those weekends you worked, she spent here with me. We christened each room of the house. The only thing I hunger from you now is your blood."

Blood ran down my neck into my hair in a warm trickle. He brushed my hair back and lapped at the blood greedily. "We even had sex right here on this table. And when you got home, you served me dinner. I could smell her scent as I ate your lasagna."

Mother Fucker!

I should have put rat poison in his dinner. I should have fucking let him kill Mandi that night! Hate churned the acid in my stomach.

He gnawed my neck once again, cradling my head in his hand as if he were holding a baby. He drank in ravenous gulps. My life force deserted my veins with each pull, replaced by smothering darkness that slithered in from David to destroy my humanity. As he ground his body into mine, I could feel his growing excitement.

The bastard was getting off on killing me. Hell no. He wasn't going to take me without a fight. I fumbled for a weapon, and my fingers hit something. A bottle of wine I'd left behind. I snatched it and smacked David in the back of the head with it.

In the movies the wine bottle breaks, leaving you with a bunch of glass spikes to use as a weapon. Real life never works the same way. The bottle made a clinking sound when it bounced off David's thick skull, but it worked. He fell off the table, taking a chunk of my neck with him.

Tears stung my eyes. I scrambled off the other side of the

table, putting it between him and me. Blood plastered my t-shirt against my skin in a warm, sticky mess. I clamped my hand on my shredded neck, trying to keep from bleeding out. The edges of the room grew fuzzy as my head spun.

"You bitch!" He growled at me and shattered the table. He tackled me to the ground. This time he didn't need to bite me. He just sucked at the gaping tear in my neck.

I yanked on his hair to pull him off me, but he didn't flinch. He made slobbery, sucking noises while he drained me. Letting go of his hair, I punched him over and over until my hands grew too numb to make a fist. My feet and legs grew tingly. I even tried to bite him, but couldn't get close enough.

Tired. I was so tired.

I struggled to keep my eyes open. Needles of cold flowed from my hands and feet like a wave. My arms and legs cramped and jerked while my heart tried feebly to pump blood into them. I gasped for air as my blood cells circulated feebly to fight oxygen starvation.

My hand hit something sharp. It was a piece of the shattered table. With the sound of David's gulps in my ears, surrounded by the coppery smell of my own blood, I gripped the piece of wood tightly and jabbed it into David's neck.

He reared back with a shriek, letting me fall to the floor. While he was trying to remove the wood from his neck, I grabbed another piece and stabbed him in the chest.

I didn't manage to puncture his heart- I wasn't Buffy after all- but it was enough to wound him. I just didn't have the strength after all the blood loss. Just when I grabbed another piece of the table, he lunged for me.

Those fangs came at me and I reflexively jammed the

stick into his mouth. His momentum was enough to force the wood all the way through and out the back of his neck. He fell to the ground beside me, gagging on the giant splinter.

Vampire blood was almost black and thick like molasses. His blood drained out in a pool around his head in a dark halo. As it grew, his struggles ceased. I crawled over him to get to the home phone I'd never gotten around to canceling. I dialed 911.

Wait. This was a trial. Would calling for help mean I'd give up? I hung up the phone before darkness engulfed me.

The cold roused me, but it was the hunger that snapped my mind alert. My tongue hit a razor sharp tooth and I tasted warm, liquid copper. It was the only moisture in my mouth. My lips were dry and cracked. My stomach convulsed, and I doubled over from the hunger pangs. I lay there, in the ruins of my kitchen and stared at my third-time-dead husband in a coffin made from our broken kitchen table feeling a hunger that bordered on madness.

I sensed someone watching. Uriel and Death were in my living room.

"Vampires are supposed to be strong. You're cheating," I croaked at Uriel.

"Common misconception. You need to feed immediately or you'll starve. Historically, the sire feeds his progeny from his own vein. They are flush with excess blood from the newly turned after all."

"Never drink from him." Brave words I wasn't sure I could keep. My shirt sunk into the hollow of my stomach. Hollow? My organs were collapsing. I could feel them shifting around inside of me. It nauseated me, despite the ravenous hunger.

"Well, obviously, not now. You killed him. Not very prudent of you while your blood drained so freely from your body,' Uriel mocked.

My hands cramped and I couldn't even cry out from the pain, because I was so parched. The bones of my fingers grew more visible under my paper-thin skin. I moaned in agony as the skin split, exposing the bone underneath. My body was cannibalizing itself. I ran my tongue along the same tooth, cutting it once again and sucked the blood greedily down my throat.

Damn David. I killed him, but he won in the end. He'd turned me into a vampire and with no one to feed from, I would starve in agony. This was my trial. Would I end up a living skeleton?

I don't know how long I lay there, dying-dead but not dead- when I heard the sirens.

"Perhaps you will be fed after all," Uriel said.

There was a loud crash as my front door was kicked open. "Sara! Sara where are you?"

Oh, God, no! It was Matt. Anyone but him.

He rushed into the kitchen and gasped in shock. "Sara, oh my God. An ambulance is coming. Don't you die on me."

Matt dropped beside me and pressed a dishcloth against my neck. I don't know why, there was no blood left to stop. I tried to push him away, but he wouldn't let me.

He smelled amazing. If my mouth could have watered,

it would have. His scent was rich with blood and life. His aura glowed white around his body like cotton candy, tempting me to taste it. Somehow, I could hear his panicked heartbeat pound its staccato rhythm.

No. Uriel would not do this to me again. I would not attack Matt like I had my sister. I ground my teeth together, to keep from biting him.

He held me close, his fingers brushed my throat. I swallowed convulsively. I could end my pain if I just bit him. My wound would heal and my hunger would end. All I had to do was turn my head, just a little, and bite his wrist.

The ambulance arrived and he gently put me back on the floor. Matt guided the EMTs in. They knelt beside me. Their blood sang to me. Their heartbeats pulsed in my ears like the pounding beat of a dance club. I was surrounded by it. I was so hungry. I couldn't resist any more.

I opened my mouth and lunged for the wrist of the EMT bandaging my neck. I missed. My teeth slammed into his watch hard enough to rattle them. The ache in my mouth amplified when he dropped my head. It hit the floor hard, slamming my jaw together.

"What the fuck! She tried to bite me. She's a freaking vampire!" Both EMTs fled like I was a rabid dog. I was so starved, I could barely move. But if one of them would just get in range, I would be able to drink.

"Get over there and save her!" roared Matt. He shoved one of them toward me, but the guy refused to budge.

"No way. We're not trained for this shit. My watch. Man, she bit my watch instead of me. She could have killed me!"

"Dude, calm down. You're freaking out. You sure she didn't bite you?" The other paramedic examined his wrist.

Matt swooped toward me. Flakes of dried blood from

my shirt and the floor wafted around me in a cloud. I pushed myself away from him with what little strength I had left. He froze and gave me an anguished look. "Sara, stop. We can help. We can give you blood."

"Uh, no. We don't have any blood on the truck."

Matt gave the guy an evil glare. "They will at the hospital. We'll take you in and get you taken care of. The government has been working on a cure."

"No way. She's not riding with us. Heck no. We don't get paid enough to risk our lives." The EMT rubbed his watch convulsively as he spoke.

"Can't control myself. Kill me." I croaked out through dry, cracked lips.

"No! I can't do that. I'll take you to the hospital myself. Please, Sara. I can't lose you."

"Go with him, Sara. I can ensure a cure is discovered so the hospital can restore your humanity. You can live your life with the one you love." Uriel was right outside the kitchen behind the EMTs.

My body screamed at me to go. Nothing, not the trials, or the world, was as important as filling this emptiness, this aching hunger inside of me. I stared at Matt. He needed me. I should go with him.

Uriel's wings were once again the blinding white they'd been when I first met him. He spread them out. The tips made scuffing noises as they hit the ceiling. They rippled like waves, scraping the paint so it fell around him like glitter. Was it his version of a victory dance? His winning was bad. I couldn't let that happen.

"I'm sorry, Matt."

"Think of what you would be giving up. You would break this mortal's heart? And for what? Sacrificing yourself for a world that never cared for you. Never wanted you. You could have love, happiness, children." Beneath Uriel's silky voice whispered a hint of desperation.

I looked at the EMTs and begged, "Please. Don't make me suffer. Don't make me kill."

They exchanged looks with each other behind Matt's back. One reached into his bag and pulled out a syringe.

Matt looked over his shoulder at the sound. "What the hell do you think you're doing?" He voice was deep and menacing.

"We're going to try to sedate her. This should knock her out pretty quickly."

"See, everything is going to be okay, Sara." When Matt turned back to me, the EMT plunged the needle into Matt's arm.

"This is your last chance to be with him, Sara. You can stop them. I can give you the strength." Uriel bargained like a used car salesman, but I ignored him. "You realize your reward for enduring these trials is death?"

I flipped Uriel off while the EMTs and Matt were distracted.

He turned his back to me to go back into the chamber. Black spread through his wings, like dye onto cloth. "So be it."

Uriel may have given up, but Matt wouldn't without a fight. He hit the EMT in the chest. The punch knocked the breath out of the guy, throwing him back against the wall. His partner stepped in front of his fallen friend to block Matt.

Any other time the guy would have been no match for Matt. Whatever they injected Matt with must have worked pretty quickly though. He swayed on his feet before swinging wildly and falling to the floor.

The man Matt had punched got up with a groan and rubbed his chest. "Go take care of her. I'll check on him." He leaned over poor dazed Matt to check his vitals.

The other EMT walked over to me cautiously.

"Please. Wood. There. Do it." My voice sounded like I was ninety-years old.

He picked up a splintered piece of wood and walked over to me. "I don't know if I can do this."

His hand shook, and his eyes were wide, dilated.

"Do it. Kill you. Your family. Please." It was a mix between a snarl and a whimper. A threat or a plea? Whatever it was, it worked.

He held the wood over my heart and said, "I'm sorry," before plunging it into my chest.

I heard Matt's anguished, "No!" before I was hurtling up and out of my house back to the throne room. Even though I knew this wasn't real, it killed me to hear his pain. This wasn't the real Matt. I hadn't just broken the heart of the man I loved. It was all a show put on by Uriel.

What choice did I have? I had to do it in order to win this trial. My brain knew that was all true, but my heart still shattered.

## CHAPTER THIRTY-FOUR

*War, What is it Good For?*

"I beat you this time, didn't I?" I said to Uriel as soon as he had repaired my body.

Uriel stood behind the Lamb's throne with his arms crossed and refused to look at me.

Holy shitballs!

Was he sulking? Add a few crocodile tears and a pouty bottom lip and he'd look like a petulant three-year-old, assuming that the three-year-old had giant wings sprouting from his back.

"So do you wanna skip this last trial? 'Cause we both know there's no way I'm not going to finish it after the hell I've already endured." I put my hands on my hips, feeling cocky. Time to end this. Uriel no longer scared me.

Except… winning in my case, meant I'd die. My hands fell back to my side as the thought deflated my good mood.

"Then finish it," snarled Uriel.

He waved his hand and I appeared in front of my house. It was dark out. The ambulance was gone. Matt's truck wasn't around. Relief washed over me. It was as though the previous trial had never happened. I hadn't broken Matt's heart. Everything had been returned to normal.

A bottle smashed in the street. The sounds of a large group of people yelling and cursing grew in volume. I raced to the end of my driveway. An angry mob of my neighbors walked up the street armed with shovels, fireplace pokers and... was that a pitchfork? Seriously? Who needs a pitchfork in the suburbs?

It was my nightmare brought to life.

Oh. Shit. This was going to get ugly real fast.

"It's all Sara's fault!"

"She's ruining the neighborhood!"

"Get the bitch!"

They were yelling for my head, but they had to catch me first. I turned and ran back to my house.

"You see? She will not finish the last trial. This is not war. In war, you fight. She has given up. It is over."

Uriel, Death and the Lamb appeared on my front porch. I would have plowed through the three of them like a bowling ball, if Death hadn't thrown an arm around my waist to lift me off the ground. For a few seconds, I looked like a cartoon character while my feet ran in midair.

Death set me down and I glared at Uriel.

"That was a tactical retreat, not a surrender. They do that in war, too." Tactical retreat sounded much better than big-sissy-run-away.

Death smirked and Uriel huffed out a breath.

Dammit. I had to fight. I could do this. They were a bunch of snobby suburbanites. How tough could they be?

I rummaged in my garage for a weapon before the crowd made it to my house. Crowbar? No, too small. I spied a pickaxe David had bought when he had decided to install a water feature in the front yard. The thing still had the price tag on it. David had swung it once, hit caliche, and gave up.

Could I actually use it against my neighbors? I hesitated. This wasn't real. Uriel had made up this fake world, but still, fighting a monster was one thing. Attacking a human being? Maybe the pickaxe would scare them away, and I wouldn't have to hurt anyone.

Suitably armed, I strode down my driveway ready for battle and nearly dropped it in shock. There were just so many of them. Smoke wafted across the street along with the smell of citronella. Someone had a torch. Sure, it was a tiki-torch but still, a freaking torch!

How was I supposed to win?

Wait.

The trial was to fight the war, not win it. Time to go on the offensive.

The pickaxe clanged loudly when it collided with the shovel Mr. Barrett swung at my head. The vibration rattled my teeth. It must have rung Mr. Barrett's bell pretty good too because the shovel went flying, along with his dentures. *Ha!* I'd lived across the street from that grumpy old man for years. Knocking out his teeth finally silenced his complaining.

Something smashed into my shoulder. Reflexively, I whipped my arm back to shove the person away. A wooden rolling pin clattered to the ground along with Mrs. Cornwell, my eighty-year-old neighbor. Oh, my God! Ten minutes into the war and I'd gotten violent against an old lady. What if she broke her hip?

"Mrs. Cornwell, I'm so sorry. Are you okay?" I knelt beside her to help her up, and the bitch beaned me in the head with the rolling pin she'd retrieved in her palsied hand. I stumbled away, rubbing the lump forming on my forehead. "What the fuck!"

Before I could recover, someone's fist bashed into my mouth, knocking me to the ground. My front tooth was broken, hanging by its roots and tickling my tongue. My lips split. Memories of my last trial filled my head at the taste of blood. I spat it out in disgust and had just managed to pull the tooth out, when someone else kicked me in the ribs. Starbursts of pain accompanied every breath.

Tag teamed by the snowbird couple from down the street. I thought Canadians were supposed to be nice. Were they hockey players?

I kicked the tall, blond doofus in the family jewels. He fell to his knees and tripped his wife in the process. I scrambled away and retrieved Mr. Barrett's shovel from the ground.

"You want some of this?" I screamed. The unfortunate answer was yes, they did.

"Bring it on!" Yelled a lady who lived in the other block.

"Go back to the ghetto!" This from a soccer mom who drove a mini-van.

"Kick her ass!" I didn't see who said this, and didn't care. There were insults and threats coming from all directions.

Surrounded by thirty or so of my neighbors, all enraged past reason, I swung the shovel. It made a metallic 'thunk' each time it connected with a head. It was almost musical, like a xylophone. A path opened. I ran up my driveway to get out of the mob. When I turned back to face them, I couldn't believe my eyes.

The riot had driven them to madness. They'd turned on each other. Neighbor attacked neighbor. Wives and husbands mindlessly traded blows. It was my chance to run away.

No. That was what Uriel wanted.

I scanned the crowd and found a familiar blonde head

fighting her way to me. Elise brandished a broken bottle like a saber. Perfect.

Wielding the shovel like a Viking battle axe, I fought my way to her.

"Violations!" she screeched. "No gatherings without a permit!"

I choked up on the handle of the shovel like a baseball bat and swung for home. It whacked her head hard enough to knock her out. "Fine me for that, bitch!"

My victory was short lived. Pain exploded along my skull. A punch smacked me in the back of the head and caused me to stumble. Swept up in the violence surrounding me, I whirled my shovel around hitting as many people as I could.

They ranted like escapees from an insane asylum. A cacophony of voices grunted, screeched and gibbered crazy things. Bodies smashed into each other. Punches flew. There was even some hair pulling. And the smell! The noxious stench of sweaty bodies and the rich vomitus stink of blood surrounded me. I no longer saw people, just body parts to attack before they struck me.

A hammer wielded by a well-manicured hand hit my elbow. A lightning bolt of pain flashed up and down my arm causing me to drop the shovel. The bone had to be shattered. My right arm was useless.

I dropped to my knees, clutching my arm. I crawled through the crowd, getting kicked and stepped on until I found shelter under a parked truck. The agony that pulsed up my arm joined with my other injuries in one miserable torture.

The crowd thinned out while they brawled. Bodies tumbled to the ground. I hunkered down to wait until they killed each other. It was a good plan, until a hand wrapped around my leg.

My attacker released me after I let loose with a few frantic kicks. I curled up my legs to my chest, hoping the person was too bulky to get under the truck to reach me. It seemed to work.

The tasseled loafers walked away. I let out a relieved breath until I felt the jab of four spikes in my back. The asshole speared me with the damned pitchfork! It didn't go in deep, but felt like four live wires burning into my back. I howled in agony and wrenched away. Hands clutched my legs once again and dragged me out, back into the melee.

The asphalt ripped the skin of my arms like sandpaper. I looked up to see Phil Jacobs standing over me in his `Dressed to Grill' apron. He raised his pitchfork, grinning maniacally.

"You asshole!" I screamed. My right arm hung broken at my side. I was weaponless and so screwed.

"You talk like a whore. That's why we stopped inviting you to our barbeques."

"Your barbeques sucked. Everyone knows your special barbeque sauce comes from a bottle, you fucking poser."

He plunged the pitchfork at my head, but only managed to nick my ear as I rolled away.

The fighting mass of bodies drifted back our way. If I could keep him distracted, he would have to defend himself. I could get away. I noticed Jeff, Phil's neighbor and drinking buddy, locked in a death-struggle with someone right behind Phil. "Jeff Reed said your beans were straight from a can. He could out grill you with one hand tied behind his back."

Phil tightened his grip on the pitch fork. Oh, shit. Had

my plan backfired? I braced for the attack, but it never came. He turned and threw the pitchfork like a javelin at Jeff.

Any guilt I would have felt at making Jeff a target faded when I realized who Jeff had been throttling. Poor Mrs. Cornwell. She must have lost her rolling pin. Jeff released her when the pitchfork perforated his back. She ripped it out of him and stabbed him repeatedly until he slid to the ground. She kicked him in the head before turning to the rest of the mob.

That crazy old bitch went on a rampage. She jabbed people in the neck and face, and she wasn't even breathing heavy. Bodies dropped all around her. Someone whacked her in the arm with a crowbar, and she didn't as much as flinch. No way a normal senior citizen could do that. I looked over at Uriel, and he winked at me.

"You're cheating!" I screamed at him.

"All is fair in love and war. Is that not what you humans say? This battle has been far too easy for you," Uriel answered.

Easy? I had been punched, stabbed by a pitchfork, and my arm had been pulverized by a hammer. How was that easy?

"Perhaps you need more motivation?" Uriel gave me a smug smile.

"Sara?" The familiar little voice came from behind me.

No! Please no!

I turned, looked down, and recognized the terror-filled brown eyes. They were the same color as Matt's. The street light reflected the highlights in her brown hair. Her lips trembled. A wave of nausea and agony hit me when Haley gripped my broken arm.

"I have to get you out of here. Come on," I looked for a

way around the mob, but people were everywhere.

"I want my daddy. I want to go home." She started to cry.

"I know, honey." We stumbled over bodies while I pulled her to the truck. I prayed they wouldn't pop up like zombies and grab us while we walked by. We made it to the door and found it unlocked. I opened it and said, "Get down on the floorboard. Don't come out unless I tell you to, okay?"

She was brave, just like her daddy. Though tears flowed down her face, she nodded and climbed into the truck. I locked the door and slammed it shut.

When I turned, I was face to face with Phil. His apron had been ripped off and gore stained his jeans.

"The girl must be important to you. Too bad you can't protect her," he said before he wrapped his meaty hands around my broken arm and squeezed it hard.

I shrieked and fell to my knees. Phil punched me in the head. My brain reverberated inside my skull. The crowd stopped fighting and gathered around us, attracted to the pain Phil was inflicting.

I curled around my broken arm to protect it while Phil kicked me in the back.

"Yeah!"

"Make that bitch pay!"

"Where's that smart mouth now?"

They egged Phil on and fed his rage.

He kicked me away from the truck and turned to tap on the window. In a sing-song voice he said, "Little girl, little girl, let me in."

The sick bastard was going after Haley. I forced myself to stand and took a shaky step toward him. Someone in the mob kicked my legs out from under me. I fell against Phil's sweaty lower back. He tried to shove me off, but I twisted a hand around and around in his shirt and held on like a rodeo cowboy. It was futile. The man had way more muscle than I did, and he wasn't wounded. He whirled around and slammed me into the truck. My head hit the window and shattered the glass.

Spotlights of pain exploded in my head and blinded me. Haley screamed. Bodies crowded against me and pulled me away. I fought blindly, biting, kicking, and clawing my way through them, but there were too many.

Haley's terrified screams grew louder when they wrenched her from the truck. "Sara, help me! Help me!"

"She can't help you. No one can help you, brat." Phil shook her in the air.

"She's just a child. Let her go!" I begged him.

He ignored me and held her like a doll, turning her from side to side making her look like she was dancing. "You want me to let the little girl go? Okay," he said and dropped her on the ground. Her head bounced off the street like a deflated basketball.

She curled up in a fetal position, a tiny ball of a girl with grown men towering around her.

I looked around, desperate for a weapon. A pickaxe was right there, within reach. Holding it with one hand was awkward, especially when I started swinging it around. I aimed for their heads this time. No way would I risk it getting stuck in someone's back. I'd taken several men down, but it didn't take much for one of the others to yank the pickaxe from my hand and knock me to the ground.

No! I had to save her. I couldn't let her die!

I struggled to stand, but someone had planted their fat ass on me and pinned me to the ground. Haley lay not too far from me. Our heads faced each other as though we were at a slumber party sharing secrets.

Everything seemed to speed up, playing in fast forward. Blink. She was crying. Blink. Phil was reaching for her. Blink. His meaty hands engulfed her thin neck. Blink. He snapped it with a crack like breaking a wishbone from a turkey. Blink. Her head lolled backward, neck unnaturally bent. Her eyes looked startled and her mouth formed an O of surprise.

"No!" I screamed and the world slowed down to normal speed. He dropped her. Her head faced me. Her lifeless eyes haunted mine.

Oh, God.

I hadn't protected her. I should have saved her. Matt would be destroyed.

"You don't. Hurt. Girls!" Mrs. Cornwell punctuated each word to Phil with a jab from the pitchfork.

Phil gave an enraged cry while he fought her off, but she nailed him right in the eyes. I gagged when she pulled the fork out, along with one of his baby blues.

The battle was almost over, but it didn't matter. I'd lost Haley. I'd let her die. The remaining combatants fought around me while I stared at her broken body. Her brown hair was tangled around her like a halo. Unable to stand up, I crawled to reach her.

I combed through her hair with my fingers, trying to untangle it. It was soft as silk and smelled of strawberries.

Mrs. Cornwell stood in front of me. I reached out to touch her, to thank her for killing Phil. She whirled and thrust the pitchfork into my stomach, and the words died in my throat.

I didn't think I could feel any more pain, but I was wrong. Blinding shards of fire pierced my gut along with a wave of nausea when she wiggled the weapon around to wrench it out.

She braced her foot on my chest while she yanked it free. I closed my eyes, not wanting to watch the killing blow. But no attack came. I cracked one eyelid and saw her in a heated battle with the last man standing, my next door neighbor, Barry.

I wrapped my arms around Haley. Cradling her tiny body against mine, her head rose and fell with my chest every time I sobbed.

Mrs. Cornwell faced off against Barry. She wouldn't have stood a chance against him if he didn't have a dislocated shoulder and a potato peeler buried in his back.

He faked right, but she didn't fall for it. The lunge seemed to use up the last of his strength. His leg gave out and he fell heavily on his knees. Mrs. Cornwell didn't hesitate. She plunged that pitchfork into his chest. When she plucked it out, he fell forward. She planted it into his back like she would a flag.

She stood panting, one hand holding on the pitchfork, cackling madly. When she stopped, the night grew eerily quiet. The only sounds were the occasional moans and labored breathing of the survivors and my sobs.

"Defeated by an old woman. Some warrior." Uriel appeared on the street along with the Lamb and Death.

*War has been waged. A victor has been chosen.* The Lamb looked over at Mrs. Cornwell who bowed her head to the Lamb. The Lamb returned the nod. She walked away muttering something about her shows being on.

Haley lay lifeless in my arms. I looked at Death and threatened him, "Don't you dare take her."

He lowered his head and she disappeared. I reached for

her, but my body spasmed in pain. My eyes closed for a second. When they opened again, I was back in the throne room, no longer broken.

# CHAPTER THIRTY-FIVE

*Unrevelated*

"Is she okay?" I asked Death.

He nodded. I knew it wasn't real. She hadn't died. But I couldn't get the image of her tiny body lying lifeless on the street out of my head.

"I would hardly call that a war. She barely fought," Uriel said to the Lamb.

Figures he would be a sore loser. I opened my mouth to argue when the Lamb spoke.

*'Wars are waged in many ways. She has fought honorably. The trials are over.'*

"It's done? Four scrolls, four trials. I saved the world, right?" I looked from Uriel to the Lamb. With superhuman restraint, I managed not to point at Uriel and shouted, "I win, asshole!" But it was a near thing.

The Lamb nodded his head, and the four scrolls, rolled up tightly, appeared at my feet.

Uriel jumped down in front of me and said, "You think you have won? What exactly do you think your victory is today? Saving a world where no one will mourn your death? A world you humans are determined to destroy on your own? You are not the victor; you are the sacrifice. What you have endured so far is nothing compared to what is to come.

I can still spare you. I can restore your life now, if you wish."

"You really think I would give up after everything I've been through? I was eaten alive for fuck's sake. You turned my family into zombies, and then turned me into a vampire. I just had to watch an innocent child get murdered and then had my ass handed to me by a homicidal old lady. Seal the damned scrolls already."

"As you wish." Uriel's voice thundered. He raised his sword and severed my arm. It felt as though lasers sliced my arm apart from the inside out.

With an agonized shriek, I sagged to my knees, vision dimmed from the pain. Warm blood poured from the stump like a waterfall. It pooled on the first scroll and seemed to solidify until the seal was once again intact. This would be when the welcome darkness should come to end my suffering, but there was no escape.

Uriel leveled his sword in front of me and slashed my chest and stomach open, just like the Lamb's. The finely honed blade made a thin incision down my front. My chest was neatly dissected. My heart quivered while it clenched and released frantically. Viscera spilled out of my body. Futilely, I tried to pull the edges of my skin together with one hand.

I wailed and thrashed my head around in agony. The stench of my bisected bowels filled the room. My intestines oozed between my fingers like steaming raw sausage. Uriel was right. This was worse than anything I'd suffered before.

My life was leaving me in a thousand tiny pinpoints of agony while blood and gore poured from wounds. It didn't end fast enough. "Please, let me die. Let me die!"

I tumbled forward, the stump of my arm falling on the scrolls.

The scrolls seemed to stir, as though alive. I could almost sense them hungrily pulling my life's blood from my body to form new seals.

"Help me!" I screamed at Death. He bowed his head, closing his eyes as if he couldn't bear to watch.

My heart practically vibrated, it pumped so hard from the adrenaline and pain. I could feel its movements with my remaining hand that lay underneath my body.

A keening sound filled the room. I realized it came from me. Time ceased to exist. It was replaced with misery, marked by the sealing of the scrolls from my blood. The fourth scroll took the longest to seal. Red oozed sluggishly across the scroll like congealed gravy until it settled into a solid crimson band.

'*It is done.*'

I heard the Lamb's voice in my head, but couldn't comprehend what it meant. Death was at my side before I could fight through the haze. He picked me up off the floor and I was healed. I gasped in shock at the absence of pain.

He cradled me in his arms while I sobbed. My voice, raw from screaming, was unrecognizable when I asked, "Is it over? I can't handle any more. God, please tell me it is over."

'*You have repaired the scrolls. The seals have been mended. The Earth shall have peace.*'

I looked up from Death's embrace, hiccupping through sobs, and realized the Lamb and I were mirror images, both carrying heinous scars from being split open and covered in our own blood. His had opened the seals, and mine had closed them. The scrolls sat stacked up beside the throne. I expected them to be covered in scarlet, but they were perfectly white, except for the matching bands of blood-red seals.

"Take her," Uriel addressed Death. The kings in white robes vanished with a wave of Uriel's hand. He no longer held a sword. Though his wings remained white, he snapped them open in a shower of anger. They spanned from one end of the chamber to the other, before he simply disappeared.

His sudden departure shocked me out of my hiccups. I hadn't expected Uriel to give me a long goodbye or anything but thought he would have acknowledged my win or maybe said I was a worthy opponent. Something.

The Lamb was the only one left, besides Death. The lamb bent his front legs and bowed before me. Despite his injuries, and the multiple horns protruding from his head, he made it look graceful. Humbled, I bowed my head in return.

'*Peace be with you, Sara.*'

My tears stopped and the hysteria was pushed down enough that when Death set me back on my feet, I was able to stand on my own. Death took my hand and a dense fog filled the chamber. All I could see was Death, who stood right in front of me.

"I am sorry I was not able to save you. If I could have spared you the pain, I would have. You were very brave, Sara. I knew you were extraordinary the first night we met."

The small amount of peace the Lamb had granted me wore off, and every ordeal I'd been subjected to hit me like a runaway train. I ran a hand across my stomach to make sure it wasn't still sliced open. Though my body seemed intact, my muscles trembled from the strain of the abuse it had been through. A headache pounded my skull and my heart still beat furiously, unaware the danger was over. My hands-both hands thank God—violently shook from the adrenaline. Even my eyes throbbed.

Several minutes passed before I could say, "So now what? You take me to meet the Big Guy?"

Death smiled, and for once, it didn't feel creepy. "I can. You would be with your family. You would have no memory of the trials. You have earned eternal peace."

Mom. Dad. Rachel. My heart soared at the thought. I could replace the last nightmare images of them in my head with new ones. No zombies, just everyone happy and together again. I wouldn't be alone any more. "You said I could go to Heaven, but that isn't my only option?"

"I have the power to send you back to your body. It was severely damaged from your accident, but you may yet survive. Though I know not how long or in what condition. And you will carry the memories of the trials with you for life."

A chill ran down my back and I shuddered. The wet dog and putrid-meat breath smell of the werewolves while they ate me alive flashed in my memory. I shook it off, but the taste of my sister's flesh and blood filled my mouth... I gagged. All the horrors that I'd endured. Could I live with the memories?

"I don't understand. I thought I had to die to seal the scroll? Isn't saving me against the rules?"

"How do we know your death was God's decree? We have only Uriel's word. If he really was carrying out God's will, then you should not have been able to seal the scrolls. Perhaps restoring you is part of God's plan."

"What am I supposed to do? What is the right choice?" I asked him in a small voice. After everything I had endured, my brain was moving too sluggishly to make a decision.

"I cannot answer that for you. I have many powers, but

knowing the future is not one of them. However, I can give you a glimpse of your life at this moment." He waved his arms and guided a way through the retreating fog.

I'd stepped right into a hospital room. Matt slumped asleep in a recliner beside a bed. A news station anchor droned on the television about the mysterious healing of those who had been turned into zombies, vampires and other monsters.

Rick walked in with two cups of coffee and set one on the table beside Matt. He looked down at the person on the bed, and I realized it was me. I looked like a mummy, with all the bandages around my head, arms and legs. My face looked purple and swollen. Rick gently brushed my hair behind my ears.

He leaned close and whispered, "Sara, you have to wake up now. I don't think this big strong guy can handle you dying. You know how fragile men can be. So snap out of it, beautiful. Please."

Rick kissed my forehead gently before straightening up and sitting on the chair on the other side of the bed.

Brandon, Rick's husband, bustled into the room wearing a white doctor's coat and both Matt and Rick jumped up to face him. He smiled his professional doctor smile at them and walked to the bed. Peeling back my eyelids one by one, he shined a penlight in each eye.

"Well?" Matt asked.

Letting out a sigh, Brandon said, "There's no change. Her body is trying to heal. She could come out of this at any time, or not at all. As long as she shows brain activity, I can override her aunt's wishes."

"I'll shoot that bitch if she tells you to pull the plug again," Matt growled.

Brandon and Rick traded a look.

Brandon placed a hand on Matt's shoulder and said, "Why don't you go home and get some rest? I'll stay with her. All my mysterious plague patients have gotten better overnight, so I have time to sit with her."

Matt shook his head. "Look what happened when I left her last time. I was supposed to protect her. I'm not leaving."

He rubbed his head, his hair scruffier than I'd ever seen before. I reached for him, but his image faded, and I was back in the fog.

"If you go back, you will have to recover on your own. I cannot say if you will suffer any permanent damage or even if you will survive. The trials will haunt your dreams. You would find peace in Heaven."

I thought about how banged up I looked. Every piece of skin not covered in bandages was purple from bruises. The accident might have left me paralyzed, or brain dead. Even if I survived, I'd suffer nightmares of the trials for the rest of my life.

"Will I be safe from now on? No more attempts on my life? Can I live my life and be happy?"

He turned to me and touched my cheek. "As safe as any mortal. I should not visit you again until it is your time to pass. And it was always your choice to live a happy life or not. I never held you back."

Death had finally offered me the choice I had wanted when I was a kid. He could take me to be with my family instead of leaving me alone in the world. I pictured a broken Matt at my funeral. And Rick and Brandon, their faces masks of sorrow.

No. After thirty-seven years I had finally found a life worth living. As long as Matt was by my side, I could deal with the nightmares. I could get therapy. Death would have to wait.

"I could visit you in Heaven when I deliver the fallen there," he said wistfully.

I looked into Death's eyes. They had at one time filled me with horror, but now they gazed upon me with an unreadable emotion. A little gasp escaped my lips. My stomach did a flip flop when the realization hit me that Death loved me.

He looked into my eyes and knew my answer. He turned away. "You are going back to him?"

Death seemed so sad. I was shocked to realize I cared for him. But it wasn't love. He wasn't Matt.

"I'm sorry," I said. I reached up before I could chicken out and turned Death's face back to mine. I stood up on my tiptoes and kissed him on the cheek gently.

The air seemed to turn solid around me and pain filled my chest. I opened my eyes. I was in the hospital bed with Matt's head resting inches from mine.

I had returned to my body and the pain, though not nearly as bad as what Uriel had done to me, was enough to make breathing a burden. My hands clenched involuntarily, and I realized they were each being held by someone who loved me.

Matt jerked his head up and looked at me. "Sara. You're awake. Thank God." Dark circles ringed his eyes, which were hollow from grief and exhaustion. His clothes were rumpled, the knees still stained with my blood. And it looked like he hadn't shaved in days.

He looked like Heaven to me.

I couldn't smile through my cracked and dried lips. I tried to speak but the bandage wrapped around my head was too tight, "gumbl muple do" was what came out.

He looked across the bed and did a double-take. Death held my hand, though I no longer needed him to guide me home.

Matt bolted to his feet, knocking the chair over and yelled, "You can't have her. I won't let you take her from me. Leave her alone!"

He can see Death?

Death let go of my hand and gently patted my arm before he turn to face Matt. "I have brought her back to you. Endeavor to be worthy."

And with that, Death vanished.

I looked at Matt and expected him to freak out. I should have known better. He rubbed his unkempt chin stubble and said, "Thought he'd be bigger. And what's with the cheesy sunglasses?"

I tried to laugh, but it made me choke. I moaned in pain. Matt pressed the call button and yelled for the nurse.

"Mad at me?" I wheezed at him.

"Damn right I'm mad. Don't even think of leaving me again. Death didn't seem so tough; I can take him."

The nurse, Rick and Brandon entered the room before I could say anything more. The nurse injected something in my IV, and the pain dulled, along with everyone in the room.

I faded in and out. Matt was there one moment, then Rick. Brandon would shine a bright light into my eyes when he would visit. Once I thought I even saw Death hovering in a corner of the room looking miserable. I drifted in my numbing fog until whispering intruded on my slumber.

Not just whispers, prayers. I opened my eyes to see Matt, head bent over his hands which clutched his St.

George medallion. He prayed desperately, reverently. His prayers sounded like demands, and I was in awe.

"Trying to save me again?" I whispered.

His head shot up. He smiled down at me. "Well, you do seem to need a lot of saving." He leaned down and kissed me gently before adding, "Looks like I'm the guy to do it."

"Nope. This time I saved you and the whole world. Girl power, grrr, argh."

A small laugh that ended with a sigh escaped his lips. "It's over then? You saved us?"

He brushed my hair back behind my ears. I didn't want him to ever stop touching me. "You can thank me later, Officer Espinoza."

He leaned down to whisper, "You can call me Matt."

# ABOUT THE AUTHOR

~~~***~~~

Rissa Watkins is a writer, mother, and leukemia survivor living in the Arizona desert. When not busy keeping her family alive (which with a super-active son is a lot harder than it should be) she can be found hunched over a keyboard working furiously on her next novel.

Rissa was nicknamed "The Ninja" by her writing friends because of her habit of taking down online bullies. When she was diagnosed with Leukemia in 2010, she transformed into a cancer-fighting ninja. She survived lethal doses of chemotherapy and radiation, a bone marrow transplant, going bald, and horrible hospital food to kick cancer's butt.

These days, she has traded in her throwing stars for a laptop, which she wields to write fiction. You can get a glimpse of her novel writing genius, or possibly nonsensical chemo-brain ramblings at www.RissaWatkins.com

If you have enjoyed reading UNREVELATIONS please leave a review online at your favorite retailer. Thank you.
~~~

www.ingramcontent.com/pod-product-compliance
Lightning Source LLC
Chambersburg PA
CBHW021943170626
46808CB00001B/13

* 9 7 8 1 9 3 9 7 7 6 1 6 7 *